THE LEFTOVERS CLUB

Book Two: Bee's Story

by

Yazhen 'Bowie' Feng
& Vincent deFilippo

Contents

ViennaRose Publishing LLC
Copyright © 2024 by ViennaRose & VJ DeFilippo
All Rights Reserved

Cover and art design by
ViennaRose Publishing LLC

http://www.vincentdefilippo.com/

Paperback ISBN: 979-8-9883420-7-6

Chapter One

The February air bit at Bing "Bee" Lin's cheeks as she scootered along the sidewalk of East Tenth and took the right onto First Avenue toward Bed Stuy. Her eyes watered to the point where she could barely see, causing her to nearly crunch a little pookie dog on a leash clutched in the hand of a woman whose cursing followed Bee through the silent, icy early morning.

That would have been only three points, Bee told herself. Wan Pi wouldn't approve of her black humor. Wan Pi, the French bulldog who had adopted Bee just after she'd moved out of the condo she'd shared with her three best friends, was snug at home in her basement studio, occupied in one of his favorite pastimes, sleeping. His name meant "naughty" in Cantonese.

She wished she could have brought him, but it wasn't possible today. Now she thought about the things that had shredded her attempts to sleep until she gave up, her phone telling her it was exactly 4:17 in the morning. Shopping bags balanced carefully on the scooter handles, her hands in the peach colored Agnelle boa gloves she'd dug out of a consignment store bin, she picked up speed, sailing off corners, gliding up and down and around.

There's no hurry, she tried to tell herself, but she felt like hurrying, because today was the day that she had been dreading for months, and she wanted to get it over with.

The cold coffee Bee swigged this morning along with a few bites of last night's poke bowl sloshed uncomfortably in her stomach. She would have felt much more chill if Alex had spent the night, but Alex had been tired from a twelve-hour shift at the hospital and wanted to sleep soundly in her own bed.

"I'll see you at the hotel early, Beetle," she whispered softly in Bee's ear as they snuggled on the flat's giant L-shaped sofa. "Take an Ambien."

Bee had *not* taken an Ambien because of the grisly dreams, and things would be weird enough when her parents and brother arrived at the Bryant Park Hotel where she was headed right now.

When she got to Fifth Avenue after zigzagging through Gramercy Park, Kips Bay, and Korea Town, it was quarter past five in the morning, and Bee saw that New York was certainly the city that never sleeps. Crossing Fifth, she dodged cabs, Ubers, and the occasional limo vying to beat the light.

After all, this was New York City Fashion Week.

As she cruised up to the Bryant Park Hotel's front doors, Bee could see people ice skating in Bryant Park across the street. This year would be her chance at the mystery of the tents, which were no longer, of course, but where she'd spent many cold and ecstatic hours hovering in the streets outside with all the other dazzle-eyed glotzers.

Now I am inside Fashion Week. Bee smiled and raised her head as she pushed through the revolving doors, ignoring the scowling doorman, rolling her scooter with the bags banging against the stem. One of them held her iron and the other a toolbox filled with sewing needs. Even though she was only headed up to the exhibit rooms to help set up her parents' pop-up shop, Bee strode through the lobby, trying to appear as if she wasn't gobsmacked all over again by the models, camera-wielders, harried seamstresses, and one or two celebrities in ball cap and dark glasses currently choking the elevators.

And it's not even six a.m.!

Bee shoved into an elevator, garnering severe looks from several occupants. But one, a young woman in a sweatshirt and yoga pants, leaned down and said, "Wow, I love your outfit."

Bee nodded a thanks, and as she was about to say, "I made this myself," the door opened and three more people carrying paper coffee cups crushed themselves inside.

New Yorkers are experts in packing themselves into small spaces, Bee mused, shoving her elbow into the ribs of a man who appeared to be napping against her shoulder.

As soon as the doors whooshed open on the twenty-fourth floor, everyone flowed out like water in a flushed toilet. Bee, with her bags, scooter, and backpack, was one of the last, barely saving her scooter from getting crushed as the elevator doors slid shut.

The Lin family's Hong Kong Lin Design pop-up store was one of five along the hotel's south wall, where a view of the Empire State Building stenciled the dawn sky. Bee and her parents, along with Bee's older brother, Hao, had been here all day yesterday unpacking clothing and accessories. They'd rented three mannequins that stood awkwardly naked against the left-hand wall. The floor was strewn with stray threads, torn labels, and the odd button. The pop-up's bland beige walls were as naked as the mannequins.

Cursing her brother's laziness, Bee went to the cramped work-room behind the pop-up back wall, where a rack held a score or more of Lin outfits. Stacked on the ironing board were hats, scarves, jewelry, gloves, and shoes. Digging into one of her shopping bags, Bee pulled out a red silk clutch and two scarves made of long ribbons sewn together, with a pair of gloves to match. She deftly mixed them into the accessory pile. The models had a tiny space behind the rack where they could change, barely room enough to bend over to tie a shoe.

Hao, who had his own reasons for slacking, hadn't bothered to commandeer a sewing machine. Thus, Bee had brought her own vast collection of threads, buttons, fabric tape, and Velcro fasteners.

There isn't room for a sewing machine anyway, Bee groused as she leaned her scooter against the floor-to-ceiling window where Midtown glinted under a skyscape of pinks and golds—two of Bee's favorite colors.

She already knew how she would dress the mannequins, and she set about heating the iron and fitting a shirt to the board. Bee didn't care for the Lin style; it was too Alexander Wang meets Tommy Hilfiger, but the clothes were popular among chic Hong Kongese, and Dad hoped to get noticed in New York.

After sweeping the accessories her dad had picked up for the styling onto a nearby chair—with her own designs added—Bee pulled a red leather belt from one of her bags. She had a pair of neon yellow Bottega Veneta heels, borrowed from her bestie, Tina Lu, for one of the mannequins. And she would use a peacock blue felt hat she'd scrounged from a thrift store—vintage, she guessed 1930s, as a little tailored glitz for her dad's line.

She had one of the mannequins dressed by the time her girlfriend, Alexis Ingles—Alex—appeared with two venti cappuccinos.

"Ah, the nectar of the gods," Bee said and safely hidden behind the pop-up wall, kissed Alex on the lips. Alex tasted like mint. She was wearing one of Bee's creations, a sweet emerald, green spaghetti-strap full-length tee, stenciled with the image of El Capitan in Yosemite. Over the tee was a black embroidered silk bolero jacket, and on Alex's feet were a pair of her own Rag and Bone ankle boots.

"You look divine," Bee breathed.

"You look like you slept for maybe one minute. Give me that iron."

Bee was in the front of the shop arranging the mannequins when her brother, Hao, appeared. In one of the Lin black linen suit jackets and Heritage jeans, without a tie, Hao slouched against the sales desk.

Bee felt the hairs on the buzz-cut back of her head prickling. She was too angry to speak. Instead she twisted off the mannequin's head.

"Good morning to you too," Hao said. "When do the models get here?"

Bee bit her lip as she removed the mannequin's gloved hand. "Eight a.m. Tomorrow." She turned to face him and enjoyed seeing his face fall. "But wow—"

Two live models glided past the shop entrance; her brother's gaze followed them.

"Wow, you're here to help. Thanks, Hao. I seem to remember something about you setting up and me helping? Not the other way around?"

"Yeah, sure." Disengaging himself from the desk, Hao lifted off a sheer black chemise from one of the racks. "How about this on one of the mannequins?"

"I got it." Bee turned back to her task.

"I knew you would. Thanks, Bee. Really, I mean it."

Bee opened her mouth to speak but shut it again. What was the point of being the broken record? Hao knew how angry she was at Dad for pegging Hao, the *son* of the family, for Lin Design leadership, when this was the last thing Hao wanted to do. It was literally Bee's life's dream to design fashions and run her own house.

"Are they here yet?" Bee asked after taking a pin out of her mouth.

Hao didn't have to ask who "they" were. "They're getting some breakfast. Or at least Mom is." Hao gave a short laugh. "You know, the restaurant here is Japanese. Dad's probably stewing in the lobby while Mom has an omelet."

Bee almost smiled. Dad despised the Japanese.

Alex came from the back room carrying a black ironed dress with three-quarter sleeves and a bell miniskirt. She glanced at Hao, then narrowed her eyes toward Bee.

Bee pulled herself together. "Oh, yeah. Alexis, this is my brother, Hao. Hao, Alexis, my friend who's helping out."

Nodding with a half-smile, Hao shook hands with Alex, giving her a thorough up and down assessment that lingered on her D cups. Alex shot Bee a pointed expression; Bee knew exactly what Alex was thinking. *When are you going to come out to your family?* This was a frequent discussion point between Alex and Bee.

Checking her phone, Bee froze when she saw the time. Only forty-five minutes before the preopening show began.

"Uh-oh." This from Hao, and Bee nearly dropped her phone.

Lin Zhen and Lin Xing, Bee and Hao's father and mother, were advancing across the event space. Zhen's chin was raised as he peered through his glasses at his pop-up shop. He was dressed formally, as if appearing in court, in a charcoal gray Lin executive suit. Xing, trailing a step behind, wore a cute baby blue wool coat and ivory-colored suit jacket with matching below-the-knee skirt. She carried a take-out carton.

Dad scowled. "Where is the sign? I shipped a special logo, custom made, to go on this wall here." He jabbed a finger on the wall.

Bee didn't respond as she slid the minidress onto the mannequin's torso. Neither did Hao.

Mom's voice, like a soft, fluffy cloud, floated in. "Zhen, I saw it in the back. I'm sure Hao was saving it for the last minute so it wouldn't get scratched."

"Time to get it up, then." Dad moved swiftly behind Bee toward the back room. He nearly ran into Alex as she came out.

Bee saw Dad stiffen. He turned to Hao. "Who is this?"

Hao opened his mouth, then deflected helplessly toward Bee. Rolling her eyes at him, Bee inhaled. "This is Alexis, Dad. She's a friend helping us out today."

"Oh. Fine." Zhen seemed to simply dismiss Alex from his mind.

Bee didn't bother to introduce them any further. Dad wouldn't remember Alex anyway, but Mom approached Alex and introduced herself, offering her hand.

"Thank you for coming, Alexis. Would you help Hao with the logo?"

Dad shouldered past Mom and Alexis with an armful of dresses, jackets, and slacks. "We don't have enough clothes on the racks. I want them stuffed full. Hao, help me with these."

Hao appeared stricken for a moment, but then seemed to remember the chemise. Bee's ire began to rise as she knew what was going to happen.

"I promised to show this to, uh, one of our models. I think I see her over there." Picking up the hanger with its filmy garment, Hao rushed away, into the growing crowd.

Sighing loudly, Bee obeyed her father's command to help him arrange the clothing on the two front racks. He had chosen, she noticed, to change two of the key outfits that she'd thought the models should wear on the runway, hiding them in the shopping racks and leaving behind a poor choice of suits and unremarkable skirts for the models. Bee didn't say anything. The first chance she got, she'd put them back.

Bee and Alex moved the logo to the shop's back wall where it got better light, fastening the framed art images of Hong Kong behind the sales counter and along the opposite wall. With Dad and Mom in the back of the shop on the laptop discussing budgets, Alexis helped Bee get the mannequins dressed, arranged, and set up.

"This looks fantastic." Alex stood back to admire Bee's work. If they were alone, Bee would have covered her with kisses. But as things were . . .

Bee noticed that Hao had reappeared—without the chemise. He stopped at the boutique entry, his back to it, staring at his phone. Stepping up behind him, Bee wiggled her fingers at him like a witch casting a nasty spell, hoping her brother would ask what was wrong. But he either ignored her or he was so engaged with what was happening on his phone that he didn't even realize she was there.

Irritated, Bee launched into a tense *sotto voce*. "Hao! Where have you been? Dad's been raking me over the coals. He's treating me like his personal child slave."

Jerking his head up, Hao turned and gaped at her.

She blazed, "If I weren't here, you guys would be half set up with your mannequins looking like suspects in a police lineup. A *naked* police lineup."

"D'you think I want credit for your work?" Hao replied, his eyes wide. "I don't want him to think for one moment that I have an ounce of fashionista in my blood. I don't want to be here. He forced me to come. At least you're into this fashion nonsense."

"I don't give a shit what you think. You're helping me. Now."

Hao surveyed the shop. The mannequins were dressed and posed, the racks ironed and crisped, and the brilliant colors of the Hong Kong skyline adorned the walls.

"What's left?" he asked lamely.

Bee pointed at the sales desk. "There. Is. A. Crate. Under the desk. It's full of brochures, swag, candy, business cards. They need to be on top of the desk, not underneath."

She didn't add that some of the business cards were her own, made up specially for this show.

"Oh, sure." Hao almost appeared relieved, but then Bee saw her brother's eyes widen when he glanced out into the crowd.

She followed his gaze and saw a stunning redhead who was chatting with the owner of the shop catty-corner to Lin Design.

"See her?" he asked Bee as she pulled him to the sales desk. "That's the girl I'm going to marry."

Bee rolled her eyes extravagantly. "Sure, Romeo."

A short time later, finished with the desk, Bee, Hao, and Alexis stood at the shop entrance evaluating Bee's work, while Bee steeped in her sense of pride. The shop popped with both old-school glamour and inventiveness, and the early visitors—press, agents, and representatives from mags and houses—were already taking notice.

Dad emerged from the back, glared at Bee and Hao, and marched up to them.

"Why are you loafing around?" he barked at Hao, ignoring Bee standing right beside her brother. "I built this company with my own two hands. You never get anything without hard work, and you don't quit until the job is done."

Bee stared at him, uncomprehending, because the booth was ready. But Dad watched Hao for a few seconds as if he thought his son had just had a stroke, then noticed the crowd of people watching.

"What are they staring at?" he asked Bee and Hao in a fierce whisper. Bee lifted a finger and indicated that he should check behind him. Turning, Dad was struck dumb. The boutique was jazzy, eye-catching—instead of the mannequins posing as if they were standing around waiting for a cab, they were grouped and imaginatively posed as if they were taking selfies. They even held mock iPhones in their gloved hands.

Beaming, Dad slapped Hao on the back. "Good work, son! This is marvelous!"

Rolling his eyes at Bee, Hao gestured as if to say, *Tell him, for the love of God!*

"Actually," Bee said loudly, "it was my design."

Dad gave her his classic blank look as if she were speaking a language he didn't. She'd seen this before. Without a word, he headed for the sales counter. "Come! Hurry! The room will open soon. Did you put out the candies and freebies?"

Following him, Bee knew it was now or never. "Dad, listen. I have some of my own designs. You know I love to draw. Well, I've made a lot of new clothing—see the cute dress Alexis is wearing— and I wonder if I could display some of them here, with you—"

Dad shot her a quizzical expression. "This is nonsense. You should stop daydreaming, Bing, and learn from your brother. Ask him about his ideas for the family business."

"He doesn't have any!" Bee exploded, to which her dad responded with a sweeping gesture at the boutique.

"What do you mean he doesn't have any? What about all this?"

Bee was shaking. "That was *me*, Dad! Those are *my* ideas! *My* booth design. *My* staging. The truth is, I have more design sense in this little mole"—she placed her little finger on a beauty mark on her upper lip—"than Hao does in his entire body." Whirling away, Bee stomped back to the front of the booth just as the ballroom doors opened, admitting a swarm of people. She searched for Hao.

He's gone, natch. Scanning the crowd, Bee saw him strolling briskly away up the aisle—in pursuit of the redhead.

Chapter Two

"Dad, you can't possibly think Lin Design belongs on the same stage with Fendi and Vera Wang," Bee argued as she zipped up the back of a Lin Design evening gown one of the hired models had wriggled into. She'd already told the model twice to lose the chewing gum, and the woman had promised to jettison it just before she mounted the catwalk.

"I'm trying to quit smoking," she explained, as if that were reason enough to risk damage to the expensive fabric.

The model, whose name was Suzy, had assessed Bee's rainbow-dyed and gel-spiked hair, spangled jacket, and neon blue leggings with chagrin, but now she exchanged that judgment for respect.

"Are you English? Your accent is so—"

"Unexpected?" *In a Chinese girl?* "Actually, I'm from South Africa. Cape Town."

"How cool is that?" Suzy rambled on about safaris and Bee tuned her out. Bee had, truthfully, spent several years in London studying at Central Saint Martin's College of Art and Design, earning the education she had fought so hard for. Getting that same question about her accent over and over was going stale.

Dad was raging—again—about Lin Designs being relegated to the back lot, so to speak. Miffed that he hadn't been granted a show at Spring Studios, he couldn't go one hour without launching his complaint. The models in the minuscule space behind the dress rack were all bumping elbows, getting their feet stepped on, and sighing. Empty cups of espresso and a dozen water bottles lined up like slouching ticket holders along the base of the window. Worse, Bee felt sweat trickling down her back; even though she had shed multiple layers of her outfit, she was down to a midriff tee, layered ruffle skirt, and flip-flops. At least she got plenty of compliments on the skirt.

"Besides," Bee called after Dad as he stomped back into the storefront, "this is one of the most coveted spaces in town for Fashion Week. You scored, Dad." Bee continued to herself, "Only you don't even know it."

Dad pushed into the space with one of his cashmere cardigans that reached nearly to the floor. The models flinched as one at the idea of wearing it on the runway.

"I feel like a boiled lobster," one of them muttered.

"Dad, we have to ask the staff to turn the heat down. The models are melting." Bee was pulling shoes from boxes, tossing them aside, and picking up the next box.

"Then you go do it," Dad told her. He picked up a Louboutin and handed it to the nearest model. "Where's the other one?" he snapped. "You are tossing these shoes around like a three-year-old with Legos."

"I'll go," Alexis volunteered. She'd come to help and found that, with Bee and her father quarreling like blue jays, helping meant staying out of the way. Bee sent her gratefulness and wished she could blow a kiss.

The models were nearly ready. Bee turned them around to check for visible Velcro strips, hanging threads, and dog hair—one of the girls had brought her pocketbook Yorkie, who sat in her tote bag growling. Bee so wished she had brought Wan Pi, despite the hotel rules. Dad was now ranting about how potential shoppers, clueless Americans who assumed Chinese names were in the same order as English ones, would read his business card and say, "Thank you, Lin. I love your work!"

Bee gritted her teeth as she brushed the wool trousers one of the models was wearing, a little distracted by the perfect roundness of the woman's anatomy. "Dad, I've told you over and over that you can solve that whole issue by changing the way you use your name. How're people supposed to find you in a business listing if they're looking for 'Mr. Zhen'?" She had made the change when she'd turned eighteen and had gone to London among the equally clueless English. She was now Bing Lin, not Lin Bing.

Dad pulled the lint brush out of Bee's hand. "Where is your brother? Hao is in charge and I don't understand why he is letting you do all this important work."

Staring at her father, speechless for a moment, Bee imagined she could turn him into a cinder using only her eyes. "Why don't you ask him?" Her lips felt stiff.

"You go find him." Turning away, Dad tilted a model's red beret.

Hands in fists, Bee turned and fled, running straight into her mother. Bee's eyes stung. She hadn't been this pissed at her father since he took Hao to Shanghai Fashion Week and left Bee behind with the excuse that he couldn't afford tickets for all family members. Xing held two paper cups, and the scent of green tea floated from them. Handing one to Bee, she guided her daughter to the front of the shop.

Sipping without thinking, Bee burned her tongue on the tea.

"He just doesn't see me, Ma. It's as if I am invisible. I'm supposed to be eternally fecund with child in the kitchen cooking Happy Family stir-fry."

Xing stroked Bee's arm, her touch gentle. "He will come around. He loves you. Your father was born in the year of the goat." This was one of Mom's stock answers.

"Very bad luck," they said at the same time.

As usual, Mom wanted Bee to stop fighting with her father. "I'll talk to him later, Bing. He's old fashioned, thinks all women should stay at home with children and noodles. He wishes that happiness for you." She smiled. "I was very happy."

Bee couldn't get that memory out of her mind, how Mom hadn't even tried to advocate that Bee go with them to Shanghai. She knew her next words would be cruel but couldn't help herself.

"Mom, he's never going to get his wish. Not ever."

"Never is a very long—"

"Mom, I'm gay."

Mom's mouth dropped open, her eyes widening. She leaned toward Bee as if trying to see this as a physical change in her daughter.

"Oh."

Setting her cup on the floor, Bee folded her arms and turned away from her mother. "I'm sorry to tell you this way, right now. But please understand. I know you try to understand. Try to understand this. This is who I am. A designer. And a lesbian."

Touching her quickly, as if she feared that Bee's skin would burn her, Mom whispered, "Whatever you do, don't tell your father!"

Bee saw Alexis standing with her back to them, straightening a blouse that had gone crooked on its hanger.

The cat is out of the bag now.

Bee felt a little sick inside. She hadn't eaten in hours. It was probably that, but it could also be that she felt bad about what she'd told her mother. Irrationally, she felt irritated with Alexis too. Alexis had told her over and over she needed to come out to her parents. Well, now she had, and it didn't feel good. Picking up a scarf, she set it down again. She was quivering so with anger that she might have ripped it apart.

Dad was herding the models out of the back. Seeing Bee standing there doing nothing, he stopped and pointed his finger at her. "Bing! Go find your brother." His face was red with rage.

The pressure of this show, Bee thought, *is making him insane.*

"You will not be a fashion designer," he continued. "That is a waste of time for you. You will come back to Hong Kong and find a husband. I let you go to school in England to find one and you didn't. I will buy you a ticket. Enough is enough!"

Sharing nervous glances, the models slithered past, while Bee cringed. Having her father berate her in public for all to hear made her see red. Literally. A red silk clutch lay on the nearest display table. She seized it and shook it in his face. "You see this? I designed this. Three people already want me to make them one. Because I'm good!"

Zhen's mouth pouched out in anger. "No. I told you no sneaky items placed here and there. Hao is in charge. He will be running Lin Design."

"Dad, how do you not see that I am the ideal person to run the design side of the business? Hao doesn't even want to be here!" Bee tried to steady her voice. "I'm going to start my own fashion line. Alex believes in me. Why can't you?"

"Alex? Ah, yes, your boyfriend," said Dad.

Turning, Bee grabbed Alexis's arm and pulled her away from the mannequins and toward her father.

Alexis tried to pull away. "Bee, I don't think—"

Ignoring Alex's protest, Bee wrapped her arm around her.

"Actually, my boyfriend Alex is my girlfriend, Alexis. Alexis, Dad. Dad, Alexis."

Then she kissed Alex in front of her parents, full on the lips, feeling proud with rage as they stared in shock. Taking Alex's arm, Bee steered her into the crowd as her dad sputtered, "You . . . you're . . ."

"The word you're looking for is gay, Dad!" Bee announced over her shoulder as they walked away.

Bee led the way to the elevators, but when she got there, she found she was alone. Pushing back into the crowd, she saw Alexis walking quickly toward the exit sign above the stairs. She caught her just inside the door, in the stairwell.

"What's wrong, luv?" Bee asked. "I did it. I told them. It felt great!"

In truth, she felt nauseous, but she wasn't going to reveal that to anyone, especially Alex.

Alex stared at her. "What's wrong," she snapped, "is everything that happened in there. What's wrong is that I wanted your parents to like me. Now they'll see me as a vice, not a person."

Whirling away, Alex started down the steps.

Bee called after her. "Wait! You're not going to walk all the way down—"

"Yes I am." Alex's voice echoed in the empty stairwell. And then she was gone.

Chapter Three

Jojo Zan sat on the toilet for so long her butt began to ache. She held the test strip wand in her hand and had to stare at it long enough, comparing it to the instructions, to be certain that what she was seeing was true. She badly wanted to call her best friend Bee, while sitting here in the bathroom so Jim wouldn't hear, but Bee would be frantically busy with the Fashion Week stuff and her parents.

There was no doubt about it. What she had suspected for more than a month now was true. She'd met three of the five reasons you should do a pregnancy test; missed her period the last two months and this month it had not appeared yet again, her breasts felt tender, and she had to hold her breath whenever Jim barely touched them, and the nausea—so weird that suddenly she hated the smell of coffee.

And she knew exactly when it had happened.

The "kids" discussion had cropped up a few times in passing, remarks like, "When we have kids, we won't be able to do this on the couch anymore" and "I'd hate to have to move out of this great apartment when we have kids."

Out in the living room, Jim was watching the basketball game. He had been cursing a lot, meaning the Knicks weren't doing so well.

I could tell him tomorrow, or the next day, at breakfast, make it a special one—he loves waffles.

But she knew she wouldn't sleep at all tonight dreading it. No choice but to get it over with. She rose, yanked on her lounging sweats, and opened the bathroom door.

"Aw, man. What's the matter with Quickley! He needs to muscle up there."

Leaning forward from the sofa, Jim was waving his arms in the air as if he was trying to get the Knicks guard's attention.

Jojo sat down next to him. "Who're they playing?"

"Portland," Jim answered without taking his eyes off the screen.

"Which Portland?" Jojo knew very well the Trail Blazers' home city was Portland, Oregon.

Just as she hoped, Jim gave her an annoyed double take, but when he saw her smirking, he relaxed. "Portland, Maine, of course. Don't you know that?"

"Oh, right. The Portland Maniacs."

The next second he was on his feet with a loud *whoop*. "That's it! That's what I'm talkin' about!"

The Knick's point guard Immanuel Quickley had just scored, the ball sailing from his upraised hands straight to the basket, narrowly missing a Portland player's leap into the air to block it.

"Impressive," Jojo remarked, staring down at the dipstick with the little blue lines in her hand. She had tested herself last week and gotten a blue, but managed to talk herself out of the reality of what it was saying.

They always say you should test twice to be sure. Now I'm sure.

When a commercial came on, Jim reached for his beer on the coffee table. Jojo, seeing her chance, stuck the dipstick between him and the can.

"What's this? A thermometer?" With concern, he asked, "You sick?"

Shaking her head, Jojo held the wand steady, unable, suddenly, to say the words. *Those words.*

Squinting at it, Jim shook his head in frustration and shrugged. "So, it's a little device with a blue plus sign in this tiny window. Okay. Plus what?"

Suddenly she realized how vital Jim's reaction to the news would be. *Angry? Over the moon? Asking for a divorce?*

She couldn't stop the tears filling her eyes. *Damn, I hope I'm not going to blubber through this whole pregnancy.*

His face changed to worry and he put his arm around her. Mutely, she handed him the test box.

Jim took it, puzzled. "Plus . . . plus a *baby*? You're pregnant?" He straightened, eyes wide as he gaped at her. "You're pregnant. How . . . ?"

"I'm sure I don't have to explain it to you." She felt a giggly laugh coming and managed to squelch it. *The hormones are making me bipolar.*

"No, I mean . . . you're on the pill."

"You remember at WindyCon, how we stayed up until two thirty for that Eye of Argon reading?"

Jim lost the thread of the conversation and grinned. "How can I forget that night? Your crowd is nuts. 'Dismiss your hand from the hilt, barbarian, or you shall find a foot of steel sheathed in your gizzard!' I totally lost it on that line." Glancing at Jojo again, he seemed to realize he was off topic. "Um, yeah, I remember."

Jojo felt relieved that he seemed to have forgotten about the game; the commercial was over. She said, "I was four hours late taking my pill, and we . . . and now . . . I'm so sorry, Jim!"

She couldn't stop a sob, and then another, and a hot stream of hyperemotion flowed from her eyes and nose, a performance worthy of Laura Petrie.

Jim nuzzled her as she wept into his shoulder. He even handed her the napkin next to the plate of hummus dip on the coffee table. She pressed it to her face.

"Shit, I think we're going to lose this one. I can't effing believe it!" His hand brushed her head. "Jojo, sweetie. Don't cry. The Knicks are still one and six."

This brought her head up, fueled by a spear of anger, but when she saw him grinning at her, one eyebrow drawn upward, she had to laugh.

"It's just that we said we were going to wait. I mean, we didn't really say that, but I was on the pill." She huffed in a shuddering breath. "I'm so busy right now, and this. And we haven't bought anything yet, or talked about which room the baby will have—"

"Babe, it's all right. Wait, not just all right. It's fantastic!"

She watched his face transform into a kind of awe and astonishment. "It's bloody fantastic. I'm gonna be a dad, and you"—he leaned in and kissed her—"you're going to be the best mom in the universe. In *all* the universes!"

Jojo felt a new bout of weeping on the threshold but managed to swallow it away. "But can we afford it? I'll have to stop working, and there won't be maternity leave pay from Gray Ghost. I'll basically be freelancing."

"Sure, we can afford a kid. I'm making good money now. Ever since I science-fictionized our wedding, I'm getting tons of work on top of my job at Empire. Your mom has even talked to me about organizing some events for TORS. And listen, you're writing a screenplay for Jackie Chan. That's money even if it doesn't end up on film. Anyway, he's probably going to film it and you'll be raking it in while changing diapers."

"Wait a minute, you're gonna be changing diapers too."

Jim slapped his hand to his chest. He said mockingly, "Who, me? Isn't that women's work?"

Jojo nodded. "It's parenting work. Parent, understand?" She dug her finger into his chest. "P-A-R-E-N-T."

This time his hug was fierce. She could feel his fast-beating heart under his ribs.

Afterward, he gazed at her with wonder. "My parents are going to be over the moon."

Oh dear. Jojo had not given a thought to her own parents' reaction.

Sighing, she watched the television screen where a BMW was snaking along an oceanside road and said, "My parents. My mother, that is. She's not going to approve. I can hear her now. 'This soon? What are you thinking? How are you going to afford Choate Rosemary Hall on your salary at the publishers?'"

Laughing, Jim rolled his eyes. "Don't worry. My parents will make up for your parents tenfold when we tell them about it."

Being the writer of a Jackie Chan screenplay didn't impress Wendy Zan. "If only Raj will buy my book, then Mom might back off a little."

His arm around her shoulders, Jim guided her to lie back against him. "You are going to sell that book. Even if Raj doesn't buy it. You are going to be sending out query letters to agents. One of them will go gaga over it."

So this is it, Jojo told herself as she nestled into Jim, contented enough, for the moment, to sit through the postgame show with him.

The biggest task before her, besides learning to be a mother for the first time, was to tell the Leftovers their news. *Not yet*, she told herself. *Let's make sure this is real. I don't even believe it.*

But the blue cross did.

Chapter Four

Wan Pi under the table asleep on her feet, Bee sat at her apartment dining table in her pajamas with a cup of oolong. Her mother had brought enough tea over from Hong Kong to keep Bee steeped in hallucinogenic caffeine for the rest of her life. Since Bee had taken today off from her job at Gray Ghost Media because she thought she would be at the boutique all day, she had little to do and a lot to think about. Nothing had turned out as she had hoped.

Outside, through the high windows of Bee's basement rental, the New York sky was concrete gray. Snow was predicted with the magical accuracy of her cell phone. Normally she liked being in the basement studio. Cathey and Gina, a couple she'd partied with when she first moved to New York from London to be closer to her best friends Jojo, Tina, and Mei, had needed someone to babysit their condominium while they were in Viet Nam—Cathey had a two-year newspaper assignment over there. But today, instead of relishing her free time to draw and sew, and take Wan Pi on a spin up to the Garment District to browse through Discount Fabrics

Truemart, Bee felt unsettled, and the black tea in her cup wasn't helping.

The events of yesterday had become a frenetic, accident-ridden Cirque du Soleil show in her head. She'd accomplished two Very Important Things, and instead of feeling on top of the world, she felt like her basement was closing in on her.

I should feel like I've won the French fashion award, but instead I—I don't know why I don't.

She'd utterly shocked her parents with the revelation that she was a lesbian—always had been, when she thought about it. All her damned life. And she'd said it out loud. Not the coming out—that was peanuts compared to the fact that she'd voiced her dream out loud. Proclaimed it for all to hear.

She shouted, her voice echoing, "I'm going to start my own fashion line!"

Wan Pi, leaping to his feet, began to bark, as if to amplify the proclamation.

"Chill, little dude," Bee told him.

He tilted his little head, then settled down again, grumbling. Bee stared into her mug, wondering what the tea leaves were telling her. Tina's mother strongly believed in tea leaves. Bee thought hers were telling her that she'd underestimated the fallout of what she had done.

First, Alexis. Alex was really cheesed at her. She hadn't wanted to spend the night—she'd made up the excuse of having an early shift today. That had never stopped her before. She hadn't answered any of Bee's texts this morning, either, and she usually did—even when she was working, whenever she had a chance.

I did what Alex wanted me to do. Why did she get so pissed about it? Is she right that I used her to get back at Dad?

Second—and in a way it was easier to think about this one— what was she going to do now about her dream? She'd made a promise to the heavens that she would begin the work toward her own fashion line, and she knew now there was no going back.

The tea was cold and Bee was hungry. After showering, she dressed in leggings, a knee-length tee, a coral-colored leather vest, and her signature rainbow wool coat. Wan Pi circled her legs, yipping his approval about a walk. In hat, scarf, gloves, and vintage Doc Martens, she went to the Blanketed Pig, her favorite breakfast café—they always brought Wan Pi a dish of water and a cookie.

In her favorite window seat, she pulled out her refurbished digital drawing pad, but it sat unused beside her plate of eggs Benedict. She couldn't stop thinking about yesterday. She didn't know where to start in developing her own brand. She didn't think she was ready. She needed more designs, more prototypes, and yes—money. A lot of it.

She needed to bounce some ideas off of someone. If Alex were here . . . But she wasn't, and Bee knew instantly who she needed to be talking to right now.

Jojo answered Bee's text right away. She'd call Bee in five minutes. Joan "Jojo" Zan had been Bee's best friend for more years than she could count. They had attended the same snobby boarding school together—Jojo grew up in Flushing and Bee had been sent to school in America when she was fourteen—another of her dad's efforts to set her aside while he concentrated on Hao. She and Jo had bonded immediately over their shared nerdism. The school had many Chinese students, but the cliques were no less xenophobic and exclusive. Bee loved that Jojo was deep into science fiction and cosplay; Bee designed and made costumes for her. Jojo had been fascinated when Bee told her she was gay. Jojo was the first female friend Bee had ever told, and it never changed the way Jojo saw her.

Jojo's call back was right on time. Wearing her earbuds, Bee took the call. "Jojo, I don't know what to do."

Lately, most of their calls started out this way. Now that Jojo had married Jim Yuhan and had left the Tribeca condo that Jojo, Bee, Tina, and Mei once shared—the legendary Leftovers Club—the tables had turned. During Jojo's roller-coaster courtship with Jim, Bee had listened to Jojo's trials and offered her straightforward advice. Now it was Jojo's turn to give advice to Bee.

Bee didn't give Jojo any opening for comments as she poured out her panicked thoughts, rambling, nonsequential, tangential.

"Hold on, Chatty Cathy!" Jojo finally interjected. "Clip your string!"

Bee was surprised into silence. "Huh?"

"It's from a movie, *Bingo*. One of my favorites, and it isn't even science fiction. A Chatty Cathy was a talking doll from, like, the sixties."

"Oh. Okay." This was classic Jojo. Bee loved her the most when she was rocketing off to Saturn, powered by some crazy idea, like speculating about murder in zero gravity. "I get it. No, I haven't seen the movie."

"Great! And now that I have your full attention, I think you've got a lot on that plate you just dumped all over yourself."

"Hmmph."

"Now, to me, it sounds like we need to call a club council."

Bee sighed. "I guess."

Jojo waited for a beat. "So, what's really wrong? You sound like you just got a fatal diagnosis."

"I'm scared, Jojo. I've never been afraid of anything in my life."

"You used to be afraid of your father."

"Yeah, when I was ten years old. I'm over that. In fact, I boasted up and down to his face about how I was going to be a success with my own line. And he dissed the hell out of me. Right in front of all of New York." Bee felt her throat close up. "And Alex."

No crying. Not allowed.

"Well, at least in front of the fashion world that is going to judge your line."

"That's helpful. Not."

Jojo's voice receded for a moment; she sounded like she was talking to someone at work. Bee stared out the window as a food-delivery bicyclist was nearly clipped by a box truck.

Jojo was back, her voice crisp and sure. "Okay. I'll call Mei, you call Tina. We'll have dinner at the condo. Tonight, I hope. Or tomorrow at the latest. We haven't had a brainstorming session in way too long."

For the first time since yesterday afternoon when Alex had called her out in the stairwell, Bee felt her twisted gut begin to unwind. The Leftovers Club would help. They would call a meeting to discuss a personal crisis, even though Jojo technically wasn't a Leftover anymore. The term derived from the Chinese concept that unmarried females of a certain age were "leftover women." Bee was still a charter member.

It also soothed Bee's soul to think about visiting the Tribeca condo that had effectively served as their clubhouse. It was like going to church.

No, temple. No, a grand old tavern where the barkeep knows you by name.

Confidence began to creep back inside her, like a timid cat climbing into her lap. The confidence she always felt when she made snap decisions, when she did what she wanted to do, and to hell with societal norms. Like the time in London when she and the girl she had just picked up at a Scrabble club walked down the middle of a busy thoroughfare, holding hands, kissing each other and singing "Girls Just Want to Have Fun" at the top of their voices.

Bee texted Alex again. *I think I need to apologize. Don't want to do it by text tho. Call me? If you're not saving a life, that is?*

Bee glanced out the window again; the delivery cyclist—a woman—was wearing goggles, an aviator jacket, and a miniskirt over her tie-dyed leggings. Huh. That was great, but better if the skirt was made of silk ribbons. Picking up her stylus, Bee began to sketch out a new design, trying to capture what was in her mind's eye in pixels. The jacket was perfect . . . except it needed some Bing Lin bling. She delved into her world of art, where time vanished and everything around her—sirens in the next street, an argument at the next table, and a couple across the street walking five pugs—faded into nonexistence. An hour later, she checked her phone.

Alex had neither texted her nor called.

Fuck it, Bee thought, slipping her pad into her backpack. *Let her stew. I'm going to get with my girl posse and plan the rest of my life.*

Chapter Five

The Leftovers Club dinner did not take place at the condo after all. Bee was disappointed until she learned the name of the new venue they planned to invade the evening after Bee's confessional with Jojo. Her eyes grew wide as she read Mei's text.

Le Bernardin. 8pm. Wear real shoes.

As soon as Bee got home from her day job as proofreader at Gray Ghost Media—where she worked with Jojo—she riffled through her closet, pulling out and discarding dozens of skirts, dresses, and slacks. As a retort to Mei's jab about Bee's shoe preferences, she eschewed her flip-flops but fixed on an outfit with a style that clashed violently with her Freebird combat boots. Wool jacket with brocaded trim, bubble-gum pink blouse with ruffled collar, and super tight mini pencil skirt. Her yellow leggings were in the laundry basket, so she settled on dove gray.

Her phone had buzzed with texts all day. Mom sent several little platitudes about forgiveness and understanding—translation: *Please call your father.* Hao wanted to talk to her about Becca. When Bee texted back, *Who?* Hao replied, *The love of my life.*

Oh, the redhead.

Jojo wanted to know what Bee knew about Bucky Gerardo, whose fashionista culture book was being edited that very moment by Raj Bhagat himself at Gray Ghost. At this, Bee rolled her eyes. *Nothing. Never heard of him,* she texted.

Nothing. Nada. Zero from Alex.

Snow flurries floated around in the sky but didn't stick. Still, it was too cold for the scooter and Wan Pi, and anyway, Le Bernardin was even farther uptown than the Bryant. Checking her bank account, Bee thanked the money goddesses that yesterday was payday. She could afford a modest plate (if there was one, she worried after consulting the menu on her phone) and still spring for an Uber. Wan Pi whined at the door as she left, and she called back that she'd walk him as soon as she got home.

She left another message for Alex, then went outside to wait for her ride. The crisp night, the odor of someone grilling, and the faint scent of a real cigarette eased Bee's irksome disappointment about Alex. It wasn't the first time she'd been ghosted, and usually she got over those girls quickly and found another. But Alex not responding hurt a little.

Okay, more than a little.

Feeling more positive about life in general by the time she arrived at the restaurant, Bee was happy to see Mei and Tina at a table near one of the back walls. The place smelled wonderful; it was packed on this snowy Thursday night. The window spots were all reserved, of course, and since Mei knew one of the owners, she had been able to get one of these prime tables.

The girls had ordered the first bottle of wine. Bee didn't care what kind of wine it was, but she usually liked what Mei chose.

Mei eyed her as she slid into her seat, after hugs and cheek kisses, European style.

Mei had styled her gleaming black cherry hair with a red barrette. She wore a green sleeveless shift, pearl necklace, several gold bangles on her wrist, and pearl stud earrings. All Mei Tang. Bee admired her sleek beauty, rather like a Siamese cat, as she lounged back in her chair, one elbow on the back. In her hand was an empty wine glass.

"You remembered your shoes. But wait, did you just join the Royal Air Force?"

Bee raised one leg straight out and wiggled her foot. "Aren't they beautiful?"

Tina leaned over the table to check them out. Her raven hair was styled in face-framing waves. In her goldenrod V-neck sheath, she showed off her curves; Bee wondered if Mei had badgered her into pouring herself into one size too small. Tina obsessed about her weight, which went up and down like the stock market.

"Well, if the city is snowed in, at least you can walk home."

They laughed together. A waiter sashayed over, picked up the wine, and paused while holding it over Bee's glass.

"For me?" Bee placed a hand on her chest and feigned happy surprise. "Aren't you a dear. Yes, please."

He barely filled the bottom of her large Bordeaux glass; after he left, Bee picked the bottle up and splashed not only more into her glass but into the outstretched glasses of her friends.

They toasted. "To the Leftovers Club. All for one and no one for all."

Tina glanced at her phone. "Jojo swears she's ten minutes away."

Leaning on one elbow, Mei swirled her glass. "That means she'll be here in twenty minutes."

"Married life," Bee said. Jojo had married Jim only this past autumn, on Halloween. The girls had given her prospective suitor a hard time. "We lost her to Jim despite all the traps we set for him. But, really, I guess he's okay."

Tina cupped her chin. "I like him, myself. He's grown on me. He's nothing like he was in college. And you can see Jojo is wild about him."

"If you like those disturbingly handsome solicitous types." Mei finished her glass and motioned for the waiter.

Then she leaned toward Bee. "So, Ms. Lin. Why have you summoned the professionals?"

"I guess I can open up the meeting, being that Jojo's already heard this."

Bee gave them the *Reader's Digest* version of her fight with her dad at their Fashion Week pop-up. When she got to the part where she told her father she was a lesbian and kissed Alex on the lips right in front of him, Mei set her hand heavily on the table.

"Hold your horses, young lady. You came out to him?"

Tina's mouth was open; she didn't say a word.

Bee felt her cheeks redden. "Yeah. I was pissed off. He was so disrespectful." She poked her chest with her finger. "I did all the work on that booth, and he ignored it. I told him I'd done it. But he still wanted to give all the credit to Hao."

Tina finally spoke. "I dropped by the Bryant, just to check out your parents' booth. It was the best one there. Absolutely! The clothes, though." She shrugged. "Fine if you're the CEO of a major Chinese noodle-shop chain."

Bee said, "Not a word of thanks from Dad. But I shocked the hell out of him. Of course, now he won't speak to me."

"Sounds like that might be a good thing." Mei eyed the waiter as he sauntered up with a second bottle, showed it to her, opened it with a flourish, and poured even smaller amounts than before into their glasses.

Bee leaned back in her chair, remembering who else wasn't speaking to her. She decided not to say anything about that. They would want to know why Alex was still in play, when normally Bee hopped from one lovely to another.

"The real problem is," Bee continued, fingering one of her earrings, "I boasted about opening my own line, saying my styles were better than his." She felt her shoulders sag. "And now that it's locked in, I have no idea where to start, like I'm paralyzed."

"It's called stage fright." Mei curled a lock of hair around her finger. The polish on her nails matched her pearls. Signature Mei. "I know. Like clockwork, at first, every time I had to lead a client meeting, I had to rush to the bathroom. I never got to one meeting early. Not ever."

Tina laughed. "I walked all the way around the campus the first time I taught a class. By the time I got back, I was too tired to be nervous. And my feet hurt."

"Yeah. Walking a tightrope above Madison Avenue seems easier."

"That's how I feel every day at work." Mei scowled. "I feel like I'm on camera, auditioning for partnership, even though I've been working at Doran and Cross for four years. Whenever I try to make an appointment with one of the partners to talk over my prospects, they call in sick. Or have to reschedule. I might have to ask one of them out on a date if I want to get any tips out of them."

"You could bring them here," Tina offered, pulling a knob of bread from the breadbasket. "Isn't a partnership all about money? They would be very impressed."

"Right." Mei didn't seem happy at the thought.

Bee asked Tina, "How are things with you and my boss, Teens?"

Since Jojo's wedding—Bee had come to think of that Halloween as something like the birth of the Common Era—Tina and Raj Bhagat, publisher and editor in chief of Gray Ghost Media, had been an item. In the last three months, they'd been exclusive to each other. Bee was careful not to remind Raj that she was one of Tina's best friends, and Raj was cautious not to mention details of their dates to Bee and Jojo.

Tina smiled. "So far, so good. A fruitful excavation."

Bee and Mei burst out laughing, catching the eyes of nearby diners. Tina was seeking her PhD in archaeology at NYU when she wasn't skiing with Raj or browsing consignment stores for half-off Miu Miu handbags. Her taste for ultra-couture fashion rivaled the Egyptians' obsession with gold, despite the fact that on her teaching stipend from NYU, Ted Baker was barely within reach.

Jojo breezed through the door, wearing a black watch cap with matching scarf and a red wool coat. Her cheeks were rosy with cold, and as hugs and kisses went around, melting snow dripped from her hair onto the table.

"What—" Mei wiped the damp from her cheek and lips. "Did you bicycle over here?"

Jojo wore a loose silk shirt patterned with midcentury cartoon rocket ships, and black velvet trousers. She was letting her hair grow out, and she was having to swipe it from her left eye.

"Oh, I forgot where the restaurant was, so I got off at the wrong subway stop. Had to walk five blocks. Not bad, though." She beamed. "It's snowing!"

"We know," Tina said, glancing warily through the window.

Jojo peeled off her blue wool gloves and blew on her fingers. The waiter was at her elbow in a flash.

"Wine, miss?" he asked, picking up the bottle.

"Oh, no thanks, but I'd love a pot of hot black tea."

The young man nodded and glided off to make tea happen.

"So," Jo said, divesting herself of her coat, "where are we in the proceedings?"

They ordered food from the waiter when he returned with Jojo's tea. Bee suspected he hoped they would get their meal finished and get the hell out of his restaurant as soon as possible.

"Catch-up time," said Mei and launched into a complaint about an office mate who chewed ice in the break room. Her audience suggested she sabotage the freezer in the employee kitchen or place a BB in one of the ice trays so he might crack a tooth.

Tina told the story of a student who texted her a love note . . . by accident. He'd intended it for a female classmate. At first she was worried but was able to piece together the error as she observed the guy in her class. She politely forwarded it to its intended target and thought they were now an item.

Bee didn't participate much. She was quieter than usual and knew it, and only pretended she was listening. Jojo knew something was definitely up with her. After the waiter cleared their plates and they asked for the dessert menu—he looked a tad disappointed, Bee thought—Jojo sat up straight and tapped her empty water glass with her fork.

"Now, I called this club council meeting so that we can help Bee out. She's having a crisis of confidence. Did she brief you on the sitch?"

Mei and Tina nodded.

Tina leaned toward Bee. "You know you have talent. We know you have talent," she added, sweeping her arm and almost knocking the artful centerpiece into the bread bowl. "You can design, draw, imagine. You can sew! That in itself is a feat I can't imagine accomplishing. It's not like you to be freaked out, Bee. It makes me nervous."

Jojo pushed her hair from her eyes. "I've been thinking about this on the way over. I think I know what we all have to do. We'll make resolutions. Like New Year's. Because Chinese New Year is next week. We'll make vows to succeed on our dearest wishes."

"Resolutions are like planned obsolescence," Mei said, studying her dessert menu. "They are meant to break down. Want to split the chocolate hazelnut mousse?"

"Only if we order a green tea tiramisu as well," Tina demanded.

The Leftovers all agreed. They ordered the two desserts and received them in quick order.

"Seriously." Jojo's eyes had a gleam of conspiracy. "If we all swear to each other that we are really going to make our dreams real, then we have to succeed."

"Do we do a pinky promise?" Bee waved her little finger at Jojo.

"Okay, I'll start." Jojo folded her hands in front of her. "I will finish the novel I'm working on and give it to Raj to read. It's a fantasy novel. No aliens or laser swords. I know this is the kind of book he's looking for."

Bee held out her hand, pinky finger extended. The girls linked together.

Jojo looked pointedly at Bee. She was, she realized, next in line.

"I will begin my preparation for launching my own line. I'll study up about finance, contacts in the business, and I'll create new designs, sew like crazy. I can talk to Cam at work—he knows everything about social media and influencers and how to get attention."

Bee winked at Jojo, who laughed. They both loved Cam Lobo —his real name was Hector Cortez—with his ultra-flaming and flamboyant persona.

Tina jammed her spoon into the tiramisu and inhaled deeply. "I'll go next. I will get my dissertation subject approved. This year." She lifted a spoonful of the dessert and stared at it as if it held the secrets of success. "And I will put my foot down with my mother about the dumpling truck. I will not work there or run the business. I got all my funding for school on my own and I don't owe her anything, in spite of what her tea leaves say."

Another round of little finger entwining.

They all stared at Mei, Bee wondering what her real dream was. Mei hadn't dated anyone since Jojo and Jim's wedding. Would she choose finding the right man?

Clearing her throat, Mei laid down her fork. "Partnership. For me. I'm going to do whatever it takes to become a partner at Doran and Cross."

"Without having to ask one of them out on a date," Bee said, then she whooped, causing heads to turn.

Fingers curled together over the artful centerpiece. The room felt bright and cheery to Bee as the snow swirled outside and covered West Fifty-First Street with a gauzy layer. Watching it, the taste of hazelnuts on her tongue, Bee made a secret second vow to herself. She would find Alex and make her talk to her. And tomorrow morning she would push Cam into a corner and pick his brain.

Chapter Six

Bee was supposed to be proofing a manuscript, a memoir from a man whose parents—both his mother and father—had become transgender. Bee wished the text had less whining and more humor about things like pronouns and dress sizes. Instead, as she sat in her cubicle on the fifth floor of the Media Arts Building, she was on her phone cruising TikTok and YouTube for adolescent influencer styling, getting ideas. She'd spent every spare hour since the "vow" dinner, as she liked to think of it, reading the backstory of new designers, how they got their start and how they built their brand.

Wan Pi, whom Raj generously allowed Bee to bring to work, lay beside her with his head on his paws, gazing up at her accusingly. She was thirty minutes late on his midmorning walk.

"Wan Pi, as soon as I figure out a good way to get a bunch of money without mugging a Wall Street trader, I'll walk you. Promise."

As soon as Bee started talking to him, Wan Pi sat up, but when his owner turned back to her phone, he gave a great sigh as he lay down and returned his head to his paws.

She'd put her phone on an open page of a tattered *Chicago Manual of Style* so that if Raj came by she could slam it shut, hiding her phone. The most daunting issue these designers wrote about was keeping up with demand, working out of their co-ops, forgetting about sleep, dealing with rejection.

Oh, that.

Bee promised herself, pinky-handshaking her two hands, that she would overcome all rejection and soldier on. One day, someone, somewhere would buy her designs. Under her desk was her portfolio. She'd brought it in every day this week to show it to Cam, but he was still home recovering from the flu.

Worse, Alex was still ghosting her. Bee worried she was now a stalker, leaving repeated voice mails and sending texts at random moments. Raj's office door opened—Bee could always recognize that sound—and she slammed the manual shut and focused on the passage where the trans mom was telling her squirming son about a girl he'd had an affair with in college. Bee felt her mind drift away, and she found herself thinking of how she and Alex had met.

One beautiful Saturday last August, on a morning bordering on sultry, Bee had taken her scooter over to the Garment District. She liked to cut across town and arrow up Eighth Avenue through Chelsea. But that beautiful sunny New York day, her ear buds playing "Yah Yah," Bee was coasting on sunshine and singing out loud, not paying attention to much of anything on the sidewalk.

A child, faster than a bullet, shot out of a shop doorway right in front of her. As she realized she was about to murder someone's kid, she jerked the scooter to the right, jumped the curb, and slammed into the back of a box truck.

Things were a bit of a jumble for a while. Bee heard voices as she lay on the tarmac where she had fallen between the box truck and an illegally parked car, after bouncing off the truck's rear fender. She was aware of cursing—probably hers—gasps of surprise, a screaming child—please don't let him be lying on the sidewalk bleeding to death —and finally a low, soft voice, quite close, asking, "Are you all right?"

"I doubt it." Bee sat up. Nothing seemed to be broken, but she could feel, and see, a couple of road burns on her left knee and elbow, and a place on her left cheek stung.

The striking young woman staring at her in a concerned manner asked, "Did you hit your head?"

It was more than an ask; it was a demand for that critical information. Bee shook her head. She had been wearing her helmet this time, fortunately, a safety measure she did not always take. "My helmet did."

The woman was luscious, Bee thought. She had tousled blonde hair, extraordinary eyes—green—and a soft, sweet mouth. *A golden fox.*

Do people always fall in love with their rescuers? Isn't there a syndrome for that?

"Okay," the woman said. "Sit here on the curb for a minute. What's your name?"

Bee felt she had no choice but to obey. "I'm Bing, but my best friends call me Bee. You can totally call me Bee."

The woman gave her a quick smile. "Listen, Bee, I'm a nurse. I saw you take that spill. These scrapes look nasty. Do you want me to call 911?"

"No way." Bee rose to her feet, as if to show the gorgeous golden fox she was fine. And she was. A little shaky but fine.

Her scooter didn't look fine, though. The handlebars were bent, and the front wheel looked flat.

She must have seemed forlorn because the golden fox said, "Okay, listen. My name is Alexis. I live just around the corner. You could clean up, and I have some stuff to put on your bumps and bruises."

Maybe the next person would have declined with *I don't want to put you to any trouble*, but there was no way Bee would let this opportunity go by. Pushing her scooter, Bee followed Alexis around said corner to a Chelsea walk-up and a beautiful little apartment Alexis shared with two other nurses. The apartment was tiny, and Alexis told Bee, as she sat on the bathroom toilet while Alexis assembled rolls of gauze, tape, and even a suture set, that this was only temporary until she found something else. She'd recently graduated from nursing school, worked in the emergency room at New York Presbyterian on the East side, and needed to save a little more money.

Bee sat quietly, soaking up Alex's honey smell and quick work as she gently cleaned Bee's scrapes, decided they didn't need dressings, and softly wiped the blood from a little "abrasion"—Bee loved that word—on Bee's left cheek.

"You'll have some bruising," Alexis said, sitting on the bathroom floor. "But you bounced pretty clean."

They chatted for a bit. Alexis seemed to have no thoughts of getting Bee to leave. Bee told her about her desires to build her own clothing design, right off the bat, something she usually didn't do when she first met a girl she might like to go to bed with. She definitely wanted to do this with Alexis, but she was careful. She was always careful when she met a woman she was attracted to, just in case they didn't share the same level of interest.

She asked, a little hesitantly, "Hey, you want to meet for drinks later?"

When Alexis smiled and nodded, Bee knew. She remembered how hopeful she was that she'd guessed right about Alex; to get to the point of sharing a bed, and a lot more, with this lovely lady, she'd taken it real slow. In the end, it was Alex who made the first move.

And now you've blown it, Bee told herself as she picked up her phone again.

"I hear you've been looking for me."

Bee let out a little yip and swiveled her chair. Cam gazed down at her, one hand on his hip, the other held toward her, palm up. He sounded a little hoarse and stuffy, but he was here!

"So where are they, your Rembrandts and Picassos? I want to see them."

Today, the Gray Ghost social media maven was wearing a long-sleeved gold shirt, a fancy Eton striped scarf around his neck, and very tight leather pants. Coughing wetly, rolling his eyes, he took Bee's portfolio and sat down on her wheeled filing cabinet.

He said, "Don't worry. No contagion."

"Glad you're feeling better, Cam."

"I wash my hands three times an hour. Let's see, now." He opened one of Bee's sketchbooks. To her great pleasure, his eyes widened appreciatively.

"Very nice. You have some imagination, *mija.*" Flipping through a few more pages, he set the sketchbook in his lap. "Do you have photos of your rags on anybody?"

Picking up her phone, Bee showed him—with a little pang—several selfies and pics of Alex wearing her designs.

Cam nodded. "You know what you should do? Enter a fashion competition. With these designs—very pretty drawings, and the clothes—and I've seen your clothes, *hermana*—you'll be accepted in a flash. Let me see . . ."

Lifting his phone close to his face, Cam began typing. This guy knew how to use the internet as if it were a SpaceX rocket; only seconds later, he said, "Oh yes. This one."

He showed his phone to Bee. "This is the NYC Fashion Award

contest for Young Entrepreneurs, open to designers under thirty." Cam squinted quizzically at her, and Bee nodded. She was twenty-nine. "Okay, good. This award is sponsored by Partners Research and Management. Says here they have big investments and much success in the fashion industry. Also, you get to work with Eighth Avenue Promotions," Cam added, seeming impressed.

Bee had heard of them too, and of several designers who'd benefited from their boosts.

Cam continued. "First prize is $100,000 and a one-year mentorship by a fashion industry maven and a business advisor to help the winner build his or her brand and business model." He read this quickly, grinning. "Maybe I should design some clothes."

Bee felt like her heart was trying to flutter out of her chest. "It's happening now? When's the deadline?"

She reached for Cam's phone, but he pulled it away, giving her a mock scowl. "Girlfriend, keep your panties on. Let's see. Ooh. It's soon. Um, next Wednesday."

Yikes! That's less than a week away. Bee thought quickly. She had the designs and some of the prototypes. There might be an entry fee, and she'd need to see the application, like NOW, to find out which ducks she had to line up.

Squeezing her hands into fists, she waved them like an excited baby. "Send me that link!"

Her phone rang. It was Hao. He had been leaving voice mails and she hadn't bothered to call him back. Feeling a little guilty, she shrugged at Cam and answered.

Nodding knowingly, Cam pushed the file cabinet back under her desk and left.

"I was beginning to wonder if you'd joined a monastery."

"Hi, Hao. What's up?"

"Bing, I'm in love."

So, what else is new? "The redhead, right?"

"Her name is Rebecca Pinterry. She's Australian. And beautiful. And smart. She's a journalist who mostly writes about fashion. She is so wonderful. You won't believe how wonderful she is."

Bee set down the phone as Hao waxed not very poetic about his new girlfriend. She rubbed her shoulders, really wanting to open the link Cam had sent her.

When she heard him say her name a few times, she paid attention again. "Yeah, yeah. She sounds wonderful."

"I'm going to ask her to marry me. I'm going to move to Australia with her."

Bee coughed. "You're kidding, right?"

"Nope. I'm going to do it. I don't want to run Lin Designs. The only way I can get out of it is to move to another country!"

Gathering her thoughts, Bee considered her brother's determination. He sounded happier than he had in years.

"I guess you're moving to another country," she told him.

With the excuse that she had to run to the bathroom, Bee ended the call, trying not to think about the coming Lin family conflagration when Dad found out. Quickly she opened the link Cam had sent her.

Just as the website loaded, Bee saw a call from her mother coming in. *How did she know I just got off the phone with Hao?* Xing's "mom-dar" was otherworldly.

"Mom! How are you?"

"Ah, Bing, you need to call your father. He's acting like a wild beast since you told that—thing you told him that I told you not to tell him."

Bee felt a little ping of worry. It wasn't like her mother to start off without a greeting and to talk faster than a three-year-old on caffeine.

"Mom, I'm not going to do that. I think he owes me an apology."

Xing was silent for a beat. She lowered her voice as if she was afraid to be overheard. Bee could imagine her shaking her head the way she did when she dared to complain about Zhen. "Last week at the boutique was difficult. Hao was like a ghost. Call his phone. No answer. He'd show up in the mornings, gone before noon, never to return. Where does he go?"

Bee had a pretty good idea where Hao went during his absences.

"Mumph, mumph," Mom added in a whisper.

"Mom, I can't hear you."

"Staff. S-T-A-F-F."

"Ohhhh. Okay. I get it. You had to hire more staff."

"Your father is hit—seal—pressure—heart attack."

Mom had a bad habit of waving her phone around as she was talking.

"Ma, Dad will be fine." Bee tried to calm her mother, who worried unnecessarily over Zhen's longevity, which promised to be very long. "I'll talk to Hao." She knew this conversation would be fruitless, but if it made Mom feel better . . .

"Okay, thank you, Bing. You are a very good daughter."

"But I won't talk to Dad. Not until he apologizes to me and accepts my career choice." Bee took a deep breath. "When he asks to see my designs, I'll be ready to talk."

After signing off, listening to her mother praising her "good daughter-ness," Bee perused the website for the NYC Fashion Award contest for Young Entrepreneurs, or the NYCFAYE. Bee began to think of it as FAYE, a fashionista that she had to impress. To Bee's relief, FAYE's application fee was a little steep, but Bee thought she could swing it. A seven-page application asked for a promotional essay, four to eight photographs and/or sketches to be uploaded to the site, and a video of the applicant describing her designs.

Bee began to smile to herself. All of this was doable, and she knew she would spend this entire weekend getting ready. Later, on her way home, all she could think about was how she would script her video, and which sketches she would use. And, after winning, standing on the runway in the flickering camera lights and cell phone gleams, shaking hands with Emma and Laura, who also had been Central Saint Martin's students, encircled by a bevy of professional models adorned in her clothes.

With a glass of wine, wearing fuzzy Acorn slippers, Bee spread her portfolio across the dining table. Her sketchbook opened to a pink dress with bell-shaped sleeves and skirt. Her mannequin wore pink ribbons wound through her hair, around her wrists, and spiraling up her legs. This one for sure, she thought.

Her phone rang. Picking it up, hoping it would be Alex, she was a little disappointed to see Cam's name come up.

"Miss Bing," Cam said; he sounded like he was in some kind of nightclub. Or one of his drag pageants. "I forgot to ask. What is the name of your line?"

Bee felt like an arrow had gone through her chest. She'd riffled through a gazillion names but had been unable to choose one.

"*Mija*, are you there?"

Bee stared at the pink dress. On the bodice she had sewn an appliqué of a sketch she'd made last year, a wide-eyed doll dressed in pink.

Well, why not?

"Pinky B. My line is called Pinky B."

Chapter Seven

"Do I or do I not enter this contest?"

Sitting on Wendy Zan's luxurious hand-knotted silk rug, her back against the Dresden sofa, Bee raised her Manhattan. She had assembled Team B Plus, demanding that this meeting take place after everyone had left work or school in the Tribeca condo owned by Jojo's parents, where Bee had bunked with the rest of the Leftovers back in the day.

Stretched out on the sofa's chaise section, Mei gently prodded her with her left foot. "Why would you even consider not entering?"

"Don't trash that carpet." Picking up one of the remaining dumplings from the dish on the coffee table, Tina leaned over the surface to dramatically take a dainty bite. She had been curled at the sofa's end opposite Mei, and between them perched Cam, whom Bee had invited to come when she found out Jojo wasn't available.

Wearing his own personalized red Pinky B T-shirt, Wan Pi

moved from guest to guest, in hopes of treats. Bee kept one eye on him at all times. He was a master at thieving food from any coffee table.

It was a bad sign that Jojo couldn't be here. Bee needed her best bestie's quirky but reliable advice more than anything. Sitting on the floor of her apartment, surrounded by photos, sketches, bits of fabric, trims, buttons, and beer, she had felt a heavy weight in her gut.

I can't do this. I can't. They'll never take me. They'll laugh or throw my sketches into the toilet or post my photos on "The ten worst outfits you'll never want to wear." Why am I even thinking of doing such a thing?

But Jojo wasn't here, and Jojo hadn't told her what she had going that took precedence over a Leftovers coven. Even so, it comforted Bee to be back in the condo with her friends around her.

She stifled a sigh. She was sick of sighing. Sigh-sick. "Don't you get it, Mei? What if I don't get accepted? Or what if I get accepted and then lose, or get kicked out after one day, or they don't like my designs?"

"The way I see it, you'll never know unless you apply. No one wins an Olympic gold medal if they aren't in the Olympics, Bee-babe." Stretching her arms over her head, Mei gave Bee a sideways glance. "In my book, entering even though you're afraid is a great success, to quote some self-help book I read a million years ago."

"Yes!" Tina added with her mouth full.

"And regardless of whether you make it in or not, girlfriend," said Cam as he got to his feet and picked up the martini pitcher, "you are too freakishly talented not to keep at it. Just remember how many times the first Harry Potter novel got turned down by every major publisher in NYC before it got published over the pond."

Bee held out her empty martini glass. "And this has to do with my fashion empire how?"

"*Mija.* Don't you pay attention? Harry Potter was so hot overseas that it ended up in a wild bidding war between New York publishers. You know how that turned out, right? Seven books, eight movies, a stage play, J. K. becomes richer than the queen—well, richer than *this* queen, anyway." He leaned over and peered at her, one eyebrow raised. "You don't give up, *mija.* You just don't. You can't be *mi amiga* if you give up."

"All I want is to get a name, and offers for my line, and the money to set up a shop."

Leaning back into the sofa, Tina asked, "Do you get your entry money back if you're turned down?"

"Oh, Tina," Mei said. "That is not helpful."

"Well, I think it is helpful." Tina crossed her legs as Cam stepped over her to resume his seat between them. "Because it makes you think about your worth. Is a chance to win a hundred thou worth throwing in 125 bucks? Are you worth 125 dollars?"

"Okay, so it's a gamble." Cam counted his fingers. "That's investing, what—10 percent—"

"Actually, that would be 0.125 percent," said Mei.

"So I'm not Einstein." Cam slid off the couch to sit beside Bee. "The thing is, J. K. Rowling didn't give up until her book sold. You miss out on this contest, there are a dozen more out there just as special."

Bee said, "Yeah, you have a point. But I don't have that much money."

"You could ask Raj for a raise."

Bee rolled her eyes at him. "I just got a raise."

Cam gaped at her. "You did? When?"

"Don't worry about the money." Tina picked up another dumpling, grimaced, and set it down again. Wan Pi watched her every move. "You can worry about that later. Besides, you've got friends with money."

"Who has money?" Jojo's voice came from the foyer as she closed the front door behind her. She wrinkled her nose. "Is there anything else to drink besides martinis?" Taking off her coat, she flung it onto a chair. She was grinning from ear to ear.

Cam got to his feet. "I'll pour you a glass of Riesling if you tell us how much Ecstasy you're on."

Jojo stopped at the edge of the living room carpet. "Um, I'm giving up alcohol for three months. A sort of cleansing. Ask me if I just had a meeting with Jackie Chan."

Bee felt her jaw drop. Cam set the bottle of Schloss Schönborn down heavily on the kitchen island. Mei sat up, and Tina reached for a dumpling. Bee didn't know which of Jojo's news items stunned her the most: having a face-to-face with Jackie Chan or taking a booze holiday.

"Did you?" asked Cam. "Have a meeting with Jackie Chan?"

Jojo's grin got bigger. She went into the kitchen to raid the fridge.

Bee said, "Spill, woman. What the hell happened?"

Beaming, Jojo pulled out a bottle of orange juice and poured herself a glass. "We discussed filming my screenplay. He's assigned me a veteran writer to help me work out the kinks."

"What does that mean?" Tina set the dumpling down again, watching Jojo as she returned to the living room and dropped into a chair.

Jojo shrugged. "It needs polishing. I mean, it is my first serious attempt. And I get to work with someone who knows screenwriting inside and out."

Bee stretched her legs under the coffee table. "I don't think I'd like some old guy messing with my stuff."

"Actually, it's a middle-aged woman, and writers always can

learn from other writers." Jojo raised her eyebrows. "You learned from other designers at school. I think of it as a great learning experience to work with experts."

Bee considered this as she tasted her drink. It was so like Jojo to be optimistic and seek out the good in every weirdness. She was the glass-half-full queen.

"You missed the fun." Mei pulled her knees up to her chest. "We've solved world hunger, developed a plan for lunar travel, and, using Las Vegas odds, convinced Bee she should enter the contest."

"That's fantastic." Jojo raised her glass of OJ. "A toast!"

"To Pinky B!" Cam added. They gaped at him. "Bee's fashion line. Isn't that the most adorable name?"

"I love it," cried Tina.

"To Pinky B." Jojo got to her feet. They all rose, holding glasses high. "The most fabulous fashion in funky NYC!"

Bee felt as if she could float to the stars as she climbed into the Uber with Wan Pi. The night was clear, crisp, and smelled like good fortune. It was barely nine o'clock, and Bee was looking forward to getting home and working deep into the night on her ideas. But as the car traveled north through Tribeca, she found she couldn't stop thinking about Alex.

Jojo's good luck with her screenplay raised Bee's hopes, hopes that she too would find luck. Before they got to West Fourteenth, Bee asked the driver to take her to Chelsea instead.

"You'll have to enter it on the app," he groused, turning on his blinker.

When she arrived at Alex's apartment building, Bee hesitated before she rang the bell.

What am I doing here? She probably won't even answer. She

might be at work. What am I going to say? And what if her room-mates are home? Do I apologize to her right in front of them?

She almost turned away. The bright, breezy night she'd seen around her seemed suddenly wrapped in heavy clouds. What did Cam say? *You can't be mi amigo if you give up.*

To her utter relief, Alex buzzed her in.

The golden fox's delicious hair was wet, and she wore a ratty plaid robe as she leaned out her front door to watch Bee come down the corridor. A smile turned up one corner of her mouth, then was gone. But just seeing that one little sign made Bee's heart sing.

Stopping in front of Alex, Bee lowered her chin and puffed out her lips. "I torry."

Alex noticed the wriggling dog at Bee's feet. "Oh, Wanna Pee came to visit me! Hullo, little handsome man. You look so dashing in your tuxedo coat—and it's over your T-shirt! Quite the fashion statement."

Ignoring Bee, Alex knelt and cuddled the dog, who avidly licked her cheek. When she rose, she folded her arms under her generous breasts and sighed deeply. Stepping back, she gestured for Bee to come inside. The roommates were home, although one of them, a graceful Latina whose name was Lulu, was dressed in scrubs and appeared like she was about to head out the door to go to work.

Lulu greeted her. "Hi, Bee. How's things?"

"Better, now."

Alex's other roommate sprawled on the sofa in front of the TV. She was older than the others with gray-speckled hair, and they called her Grammy. She tiredly waved one hand in Bee's direction.

Alex asked Lulu, "Are you done in the conference room?"

"Yeah. Off to the salt mines." Lulu grabbed her coat. "You two behave now."

"I don't wanna 'have!" both Alex and Grammy shouted, startling Bee. She wondered what the neighbors thought about this.

As Lulu breezed out the door, Alex pointed at Bee, then gestured with her finger that Bee was to follow her.

The "conference room" was the bathroom. Besides the single bedroom, which belonged to Grammy, there was nowhere else to have a private conversation.

Alex sat down on the toilet, the same throne Bee had occupied all those months ago as Nurse Ingles stitched her up after she crashed her scooter. She looked solemnly up at Bee.

Lowering herself to tile floor, Bee sat on her coat and unzipped Wan Pi's little tuxedo jacket that she had sewn for him to wear on cold winter nights. It took her a moment to get her words in order, but she finally said, "That was a shit show, last week. I'm sorry I dragged you into that drama. I was mad as hell, but I know there's no excuse for it. I really am sorry. I know this isn't the first time I hurt your feelings, and it won't happen again. At least, I'm going to really, really try."

She waited, wanting to say more, but she knew she was in danger of contracting foot-in-mouth disease. Her heart raced, and she hoped Alex couldn't see it hammering under her ribs.

"You know what your problem is?" Alex gazed down her nose at Bee shaking her head. "You have Luke Skywalker syndrome. You are always trying, and then you yell, 'It's impossible!' As Yoda says—"

"Judge me by my size, do you?" Bee joked.

"'All his life has he looked away,'" Alex quoted, poking Bee just as Yoda poked Luke. "'To the future, to the horizon. Never his mind on where he was . . . what he was doing.'"

"I promise." Bee couldn't stop herself from smiling. She crossed her fingers. "I will try to keep my mind on where I am and what I'm doing and who I am doing it around."

Alex smiled primly. "'Do or do not,'" she intoned. "'There is no try.'"

Slipping to the floor in front of Bee, Alex leaned in for a kiss. Bee felt as if the bathroom was rising to heaven as she tasted Alex's sweet, moist lips. The touch of Alex's damp hair was like stroking thick mink.

There is no try. There is only do. Do and do and do.

Chapter Eight

By Sunday, when Alex was available to help, Bee filed several photos of skirts, including the ribbon skirt, a version of Alex's spaghetti-strap long tee with a silk screen of the Singapore skyline, and lavish floral-print bell bottoms. She festooned her body dress form with lace trim, filmy silk-screened scarves, and items from her thrift-store scrounging: gloves, leggings, slouchy mismatched socks. She hastily designed two new hats, a vagabond embroidered with secondhand beads, and a bucket style sewn of multiple fabrics and feathers. She had to safety-pin the parts together for her photos.

All this was the easy part. The hard part she had kept avoiding until today, Sunday, but she knew she had to face it. Alex was here to act as director and voice coach while Bee recorded herself on her phone.

It was a rainy, unseasonably warm winter day when Alex arrived with the anticipated venti cappuccinos. Bee wanted to sit in the middle of her living room amid a sea of sewing materials and talk about herself, picking up a hat or a yard of silk, but Alex talked her out of that. Bee had to agree that it would be better for an edited video of Bee close-ups—hair rainbowed and gelled, wearing earrings that Alex had made from repurposed beads, a ribbon tied around her neck, and wearing one of her silk-screened tees.

"Better to not take the attention away from your creations so it's all on yourself, not them," Alex told her after Bee said she would wear one of her bright, puffy-sleeved print blouses for the shoot. "Be subtle. Let the fashions talk."

Bee was grateful for Alex's calm. Inside she felt more jittery than a chihuahua at a clog dancing contest.

"And talk slower," Alex ordered from behind the phone, propped on the dining table against a stack of fashion and art books.

Referring to her notes, fussing with her hair, licking her lips, and then having to reapply her lipstick, Bee fumbled over her opening. Alex stopped the recording, and by the third time around Bee had filmed the first section, describing her line and the rationale for the name.

After introducing herself, Bee explained that the engine behind her creations was instinct, a quality she greatly cherished. She described the purely emotional reaction to "a look" as arising from an unspecified place within—a feeling, a knowing. Being a fan of bright colors, Bee loved all shades of pink as a child, until her mother began to tease her with the nickname "Pinky."

Alex raised her eyebrows. With a mocking smile, she shook her head. But Bee pretended not to notice, ignoring Alex's reaction to this little secret, pressing on, describing that color is infinite.

"We haven't even seen all possible color combinations or bothered to try to name them. In my styles, I think those enigmatic combinations speak to the person who looks at them, creates feelings of well-being, fun, and even hope."

Nodding, Alex turned off the phone. Next, they filmed Bee standing next to a dress form. After that, a layout of her trims and hats as Bee talked in the background, describing her techniques, the fabrics she loved best and why, and her love of ideas.

"Despite what the haters say, fashion is art. We adorn ourselves every day, giving thought to each garment, even without realizing it. Not only that, fashion is fun. And best of all, it makes us feel real good!"

They finished with a shot of Bee sitting cross-legged on her coffee table, beading a repurposed denim jacket. Alex panned in on Bee's hands as she threaded the bead and pushed the needle into the felt.

After she turned off the video, Bee said, "I wish we had time to add a soundtrack. Something like 'Taco Cat.'"

Chuckling, Alex fell onto the sofa. By the time they had completed the finished product, it was late afternoon. Squall after squall had hit Manhattan. Now, briefly, the setting sun was out. "I think it's better without music. Music feels manipulative, maybe, huh?"

Maybe, Bee thought. *WWJD? What Would Jojo Do?*

Doubts crowded her mind again. But she remembered what Jojo had said when Bee panicked about being so late to enter.

"Well, look at it this way. Your application will be one of the last ones the judges see. This way it's bound to stick in their minds."

Swinging around, Bee climbed onto the sofa beside Alex. She snuggled against her, thinking how much she liked it when her golden fox was around. Wan Pi, who much to his displeasure had spent a lot of the time during the filming shut in the bedroom, pushed his way between them.

"Hey," Bee said, "we're going to gang up and subway out to Flushing to visit Tina's parents' dumpling truck. Want to come?"

"I thought you'd never ask. Good job, Luke."

Reaching over to tickle Alex, she saw Alex gazing up and out the window to where, at this angle, a shred of sky was visible. "Look at that," she breathed.

Bee gasped as she followed Alex's pointing finger. A rainbow arced over the eastern sky against a backdrop of silvery-gray clouds.

"Talk about colors," Bee said, filled with awe. "That is so beautiful. If only I could capture something like that."

Alex leaned her head on Bee's shoulder. "Now I know you're going to get into the contest."

Bee sat before her laptop for several minutes before she hit SEND early Wednesday morning before she left for work. She'd loaded the photos, video, and essay to the contest website. She reviewed her checklist for the sixth time. She hoped all her T's were crossed and her I's dotted.

It was late. Alex had gone home. Night appeared in her window —the apartment building across the street showed few lights. Most people were in bed by now.

All this work. What if it's for nothing?

Team Bee had told her over and over, each time they met for coffee, cocktails, or to see the newest exhibit at the Met, that she must press on, put this insane prepping period behind her, and continue to develop her look.

I could work on the Alex brand, she told herself. *I could call it Golden Fox, open a store selling only her look. Silk-screened tees, denim shorts repurposed with ribbons and trims, large-brimmed hats. Hiking and climbing skirts sewn of strips of patterned fabrics from Malaysia.*

It felt good to take up her pencils and begin to sketch her ideas. As she studied a finished drawing, she smiled to herself.

"I'm good," she said to the page. "To hell what some judge says."

In the following days, Bee tried to keep busy at work, focusing on proofing, recalling how much she used to like mining words and digging up mistakes, and browsing through the web for inconsistencies in citations and misappropriation of phrases. The contest was due to start on the eighth of March, giving the competition managers only nine days to choose fifteen participants.

She made a rule for herself not to check the FAYE website for updates until the end of each day at exactly four thirty. Cam and Jojo annoyed her with questions: Did you hear yet? Any news? Jojo sent her cheerful messages of lines quoted from science fiction movies.

I'll take the Ring to Mordor, although I do not know the way.

I am one with the Force. The Force is with me.

Neo, sooner or later you're going to realize, just as I did, that there's a difference between knowing the path and walking the path.

Bee finally sent one back: *I'm sorry, Dave. I'm afraid I can't do that.* Which was the only science fiction line she could dredge out of her memory.

Friday, February 26, brought in a heavy storm, blanketing New York City with a lush robe of snow. Waking up early to the special glow through her bedroom window that signaled snow everywhere, Bee dressed carefully for the walk into the office. She decided to wear her red wool coat, a masterful find at Goodwill. She had a yellow watch cap that the mother of one of the girls in her Scrabble club had knitted for all of them. With a kelly green scarf and her favorite gloves, Bee laced up her Doc Martens, dressed Wan Pi in a matching red wool jacket and red nylon foot cozies, and crunched through the drifts. On the sidewalks before the Christodora House lay a carpet of ice-melter—the management had gotten on it early. But Bee loved the sound of snow under her boots, so she was happiest when trudging along sidewalks where few had gone before.

She was the first one in the office. As she peeled off her layers, warm from her hike, Bee felt a little nauseous. Last night Jojo and Alex—she'd called both of them—were able to talk her down from her certainty that she had been rejected. But this morning the unease was back, gnawing at her gut. To assuage this, she turned on her computer and began browsing for more contests. There were dozens, she saw with relief, and she felt way better prepared than she had when she decided to try out for FAYE.

People began to file in. Noisy Jojo breezed in, thumping down her Winchester Coffee travel mug, unzipping and bumping and jingling. She opened and closed her file cabinet. Bee slipped on her headphones.

Jojo's head appeared around the corner of Bee's cubicle.

"Any news?"

Bee wished she could ignore her friend, but she didn't want to. Slowly she shook her head.

Jojo made a pouty face, then handed Bee a cheddar/mustard/bleu cheese scone from Third Rail Coffee.

Taking it, Bee blew her a kiss. She had no appetite at all.

Today, for some reason, dragged endlessly. The clock on the wall next to Raj's office acted like it was broken. Bee read the same paragraph three times, trying to understand what was wrong with it. She knew there was something, but her brain felt too foggy to figure it out.

Cam breezed by in a flowing black cape. The scent of cold air wafted over Bee as he stopped beside her cubicle.

Keeping her chin tucked, Bee made eye contact with him and shook her head.

Shrugging in an exaggerated way, Cam leaned down and gave her a kiss on the cheek before he continued to his office.

By three o'clock p.m. Bee was ready to go home and to stop in at Molly's on the way for a stiff drink. Her chin in one hand, she scrolled through the manuscript she had been struggling with all day to see how much further she had to go. Another twenty pages.

Okay, I can do that, then Molly's.

At 4:25 precisely, Bee started to log off her computer when an email alert message she'd tried to ignore flitted away. She froze, then swiftly poked up the mail program.

Gulping, she read the subject line: New York City Fashion Award contest for Young Entrepreneurs.

The judging panel of the NYCFAYE is pleased to accept you as a contestant in the Young Entrepreneurs lineup of exciting new talent . . .

Bee must have made a loud noise, because even Cam heard it from wherever he was, and both he and Jojo appeared like magicians at her desk.

"What. What?" Jojo was practically jumping up and down. Cam fanned his cheeks.

Falling back in her chair, Bee whispered. "I'm in."

Jojo bent down to read the email. Cam engulfed her in a big cuddling hug.

"You go, girl!"

"Oh my God, Bee." Jojo read the email, muttering the words to herself. "They say there's a welcome packet in the mail, and they have a special contestant login here, and oh my God, you're going to be famous!"

Raj's office door opened, and he came over also. "What's all this then?"

Bee opened her mouth to speak, but her throat wouldn't work.

Jojo and Cam excitedly filled in Raj. He regarded Bee with a half-smile.

"I wondered what all the visits to your cubicle this past week were about," he said. "Congratulations."

While Cam proposed celebratory drinks in the Village, Bee's shock began to drain away. Her number one wish was within her reach. She was really going to be able to launch her own show. Then, reality began to sneak around her feet like a hungry rat.

Now the real work starts. Now that you've bitten, you have to chew.

Chapter Nine

Alex woke up tired. She'd promised to be at Bee's apartment before eight, but she'd somehow missed the alarm. The last two twelve-hour shifts in the Presby emergency department had been brutally busy, and as she climbed out of her bed behind the shoji screen that shielded it from the living room, she felt mortally grumpy. Maybe she should have spent the night with Bee, as Bee had begged her. But she wanted to get a good night's sleep, and that wouldn't have happened if she was in Bee's bed.

After picking up a latte at Starbucks—it was her lazy way of getting morning coffee, and she always poured it into her travel mug, so she wasn't carrying the mermaid around—she settled into the subway. The crosstown L train was an easy ride to Bee's building in Alphabet City. Usually, Alex felt warm and happy when she was on her way to see her crazy girlfriend, but today she felt oddly miffed. Today the men and women in the model pool from which the designers could choose their models were scheduled to audition for Bee's contest fashion line. One of Bee's many faults, but the only one Alex had a hard time overlooking, was that she was a shameless flirt.

Add to that the fact that Alex was now an hour late and she had promised to come early to help shift the furniture around to provide room for the girls to show off their struts. The first model was arriving at ten o'clock.

"Huzzah," Bee sighed dramatically as she let Alex into her apartment. "She makes her appearance."

Alex received no kiss, not even a cheek peck as Bee whirled away. Wan Pi did greet her, though, and kneeling, Alex hugged the dog, accepted some licks to her ears, and swallowed her disappointment. Bee was understandably wound up tighter than a two-dollar watch. She set Bee's venti on the kitchen counter, pulled off her coat, and said, "Okay, what's first?"

Bee had been busy, Alex could see. Bright clothing cluttered the sofa, coffee and dining tables, chairs and doors.

"Did you sleep at all?" Alex asked, picking up a dress and hanging it up on the clothes rack next to the hall doorway.

"Nope. Help me move the sofa, will you?"

They spent the next forty minutes readying the apartment great room—a large cavern of a room with a Swedish finished wood floor. They moved her worktable and racks closer to the walls, shaded the windows, and set up the spotlights Bee had rented.

Bee pinned sketches on the plain screen, a selection of outfits she would ask the models to wear. She'd spent the last forty-eight hours making adjustments according to the girls' measurements. Bee's boss had given her three weeks off—one of them without pay —when he learned she'd been accepted. The contest schedule was brutal, probably squeezed tight to give the contestants a taste of runway show pressure. To save time, Bee had asked her models to bring their own makeup and extra pairs of shoes and boots; the footwear didn't matter so much at this stage. What mattered was the look and how they wore it.

Alex had been in awe of the models' websites as she scrolled through them while Bee was model shopping through FAYE's offerings. Bee had pegged ten models to interview, six women and four men. The requirement was two men and three women, one of them a plus size. Six were coming today and four tomorrow. Getting a sense of how exhausting this work would be—just being around Bee when she was so buzzed was exhausting—Alex couldn't decide whether she was happy or not about turning down an extra shift the next day so she could help her fashion designer girlfriend.

When the door buzzed, they were pretty much ready. Bee, barefoot, wearing silk palazzo slacks and a form-fitting tie-dyed tank top, raced to open her door. Alex, in her El Capitan tee and Chinese-style Mary Janes, rounded up Wan Pi and sequestered him in the bedroom. It was hard to ignore his whining.

Through Bee's door strode the tallest girl Alex had ever seen. She had long hair the color of white gold and wore jeans and a black sweatshirt with a Givenchy logo.

Grinning up at this Amazon, Bee offered her hand. They shook, and the girl smiled after a quick—and maybe disappointed—look around Bee's great basement "loft." Behind the girl slouched a man barely meeting the model's height, with a mop of black hair over one eye and already looking super bored.

The girl was on time, Alex thought. That's one check. Bee led her over to the rack and began to pull out pieces of clothing she thought would match the girl's Nordic coloring.

"You'll be delicious in this," Bee said as she handed the model, whose name was Tamarin, a deep green-and-blue puffy-sleeve cotton blouse and a stiff matchstick striped skirt of linen with a petticoat to fill it out.

Tamarin gazed raptly at Bee. "Is that an English accent? Are you from England?"

"Sure," Bee said as she fluffed up the sleeves. "By way of Camelot. You heard of it?"

"Sure. That's in England, right?" Tamarin said, feeling the fabric of the skirt.

Bee almost said Hong Kong, but she held back. New York City, with its smell of fresh paper, street canyons ringing with blaring horns, and bejeweled evenings, was Bee's anecdote to bad memories of Hong Kong.

Tamarin had no qualms in stripping to her undies—no bra, of course—and standing patiently as Bee dressed her. Then Bee led her to the bathroom where Bee also directed makeup color and placement.

On the dining table, pushed against a wall underneath one of the daylight windows, was bottled water and an array of finger food, which Bee told Alex the models wouldn't touch. It was mostly for whomever they brought with them. The slouchy boyfriend was already there, idly chewing a slice of rolled-up ham.

Tamarin looked beautiful when she finally emerged. She'd pulled her hair away from her forehead, as Bee had asked. Bee clapped her hands, then proceeded to adorn the model's striking white hair with tiny fan-like ornaments. She added bangles and ribbons and offered ankle socks with beaded lace trim. Tamarin slid into her brown ankle boots; brown was not the ideal color, but at least they had the look.

"Okay, my assistant here is going to video you as you walk up and down." Bee threw Alex a swift glance, and Alex realized she had been demoted to assistant for this fantasy of Bee's. Giving Bee a strained smile, she picked up her phone.

"Okay, go for it. I want smiles. No frowns."

Nodding obediently, Tamarin got into her runway style, strolled toward the screened end of the room, whirled around with a stylish turn of her head to catch Bee's eye, then sashayed back to the hallway entry.

"Very nice," Bee said.

Alex showed Bee her video; it was a little shaky, and the light wasn't quite right.

Bee scowled, just a little, but she tried to smile. Alex wanted to do a good job and felt grateful Bee didn't say anything snide about her work.

"Would you mind, Tamarin, one more time?" Bee asked after she'd adjusted one of the light stands.

After the third girl of the day had come and gone, Alex had a pretty good feel for her filming. But she wasn't happy. As each girl entered, brooding brunette, ravishing redhead (Alex stopped trying to remember their names), she felt more and more like a lumpy burlap sack next to a display of elegant silk purses.

To make matters worse, Bee was acting in a way with these girls that Alex had never seen before. Watching Bee flatter, fearlessly touch, and fawn over the models made Alex itchy in a way that was uncomfortable and unpleasant. When they went to clubs together, there was flirting, sure, but Bee always stayed close and danced only with her.

When girl number four oozed in through the door, dread filled Alex's soul. This girl was stunning, with luminescent blue eyes, thick dark eyebrows, and black hair shorn buzz-cut tight. Even Alex felt a little sting of attraction as she watched the model, in a body-tight shift over leggings, give Bee a beautiful smile.

"Ooh la la, you are a fox, darling," Bee gushed as she offered a hand. "Come into my boutique and show me what you got."

The girl laughed and gazed at Bee with what—to Alex anyway—seemed to be appreciation. Bee was endearingly cute, small, pert, and sardonic all at the same time. All of these were reasons

Alex loved her so much and were huge contributions to Bee's charisma.

Bee obviously had been expecting Bettina "Call me Bettie." She handed Bettie the party dress, an embroidered fantasy of silk, lace, gauze, and lamé, three-quarter length, long-sleeved, and all shades of pearl and ivory. It had taken Bee two full weekends to make this dress, which she promised she would give to Alex to wear at the next gala they attended—as if they got invitations to such events every week.

Alex felt as if she had been punched in the stomach. She was being betrayed, out in the open with everyone to see. Slapped in the face. Turning away, she picked up a hazelnut cookie, broke it in half, and took a bite. It tasted like ash.

You're jealous. You are acting like a jealous shrew.

The depth of this feeling was fierce, making Alex wonder at herself. *What is the matter with me? Bee loves me, right? Doesn't she? Wasn't her use of the possessive "my golden fox" an expression of love?*

Yet Alex knew, just as deeply, that she didn't exactly know the answer to those questions. Bee had never said the L-word out loud or in any degree of seriousness. It was always and ever "luv ya!" and she said that to everyone.

"Call me Bettie" rocked that dress. And she knew how to model it. She drifted across the living room, swirled, smiled just as Bee demanded, and floated back again. Still fuming, Alex filmed it all and had to admit with regretful forgiveness that Bettie was a perfect model for the look.

"Oh, honey. That was fantabulous." Bee crossed the room to Bettie, took her hand, and gave her a swift kiss on the cheek. Bettie flashed those unearthly eyes at Bee, and Alex gritted her teeth when she saw the expression on Bettie's face. Whether Bettie was gay or not, she was coming on to Bee big time, and Bee was enchanted.

"You'll call me, right?" Bettie whispered to Bee, but Alex could hear everything. "Your clothes are amazing. Just wearing this dress makes me feel like an angel. Divine, right?"

Bee ran her hand down Bettie's sleeve. "You bet I'll call you, luv. You can count on it."

After Bettie was safely out the door, Bee stood for a moment and sighed deeply. "Oh, mama. Wow." She turned to face Alex, who pretended to be staring into her phone. "Wasn't she beautiful? Crikey!" Bee fanned her face.

Shrugging, Alex cleared the dining table of leftover strawberries. "Who's next?"

"Oh God, two more. After the Blessed Bettie, I can't even go on."

I'm not sure I can either, Alex told herself, crumpling up a paper plate and hurling it into the garbage can.

Protestations aside, Bee seemed to find it in herself to flatter and fuss over the next male models, one a winsome wheat-colored blond and the other with gorgeous *café noir* skin. The blonde appeared impervious to Bee's compliments; two men accompanied him, roughly thirty-something, well dressed, checking their expensive watches as the model traipsed up and down the room in a woven ribbon kilt and silk-screened muscle shirt.

Black Coffee was sweet, but was trying too hard to please, Alex thought, praising the outfits in a giggling voice, chattering nonstop about the quaintness of the Christodora House and how he *adored* Bee's hair and *adored* the taste of the bottled water.

"My favorite!" he exclaimed, snagging two more bottles before he bustled out the door.

Bee flung herself onto the couch, spreading her arms along the sofa's back. "Even the guys are delicious! I'm going to love this." She wrinkled her face when she heard Wan Pi barking from the bedroom. "C'mon. We really need to walk him." Bee hopped to her feet and trotted down the hall to let him out.

I'm not going to love this. Alex had started to pack up the food, but she knew a walk would do her good.

The city evening was briskly cold; a breeze chilled the air, but the sky was clear. Once they'd crossed Avenue Bee to Tompkins Square Park, Alex said, "I think I'm going to work tomorrow. I got offered an extra shift and I can make a lot of overtime."

"Wait. You said you'd help me tomorrow, too."

"No. I never committed to tomorrow." Alex was sure that she had told Bee Sunday might not be possible; before today she had decided she was going to turn down that shift. She stood behind Bee as Bee scooped up Wan Pi's turds. "I don't think I can take another day of watching you drool over these women, one after the other."

Bee stared at her as if she was taken aback. "Huh? What are you talking about? This is how it works. You schmooze. You kiss ass. They need to like you as much as you like them. These guys need the work, otherwise their agencies wouldn't send them to the hedge funders to hire them."

Alex felt stung. She'd hoped Bee would respond with a laugh, saying, "Yeah, I'm a bit covered in saliva."

"Don't you think you went overboard with the ass kissing? I suppose models are used to being man, I mean, woman-handled. But is that a respectful way to do it? Is your touching and kissing professional? I don't think so."

Bee stared at her goggle-eyed, as if she had just grown two horns. In fact, Alex felt as if she *had* just grown two horns, both fed by jealousy. She watched Wan Pi stand politely as an elderly man petted him. She replied, "I'm going home now. This scene is just not for me."

"No you're not. Wait a minute." Bee was across the sidewalk

beside her. "Okay, so, maybe I don't know what I'm talking about, but in the fashion world people need to like you. They need to want to work with you."

Alex shook her head, sliding a hand into her backpack front pocket to find her subway pass. "You are likable, Bee, very likable, except when you're faking it up with the schmooze. It looks bad, that's all. I just think you need to tone it down."

Alex felt Bee touch her hand and allowed herself to be gently pulled to face Bee. "Hey, okay, maybe I played it too high." She shrugged. "You know, I was so nervous, I would have kissed a statue covered with pigeon shit."

Reaching up, Bee dug her fingers into Alex's hair. "I'll try to do better. Tomorrow. You'll be here, right? You'll see."

Alex felt herself lean into the touch of Bee's hand on her temple. "Remember what Yoda said."

Bee pressed herself against Alex, who felt all the icy green resentfulness inside her melt away.

"I remember," Bee said. "I will do better. I am doing better already." She slid her hands under Alex's coat and around her waist.

The old man, now walking away, turned back to stare.

Bee kissed Alex, long and deep. Afterward, Alex pulled her phone from her coat pocket.

"I have to call the hospital." She hoped she sounded solemn, and it must have worked because Bee appeared worried.

When the supervisor answered, Alex asked if he'd found someone for that shift tomorrow. Bee's hands dropped to her sides.

Listening, Alex began to smile. "That's great. What a relief. Okay, bye."

"So you're going?" Bee's shoulders sagged.

"Who, me?" Alex pocketed her phone. "They found someone else. I was just checking. Professionalism, you know."

Alex put her arms around Bee as Bee fell against her like a purring cat.

Wan Pi was tugging at the leash as if to say, *Okay, you've kissed and made up. Let's go home. It's cold out here!*

"Hey, what's for dinner?" Alex breathed into Bee's ear. "Shall I order something?"

Bee shook her head, straightened, grabbed Alex's hand, and pulled her toward Avenue B and the Christodora House.

"Dessert first," she said.

Chapter Ten

Saturday's Parade of Beauties had been stressful enough for Bee, but Sunday was a disaster. One of the models cancelled at the last minute, and the next three were pretty, but one was hungover, another was in a very bad mood, and the third had lied about her measurements and didn't fit into any of Bee's outfits.

All through this torture, Bee sensed that Alex was moody too, but she brushed it off to weariness; last night had been loads of fun, but sleep had not been in the cards. The last model, the one who had eaten one too many cannoli over the past week or so, had a temper fit when she felt a seam rip in one of Bee's silk blouses.

"You told me these clothes would fit. See this seam? These are lousy, sloppy." She waved one of the sleeves after she struggled out of the shirt. "This cuff isn't even straight."

This one had brought her husband. He joined in defending her as Bee scowled over the ripped seam—and the insults.

"Who are you, anyway?" The man, tall and entitled and with a layer of fat around his middle—he looked roughly a century older than his wife—waved his arm to take in all of Bee's living room. "This isn't a studio, it's a basement. A cellar. If you want my girl to work for you, you need to have quality. Quality clothes, quality sets, and—" He picked up one of Bee's ribbon miniskirts. "What is this, anyway? A circus outfit? Who's going to wear this stuff?"

"It's up to the judges to critique my designs," Bee began to explain, feeling confused, which made this guy irritate her even more.

"Sam, they hired me for this contest. You knew that," blurted the model. "Ari didn't tell me anything more than that." She stomped across the room toward her coat.

Her husband followed. "Ari is a schmuck. He also didn't tell us this contest is full of dykes."

"Hey, hold on there, partner." Bee closed in on the man, hands in fists and ire rising greatly in her chest. Wearing what Alex called her "Chinese demon face," Bee raised a finger and pointed it at his chest. "You are way out of line, arsehole."

Wifey, who had sidled over to the table, elbowing Alex aside, picked up a plate of cookies and said, "You saw what she did, honey, didn't you?" She folded up the plate and slid it into her capacious purse.

The man's upper lip curled. "Yeah, I saw it. I saw you run your hand down my wife's ass. I don't know what you thought you were doing, but—"

"I was pulling wrinkles out of the skirt!"

"Yeah. Sure. Let's get the fuck out of here." They swung away, stomping mightily on Bee's Swedish finished floor.

After the door slammed shut, Bee said, "I think we just had a close call with Housewives of The Hamptons." She was shaking. If there was one thing that blew her top, it was anyone but another dyke calling her a dyke.

Without a word, Alex began to clear the table. Bee's phone rang and she nearly dropped it as she picked up. The model who backed out had changed his mind, saying the conflicting appointment he'd made was cancelled—how about that, Bee thought—and could he drop by for an audition now?

"Sure, honey. Come right over."

When she got off her phone, Bee saw Alex buttoning up her coat.

"Aw, you can't desert me now. The one who cancelled is on his way." Bee was tired too, and she almost didn't have the energy to sweet talk Alex into staying, but she had to try. "Come with me to walk Wanna Pee."

Shaking her head, Alex picked up her hat. "Nope. I'm tired. And besides, I also saw you run your hand down that woman's butt."

"I wasn't—"

"No. Bee, I'm just over it, okay? I'm going home to sleep for the next day and a half before I have to go back to work."

"Brilliant. Yeah. Abandon me when I really need your help." Any thought of cajoling Alex flew from Bee's mind. She felt like if she said anything more she would spit fire.

She watched as Alex lingered at the door shaking her head, hoping that her girlfriend would smile, sigh, and take off her goddamned coat. But instead, Alex turned the knob and left.

Bee looked around her empty apartment. Clothing that had in the first few hours been hung back up neatly now hung on the backs of chairs, floor, doors, and the radiator. Crumbs and half-eaten cheese triangles littered the table. And shit, she hadn't gotten today's videos from Alex. After picking up Wan Pi to give him a hug, she quickly walked him and came back, shivering from the cold outside.

She picked up her ribbon miniskirt from the floor and clipped it to a hanger, but the last thing she wanted to do right now was clean.

Or go through the list of available models and schedule more interviews for some evenings next week.

Jojo answered the phone on the first ring. Bee could hear a
basketball game on in the background—Jim loved basketball.

"Hey, I'm glad you called," Jojo said. "Jim is in hoops land and
I am stuck on a scene in my female warrior novel where one of my
Nǚ zhànshì is supposed to have an argument with her best friend."
She sighed. "I need distraction! How did the model interviews go?"

"Exhausting. The big designers have other people to deal with
this, but I have to do it myself." Bee lay on the couch, head
dangling off the edge, feet on the back. She hoped the position
would help ease the pain in her neck.

"Will you be judged on this, too? The quality of your models?"
Jojo's voice sounded gleeful.

"It's the look, Jojo. If it didn't matter how the model wears the
clothes, then I could use dress forms on roller skates."

"What were they like? Were they all beautiful?"

"Uh, yeah. This is the first time I've worked with professionals
like these." Bee sighed yearningly. "It was like I had just been
elected the queen of the Amazons. The men weren't bad, either. But
this *one* ducky—too beautiful to live. I'll definitely use her. She had
eyes like the Caribbean Sea—"

Bee stopped herself. She heard the sound of a spoon stirring the
contents of a glass or a mug.

"You having iced tea?"

"Brrr. No, idiot. Hot chocolate. Mexican hot chocolate, to be
exact."

"One thing, though," Bee began, remembering the beautiful
Bettie and how she felt like they clicked. "Alex got all pissy with

me. She didn't like my method. She said it looked bad when I flattered them and got all girlie. That I wasn't professional. Sure, I was having fun with them, but that's how it works. They might need the money, but if they don't like you, they won't work with you. I didn't get Alex's problem. So what if I flirted with them. Big whoop."

"You flirted with them in front of Alex." It was a statement, and the way Jojo said it felt like a rebuke.

"Sure. I did. It was a lot of fun, too."

"What do you mean you don't get Alex's problem? You were ready to turn my husband into a soprano because he once got paid to dance for strange women. You weren't even his girlfriend, and you were all, 'Dude, how can you marry this geezer?' He was flirting. For money. With strange women . . . *Fifteen years ago.* You think Alex is being too uptight about your fixation with flat chests? She wears a D cup, at least, Bee. Imagine how that makes her feel."

"Ouch." It was humbling to think Jojo was right. Jojo usually was right. "But jeez, Jojo, we're not a thing, Alex and I. Yeah, we like to party together. She's sexy and great to talk to and real funny and smarter than God. But I've never promised to be monogamous with her."

"Maybe she has a different idea about that. Maybe she's—oh, gasp—actually in love with you."

Bee thought about that, and it worried her. She replied defensively, "That's her problem, isn't it? Those girls liked me. I surprised them because I wasn't like any other designer they'd met, you know, a rebel. A challenge."

"Yeah, Che. You're a renegade. But you need to talk to Alex about this, not me. She's something special, I think."

"You said that about Janelle too and look what happened." Janelle was two years ago. She was special, but not at all in the same way Alex was.

"She was real nice, at first." Jojo's mug clicked against the phone as she took a drink. "Who knew she was stalking you?"

"Yes. And slashed my scooter tires and followed you and me along Fifth Avenue screaming her lungs out because she thought I was cheating on her with you." Bee could even laugh about it now, but at the time she didn't feel amused. "Still, I think I can run my business the way I want. Edgy, breaking the rules of design and color. That's Pinky B."

"I don't know, but you might want to think about what might get back to the judges." Jojo was silent for a beat. "Besides, that's business. Alex isn't business. I think you need to figure out where she fits and then talk to her."

They signed off shortly after Jojo said she needed to get back to work. Jim was cursing in the background as the Bulls scored against the Knicks. Disgruntled, feeling that Jojo hadn't been as sympathetic as she'd hoped, Bee retrieved her coat. Strolling the streets of New York in a Sunday dusk with Wan Pi was the perfect activity to get her head straight. She just might stop in at the Phoenix and take in the drag show. Maybe strike up a chat with a lovely stranger.

Alex would be back. She was like Lassie; she'd always come home.

Chapter Eleven

By the following Saturday, Bee had her roster, which was good because the contest started Monday. Her lineup was Beautiful Bettie, Halemé, and Dot. Also, Felix and Simon —the last-minute cancellation/reschedule. They all seemed easy to work with, appeared to love the clothes, were available for every semifinal run, and had stunning bods. She felt gloriously happy, as if she were not only over the moon but living on it.

That evening, the Leftovers Club and plus ones were joining her for celebratory drinks at Wilfie and Nell's in the West Village. It was Bee's job to arrive first to secure the big booth; the trendy pub was a cheek-by-jowl flirt club and always busy. She'd invited all the models, but they demurred—what busy people they were!

Bee, Alex, and Wan Pi arrived ten minutes after six. Wilfie and Nell's was Frenchie ready, with water bowls on the floor and doggy treats handed out by the waiters. Happy hour was over and the place thinned out briefly before the dinner crowd shoved their way in. She took it as an excellent sign that the booth was just emptying

—she hovered near as jackets, hats, and scarves went on and the men—sweet boys all—filed away.

Diving into the booth, she prayed for the appearance of Jojo and Jim. She and Alex spread their coats and bags over the canvas seat and ordered a Manhattan for Bee and an India pale ale for Alex. Mission accomplished, they blissfully held hands as pub-goers drifted past with envy on their faces.

Leaning over, Bee gave Alex a kiss. Alex had returned last night, but only after Bee begged her and swore there would be no more fawning over models or anyone else.

"What I'm wondering is when are you going to sleep?" Alex pulled her hand away when the drinks came. "You have less than one week to the first semifinal."

Bee took a long sip. The first sip of a Manhattan was like breathing fire. "Practically an eternity. Not. It's like a Call of Duty: Modern Warfare 3. First they watch you sketch out an idea, then— oh, saved. Here's Tina and Raj."

Tina, Raj right behind her, wove through the growing crowd. Grinning, she sighed in relief. "Oh, the booth. Bee, you are Supergirl!"

"You should have seen Alex pick up the guy who tried to steal it from us by the scruff and carry him outside."

Alex gave her a cute smirk. Bee watched, amused, as Raj helped Tina out of her coat. *What a gentleman.*

"Kudos to Alex." Tina slid in beside Alex. She wore a fisherman-style sweater and jeans. She lifted up one of her feet before Raj could sit beside her, so that Alex and Bee could check out her new ankle boots. "Check these out. Stuart Weitzman. Nabbed them at consignment."

Bee nodded her admiration. "At least these are more in line with what an archaeologist might wear to a dig."

"Right, aren't they?" Tina straightened up, and Raj, still in his office uniform of well-fitted shirt and Ted Baker gray jacket, sat down beside her. To his credit, Bee hadn't seen him in a tie since Jojo's wedding.

After they ordered drinks from a tattooed waiter in muscle shirt and tight black jeans, Raj, lowering his eyebrows mockingly, said to Bee, "As your boss, I am concerned about your work ethic. I understand you sewed ten outfits in five days."

Bee saluted. "Alex was just remarking on that."

Jojo and Jim arrived next, sliding in next to Bee. They were out of breath as if they had been running. Jojo gasped, "We were trying to get here to help you hold the table, Bee, but the warp engines in the shuttlecraft are on the fritz."

Jim smiled sheepishly. "In other words, the husband had to catch the end of the game."

"Did the Knicks win?" Raj asked eagerly.

"No." Jim and Alex spoke at the same time.

Bee stared at Alex. "What, you watching the semis?"

Alex shrugged, her lips in a sly smile. She raised her phone. "Pretty easy to follow the scores."

Another round came for Bee and Tina as Jojo and Jim ordered. The IPA was gaining popularity at the table. Just as the drinks were delivered, Mei slid in next to Jim.

"Well, at least it's not dark and silent in here, like a church or a funeral." She was still in her work clothes, a charcoal gray Armani wool suit with a yellow bow blouse. As she shrugged out of her jacket, she picked up the drinks menu.

"This is interesting," she told the waiter, whose smile looked a little strained by now. "This McQueen: Union mezcal, Monkey Shoulder scotch, agave, orange bitters—is it good?"

The waiter's grin widened. "One of our most popular. I highly—"

"I'll have one." Smiling at him in return, Mei set down the menu.

Glasses were raised to Bee's success with the competition, which Jojo christened as Pinky B's Bonanza Bazaar. Bee amused them by describing the incident of the model who fudged her measurements, editing out the part about bum brushing and lesbian bashing, but embellishing the cookie thievery.

For the next round they ordered a pitcher, Bee, Tina, and even Mei filling their pint glasses. Jojo rather conspicuously ordered her beer separately. When Bee raised a questioning eyebrow, Jo said, "I was jonesing for a *hefeweizen*. They have Erdinger—my favorite!" Jojo didn't wish to advertise that she had ordered a non-alcoholic drink.

"Shit like that," Mei told Bee, almost shouting over the cacophony of voices in the increasingly packed bar, "comes with the territory. And with a price. I swear I have lost count of the times I've introduced, or reintroduced, myself to some Gucci-wearing brief-cake as 'Mei,' only to have him say, 'Pleased to meet you, My. You're very pretty, aren't you?' Like to be the office ornament is my stock in trade."

Picking up her glass, she tilted it toward Bee and Alex. "I guess I'll have to start adding, 'Mei, as in the month of May, you know?'"

Mei leaned forward toward Jim, who was sitting next to her. Bee felt a little alarmed, remembering the uncomfortable past they shared.

"Kudos to you, Jim. At least you could pronounce my name correctly. But I swear, most guys were reading from the *Mad Men*'s playbook." She began to tick off her fingers. "Rule number nine: Compliment her hair. Rule number thirteen: Ask her to help you with a spreadsheet, and when she sits in your office chair, reach for the keyboard and 'accidentally' brush her breast with your hand."

Bee and Tina managed to laugh, and when Bee glanced at the

men, she saw Raj smiling uneasily at his drink while Jim seemed to have found something objectionable on the ceiling.

Mei fingered her chin. "What's rule number three?" She snapped her fingers and angled her face Jim's way. "Oh, right. Never ask her about case law, because she might know more than you and then you'll feel emasculated. Spreadsheets or recipes are always safer."

Every female at the table laughed this time. Bee knew that every woman sitting at this table had been in this position more than once.

Jim turned from Mei to Jojo. "I gotta go to the john," he told her, making a face that asked, *Will you ask her to let me out?*

Jojo had been staring at Mei with empathy on her face. "Oh, me too. We need to get out, Mei."

"Oh, sure." Mei slid out of the booth, letting the two escape. A few minutes later, Jojo returned first and seated herself beside Mei, who had scooted over next to Bee.

Settling at the table, Jojo leaned forward and told them in a low voice. "I'm glad I went with him," she said. "Some guy just tried to pick him up. I guess it's the hair."

Bee rolled her eyes. Jim's unique hairstyle—a long, side-parted curtain cut—looked great on him but seemed to attract other men as much as it did women.

"Well," Tina interjected, planting her hands on the table, nearly knocking over Alex's beer—still her first, "I have to tell you the craziest thing. Raj and I went snowboarding up at Whiteface Mountain resort last weekend."

Glancing at Raj, Bee thought her boss seemed worried, but this only made her more eager to hear what happened. "Do tell," she said.

"It was like flying." Tina stared toward the ceiling as if she saw angels up there. "What a rush. I took a wrong turn on the slope and literally flew through the air for twenty feet! It was like a near-death experience," she babbled, having received the requisite ohs, my Gods, and wows.

"You're lucky you didn't get a head injury," lectured Alex.

Tina shook her head. "Yeah, I know. I mean, I really could have died. But it was so, so life-affirming, you know? When Raj dug me out of that snowbank, I was so turned on. Who knew almost dying could be such an aphrodisiac."

"Every jaded scriptwriter in Hollywood?" offered Jojo helpfully, but Tina rolled into a vivid description of how she and Raj made love in the sauna at the spa without anyone being the wiser.

Raj coughed and looked away. Jojo's mouth hung open. Even Bee smelled a whiff of TMI.

"I've never done anything like that before in my life!" Tina enthused. "I got a real thrill out of wondering if we'd get caught. You should have seen Raj's face when I—"

Jojo stood up. "I'm wondering where Jim got to. I hope he wasn't kidnapped. Hey, Raj. Come with me. I might need some heavy muscle." Without another word she disappeared into the crowd. Raj leaned over and kissed Tina on the cheek. "I'll be right back, love."

"Tina, listen." Bee felt a new regard for her egghead, PhD-driven friend. "I know exactly what you mean."

She felt Alex nudge her gently in the ribs.

Mei was close to laughing. "And what dirty little secret are you going to spill?"

Bee's thoughts had gone straight to Bewitching Bettie while Tina told her story. "You have no idea. I've just been through a week of torture, with some of the most beautiful girls in the universe traipsing through my studio."

Bee could see Mei and Tina meeting eyes. They leaned forward to listen.

"I hired the hottest of the hotties. I was lucky to get them," she breathed, remembering Bettina's eyes, Halemé's silky chocolate skin, and Dot's lips. She described each one.

"Bettie looks like an Irish queen, one of the Fae. Creamy skin, mind-blowing eyebrows. And her smile just lit me up."

Bee felt Alex slide a few inches from her side, but she couldn't stop herself. Besides, it was Alex's problem if she couldn't see that Bee had been only flirting with Bettie, nothing serious. Not really.

Also, Bee loved an audience. "And the curvy girl, Dorothy, has more hair on her head than Michelle Pfeiffer, you know, in that one movie. She's a plus model. Incredible proportions. And Halemé looks like she just walked out of a palace in a lost civilization in Zambia. She has hazel eyes, like twin tourmalines."

The girls showed Bee a gratifying amount of interest and adoration, and peppered her with questions about clothes, makeup, boyfriends—girlfriends?—and whether the models were arrogant and self-entitled or sweet-tempered lambs. She vaguely remembered hearing Alex say, "Excuse me" and seeing Mei shift to one side but forgot about it when she dug out her phone after Tina and Mei demanded photos.

By the time Bee was done describing her time with the models, sharing the photos, and finishing her third Manhattan, the club was thinning out. The early-evening jam was over, and now it was time for serious drinking and hooking up.

"Whew." Bee blinked. Her surroundings were fuzzy. "Maybe it's time to split."

Tina was half asleep, chin on one hand. Mei leaned back in the booth, feet curled underneath her. She held a bottle of wine.

When did that come to the table? Bee wondered. *And where did Alex go?*

Jojo and Jim were MIA. Raj hadn't returned to the table either, and if Tina worried about that, she had made no sign so far. Alex would have had to levitate over either Tina on one side or Bee and Mei on the other.

"Where did Alex go?" As if to accentuate this quandary, Wan Pi jumped onto the bench and wagged his tail.

Mei had stretched her feet out on the booth's wooden bench. "I guess she went to the bathroom."

A sick feeling came over Bee. "Let me out."

Raising one eyebrow, Tina scrutinized her. "Didst thou speak?"

"Yeah." Bee felt an itch of panic. "I said let me out."

"Okay." Tina got to her feet and crab-walked from the booth. "Where's my Uber companion?" She squinted down the length of the bar.

Bee scanned the bar where, hours ago it seemed, Jojo, Jim, and Raj had been huddled together. They were gone. She didn't see them at a table, and damn, they couldn't all have gone to the bathroom at the same time.

Mei was pulling her coat on. "I think we got ditched."

Bee's heart sank. Alexis was gone too. Maybe they all had shared a cab home, or Raj had called his car.

Now I've done it.

"Why would they take off like that?" Tina muttered, scrabbling with her phone. "Where's that frigging Uber app?"

Bee tried to remember what she had been blathering about for so long. She remembered laughing hysterically, shouting, clinking glasses together in toast after toast, but what was it all about anyway? Oh, right. Those damn models.

Lassie ran away again. I'm going to have to put a tracker on her.

Chapter Twelve

The slamming of a dumpster lid woke Bee from her dream, where she, Beguiling Bettie, and Alex were riding horses down Fifth Avenue. They were in some kind of parade with colorful banners, marching bands, and convertible Cadillacs. Bee's mount was ploddingly slow, and no matter how many times she kicked the beast's flanks, she couldn't catch up to Alex and Bettie, who surged forward into the crowd. The horses' lovely round rumps glided farther and farther away, tails sweeping the asphalt like feathery brooms.

Staring up at her bedroom window that had a view of the alley where the garbage cans were, Bee reminded herself that while she was in this contest she had to start sleeping in the quieter living room. She unwrapped herself from her bedspread, which had somehow turned her into a human burrito sometime during the night. She was encumbered in this effort by Wan Pi, who had dug himself a comfy den on one side of the burrito.

Oh, goddess, what had happened last night? She'd slept in bra, panties, and leggings; at least she had been conscious enough to get out of her skirt and top before falling into bed. She shook her head, trying to remember how she had gotten home.

In the bathroom, as she perused the smeared mascara and lipstick on her face, the memories hit.

When had Alex left the booth? *While I was yakking about Bettie's eyes? Or—ouch—where I was planning a threesome with— oh my God.*

Bee felt a little sick, rather intensely sick, enough that she knelt before the open toilet for a few minutes until the nausea passed and while Wan Pi stared at her curiously. After washing her face, sliding on her robe, and retrieving her phone from under her bed, she set the tea to boil.

By the time Bee had the mug of tea warming her hands, she had reconstructed the nightmarish celebration, starting with Mei sniping at Jim, Tina embarrassing the hell out of Raj, Jojo—her rock, her bestie—abandoning her, and worst of all, Alex ghosting her again, which she hadn't even noticed at the time.

After forty-five minutes of self-flagellation, while the sky turned concrete colored, she picked up her phone and called Alex. As the phone rang, Bee ashamedly realized that she didn't remember whether Alex was working today. When Alex answered, Bee felt a mix of both relief and fear. She stared out the window as she said hello, as if somewhere out there she would find courage.

"I'm on my way to work right now," Alex said, her voice sounding flat. "Someone had to go home sick, and I agreed to finish his shift."

"Alex, where'd you go last night?"

After a beat, Alex responded, "Where did *you* go? Mars?"

"Yeah, did I? I don't really remember, but, if I said anything . . . uncool or whatever, I'm sorry. We all got a little too lit up."

"You, Tina, and Mei hit the stratosphere."

"I feel terrible. And not just physically. I wouldn't hurt your feelings for any money."

There was a long pause. "Yoda."

"Yoda. I mean it. I'll Yoda all over the place."

"Okay, listen. I really have to get going."

"Come over after work?" Bee wished she had more time. At least Alex was talking to her, even though Bee could tell she was not forgiven. "Or I can pick you up and we can have dinner out?"

"We'll see," was the tepid response. "Maybe I'll drop by later."

Bee wrapped Wan Pi in his yellow fleece Pinky B embroidered coat and took him to the park. The morning sun was still way too bright, even for sunglasses.

"A little too much to drink last night?" Jojo asked when she answered Bee's call.

"Ya think?" Bee slid Wan Pi's leash around one wrist, pulled her travel cup from her backpack, and swigged her quadruple espresso.

"Jim bet me that if we went in to Wilfie and Nell's today we'd find you guys sacked out in the booth. I was pretty sure they'd have tossed the three of you into a dumpster."

"Mei managed to get us into an Uber." Wan Pi was dragging her to the off-leash area and she had to move quickly. "So, did you guys all leave at the same time?"

"Yeah. Raj gave us all rides home."

"Alex too?"

"Uh-huh. Alex too. Did you . . . ?"

"Okay, yeah. I talked to Alex." Bee fumbled with the off-leash gate.

"And?"

"I apologized, and she said she'll try to drop by tonight."

"Okay! You get three gold stars for that."

Bee followed Wan Pi into the off-leash area and freed him. "I owe Raj so many thank yous for the time off. I mean, Joey, he is the best boss ever."

Jo gave a snort. "Yeah, he is. And Tina would totally strangle him if he hadn't let you go work on your contest. Then she'd have him drawn and quartered and trampled by feral ponies and then she'd break up with him."

Bee laughed. She loved that Jojo could always surprise laughter out of her with the stuff that came out of her mouth. Feral ponies. "You know, Joey, if you weren't married, and straight, I'd marry you myself." Her phone alerted her to another call coming in. It was Cam. "Hey, Jo, gotta go. Cam is calling me on the bat phone."

"No worries. Tell him hi for me."

She took Cam's call and said, "Jojo says hi," then leaned against the fence and watched Wan Pi instigate a chase game with a bullmastiff.

"Sorry I couldn't make the big celebration last night," Cam said. "First date with a new man. You understand."

"No, not really. I don't date men."

Cam snorted. "Well, aren't we a pair?"

"You didn't miss much anyway," Bee told him. "Mei and Tina and I got pretty lit and made fools of ourselves. I may have lost my girlfriend, but hey, that's life, right?"

"Dunno, I've never lost a girlfriend."

Wan Pi was now picking on a golden standard poodle. He definitely had short-man syndrome. "You still coming by tonight to help me figure out my life?"

"Oh course, *mija*. I'll be there. You going to feed me?"

"Korean?"

There was a pause and a huffing noise. Bee could imagine Cam wearing his squinchy face. "Honey, only chicken tingo tacos from Maya will do."

Bee ordered from Maya, including enough food for Alex, if she came. On the way home from picking it up with Wan Pi, she'd nabbed a six-pack of Tecates. Spreading the FAYE booklet on the dining table, she reviewed the schedule. It seemed brutal.

"I'm not going to survive the first week, even," she complained to Cam as she let him into the apartment. "Look at this: Monday is a big yawn: Meet the judges and make real nice. Sit through a lecture on the goals of fashion. They make us do this first, thankfully. Next is lunch! Only after all this torture do we get to tour our workspace!"

Cam opened two beers and handed one to Bee. "*Mami*, you need to climb down from the ceiling. Okay, let's review supplies." He settled on one of the chairs and started thumbing through the contest materials while Bee paced the floor, sipping her beer, and trying not to wonder whether Alex was going to come over.

"They are supplying sewing machines, right? Thread? Scissors?"

Cam's voice faded into the background as Bee dove into imagining her life after winning the contest, fans stopping her in the street, their posts overwhelming her Instagram, standing on the runway with her models before a gazillion camera flashes.

Cam's voice broke loudly into her daydream "Oh my God, they're supplying free back-stabbing knives!"

Bee came to a stop then came back to the table. She felt like Cam had just thrown ice water on her.

"Want to tell mama what's on your mind?" he asked as she fell into a chair and pulled the guacamole dip closer.

"Why do I feel like I've been condemned to death?"

Cam stuck a tortilla chip into the guac. "Where is your lovely *chica*? She working tonight?"

"Not here, obviously."

"There's a source for your anxiety right there. It's not like you, Bee, to fuss about a girlfriend."

Bee sighed, wishing she could unwind herself and melt onto the floor. "I know. It's weird, right?"

Cam leaned his chin on one hand. "Could this possibly be because she's running away from you, instead of the other way around?"

Bee felt like Cam had just bitten her. "What do you mean?"

"That you aren't comfortable doing the chasing, girl."

Bee froze as the truth of what Cam was saying soaked in. She picked up a tortilla chip, scooped up a bolus of guac, then set the chip down. "Jesus."

After he left, Bee settled on the couch and turned on the TV. She didn't have the cojones for any more competition planning. She felt completely and utterly knackered, but maybe she was still hungover from last night. She found herself feeling angry at Alex but didn't understand why.

No, she understood it, all right. Cam was wrong—it had nothing to do with not wanting to do the chasing. Alex didn't accept Bee for who she was; that was the problem. She liked to have fun, she liked new things, she liked new girls, and she liked Alex. What was so hard to understand about that? Alex just needed to lighten up, enjoy what was right in front of her. That was it; that was all.

Wasn't it?

Chapter Thirteen

Tina Lu wished she had brought a heavier coat, but the March evening being so silky warm, she told Raj to book an outdoor table at the Merchant River House. The clear, breeze-swept sky made the Jersey City skyline across the Hudson resemble a lost city from a fantasy novel.

Raj was already seated by the time Tina got there after catching an Uber from the campus, where she'd spent the afternoon in the library working on her thesis. Her favorite Merchant cocktail, the Airmail, was waiting for her. She leaned over to kiss him, but his smile seemed a little stiff.

As she sat down, Tina pulled her feet partly out of her new, gently used Manolo Blahniks and raised her glass. "Here's to whatever is bothering you today and hopes that I can make it go away."

Raj's smile got a little fonder. He touched his wine glass to hers and drank.

She gave herself a few seconds to simply admire him. Full-lipped, with glossy wavy hair and big, dark chocolate eyes, he was a stunner. And it didn't seem to matter whether he was just crawling out of bed or wearing a tux at a fancy party, it was so easy to drink up his loveliness.

"How is it you always look so good?" he said to her, as if he could read her mind but turned her thoughts around on her. Ever the gentleman when he was with her, thoughtful, caring, complimentary Raj knew how to charm.

Feeling warmed under his gaze, Tina was glad she had dressed up a bit. She'd found the draped shoulder yellow wool top at a consignment store, and paired with tight black velvet slacks, she felt she'd scored. She'd lost weight since she'd been seeing Raj and had never felt so good about her body.

They ordered, and Tina fearlessly selected the Bolognese pasta. Since Raj still appeared to be distracted, she told him about her day, trying to keep her students awake and her awe in reading about the discovery of the earliest sheet music—only the sheet was stone and the notes hieroglyphics.

Finally, when the dishes arrived—Raj ordered the lobster roll— she stabbed her fork into the pappardelle and pointed it at him. "Okay, 'fess up. What's wrong? If it's about last night, I'm really sorry. I seem to drink a bit too much when the other girls are in celebration mode."

Setting down his sandwich, Raj shook his head. "I had to turn down Jojo's book."

Tina set her fork on her pasta dish. *Poor Jojo!* She knew Jojo was a good writer; when they were roomies, she had snuck a peek at one of Jojo's short stories but hadn't been able to finish it before Jojo returned from the swimming pool.

"Why?" she asked incredulously.

Sighing, Raj looked truly disappointed. "She's a good writer. With a little polish by an editor, at the right house, this book would sell. But not through us."

"You publish books, don't you? Fiction too, right? Not just fashion and food?"

"Yes, but I can't help her right now."

They sat in silence. Tina stared at the artistic swirls the pasta made in her dish. *Jojo will be heartbroken.*

She asked, "But why, exactly? If the book is good—oh, wait, is it because it's a fantasy? Is that it? Too genre ghetto for Gray Ghost?"

Raj was taken aback. "No. We've got fantasy in our catalog. I thought you knew that. Science fiction, suspense, thrillers." He hesitated. "It's more a business decision."

Tina felt a twinge of shame for not knowing what sort of books her boyfriend bought and edited but suppressed it in favor of defending her friend. Jojo needed someone on her side. This book meant more to her than the Jackie Chan screenplay, because this book was deeply personal.

"A business decision. What does that mean?"

Tina could see that Raj felt conflicted, but Raj was, first and foremost, in this situation at least, the chief editor of a small but prestigious press. It wasn't easy running a small press in this economy of giant publishing houses consolidating like crazy.

"I wish it were different," he said, swirling the last bit of wine in his glass. "But look, Jojo has no name to bank on, no previous publications or big sales. New writers are a risk to any publisher." He spread his hands, almost knocking over the water pitcher. "It's not even finished yet, she tells me. The chapters I read are good, believe me, but how do I know she'll finish, especially if she's working for me and writing a screenplay for Jackie Chan?"

Tina straightened in her chair, a little shocked at what she was hearing. "But if you told her to send it over when it's done, that it's got a good chance—"

"Tina, love, it doesn't work like that. Whenever she finishes it, the market will be different. What is hot right now might be dead cold in the nine months it would take me to get her book out."

"But if I know Jojo, if she knew you wanted it, she'd get it banged out in record time."

Tina saw a stiffening of Raj's jaw, which meant he was nettled by what she was saying. But this was her best friend he was disappointing, and she didn't plan to let this go.

She reached for his hand. "Just give her, say, a month to get the finished book back to you. You know, we—Jojo, Bee, Mei, and even me—made vows to each other. Jojo's was that she was going to write this book and bring it to you. She's done that. Don't disappoint her like this."

"Tina, I am running a business. If every small press bought and marketed their best friend's book, there would be no small presses anywhere. Marketing is expensive. More to the point, if she rushes the end of the novel to its detriment, and I've contracted to publish it . . . that doesn't serve either of us."

"Bottom line. Money. Fuck art." She knew the diners at the next table shot her a glance, but she didn't care. She picked up her fork again. "That's the trouble with running a business. You'll publish that fashion guy, that influencer who has a jillion followers on Instagram before you'll bring out a truly worthy book."

"That influencer guy's jillion followers will buy his book. What does Jojo have to offer? A handful of Facebook posts? A blog? Has she ever schmoozed with other writers and editors, other than going to sci-fi cons to cosplay? Reviews? Interviews?"

Tina's fork fell onto her plate with a clank. Now everyone was looking. "I can't believe what I'm hearing. You're saying this about Jojo? How can you overlook that she got Jackie Chan interested in her screenplay?"

Raj's eyes darkened. He glanced around, leaned forward, and whispered fiercely, "I am a publisher. This is what I do, and you know I'm damn good at it. Listen, I'm not going to tell you how to dig up pot sherds, so I don't think it's unreasonable for you to oblige me by not telling me how to publish books."

Tina pushed her chair back. This was a side of Raj she had never seen before. The thoughtful gentleman had turned into a privileged prick right in front of her.

Standing up, she yanked her coat off her chair. "When are you planning to tell Jojo that you are turning her down?" She hoped her voice sounded cold.

"That's the other thing," Raj said, getting out his wallet. "I hate it. I hate telling people I can't take their work. Okay? Especially face-to-face, as I'll have to with Jojo."

"You could just send her a form rejection letter."

"Tina, stop." Raj counted out some bills and laid them on the table.

People were noticing their argument. Tina wished she had the balls to flip them off. Turning, she stalked out of the restaurant, pulling her phone out of her pocket so she could call an Uber—even though they were scheduled to spend the night at Raj's apartment.

The sky was dark enough for a handful of stars to show themselves, and the March spring air was cooling rapidly. Shivering, Tina couldn't stop shaking her head, unbelieving that Raj would do such a thing to sweet, likable, funny, smart Jojo. She was tipping her location into the Uber app when Raj caught up to her.

"Put that away. Aren't you coming over?"

"I'm too mad at you."

Tina could see his disappointment even as the shadows fell.

"I'm sorry," he said, caressing her cheek. "I feel shitty about it. I wouldn't hurt Jojo for the world, but—"

God he's handsome, and she could see that, underneath his suave facade, he was telling the truth.

"Oh, shut up," she said and, putting her hand behind his neck, brought him in for a kiss, because this is what she'd wanted to do all day.

A scattering of applause echoed from the restaurant entrance. The two diners next to them, a man and a woman, stood beside the door, clapping and smiling. It was nice to hear Raj's laugh.

Chapter Fourteen

Below Alex, the Rockefeller Center ice rink was full. Being an ice-skater spectator was up there with all the other activities she loved to do. She could hang on a cliffside that she had just free-climbed in the Shawangunks, also known as "the Gunks"; she could descend a Cunningham Park mountain bike trail without touching the brakes; and she swam a half mile nearly every day at the Chelsea Pool. But she had no urge to learn to ice skate.

She loved watching, and this Sunday night, after a twelve-hour shift, she came to watch. The music, swirling figures, and gales of laughter soothed her, eased her aching feet. Clouds reflected the city glow, but the night was dry and crisply cold. Holding a cup of hot chocolate, Alex strolled along the barrier, inhaling the cool air.

She had also come tonight because she didn't want to go home where the girls would be stepping over each other, and she wanted to put a dagger in the crazy idea of dropping by Bee's apartment.

Trees draped with golden lights illuminated the iconic Manhattan open space. The onlookers crowded against Alex as she leaned on the railing, but she loved the feeling of being lost inside the crowd. This was her comfort zone, going to places alone to people-watch. Her observations always made Bee laugh as Alex described restaurant diners and subway riders.

By the time her phone rang with Bee's ringtone, Alex was feeling better. Maybe this was the reason she answered, when she had vowed she would let Bee stew all week before she'd talk to her. She slipped off a glove and tapped the Accept button.

"Oh, thank God you answered." Bee sounded breathless, and her words shot out as if pressurized.

Alex took a breath. It surprised her how happy she felt to hear Bee's voice. "You sound pretty buzzed."

"Yeah, well, tomorrow's the big day and I've got an insane idea and you need to talk me out of it. Although I don't think you can."

Tucking her cell under her ear, Alex slipped her glove back on. "Try me."

"Listen. I want to do a fashion show. For us, the Leftovers Club. I've got the clothes, and I've made some Pinky B swag, and I think it will be like a rehearsal for the first contest runway show, which is next Saturday."

Alex felt a twinge of foreboding. She knew how manic Bee could get when it came to her art. She'd had enough of it during the model auditions. When Bee was spiraling like this, sound decision-making went out the window.

"Mmm," she said. "Are you going to have time for this? What kind of schedule do you have for meeting contest goals?" *Jeez, I sound like a college advisor.*

"Crazy nuts. After an introductory morning, we jump straight into the soup tomorrow afternoon. They give us an assignment—I think the first one is street wear for a man and a woman. The first cut is Thursday. They're going to slash us by five."

"Then, really, how do you think you'll have time for a fashion show?"

"I don't know!" There was a silence; Alex heard the clink of a glass against Bee's phone.

Uh-oh—she better not be drinking.

"But I want to do it," Bee added. "I think I need something, like —support from my friends."

Support from my friends. Not just me. Am I just another friend, like Jojo, Mei, and Tina?

A burly man wrapped in a shiny down jacket shoved Alex to one side as he made himself a space for a selfie. Alex suppressed an urge to stamp on his sneakered foot. The beauty of the Center turned sour. Breaking away from the crowd, Alex started across the plaza, aiming for the subway station.

She said, "But they do support you, you know that."

"Yeah, I know. But I worry. I'll be too busy to spend time with anyone."

Alex listened, perplexed. This was classic Bee—running full speed on her worry treadmill. "It's only two weeks. You can do the show when you're done. Show off your newest creations, ones you've made for the contest."

After a momentary silence, Bee spoke, barely audible as a delivery truck roared past Alex while she waited at a crosswalk.

Pressing her phone against her ear, Alex asked, "What was that? I couldn't hear you."

"I said I miss you, damn it. Don't you get it? I want to see you and you're ghosting me again."

Feeling a twinge of guilt, which she shot down with a cold dart of reason, Alex said, "I just couldn't stand it last night. When you were talking about those girls, right in front of me. It's like sometimes I think I'm not important, or maybe . . . shit, I don't know."

She couldn't say it, because it might signal the end. She

couldn't tell Bee how much she loved her, how much she meant to her, how she felt as if she'd met the soul mate she had always been seeking. This woman, rebel-crazy but more generous than anyone she'd ever met, was her perfect opposite. This woman liked her back, just not to the same degree. Maybe that was just something Alex was going to have to accept—that they'd never be on the same page in that way. Maybe Bee simply needed casual adulation from many different people instead of a deep, solid relationship with one person. Maybe she just wasn't capable of being monogamous.

Can I live with that?

"I'm so sorry about that," Bee was saying, "but I was drunk. Period. Stupid, I know." Alex could hear her coughing.

I hope she's not getting a cold.

Bee continued, not allowing Alex to respond. "I am trying. I'm like really, really trying to put a lid on myself. I promise I'm trying, just—"

"Beetle," Alex interrupted, "I think you won't allow yourself to be vulnerable. You can't ask for help. So you make up this nutzo idea for a fashion show right in the middle of—"

"I know. I know."

Alex felt a little shock, thinking she heard Bee trying not to break into tears. Oof, that would be weird.

"Okay," Alex said. "Here's what we'll do. We'll talk Tuesday, after you've had a chance to see what kind of mess you've fallen into. If you really think you can pull together a private showing, then I'll help."

Nurse Alex, she told herself. *Summing up the problems and forming a plan.*

"Okay! Wow. Babe, you're amazing, astonishing, astronomical! Yes, yes. Oh, thank you. You always know how to pull my bum out of the fire."

Then Bee ran down the list of things she needed to do while Alex descended into the subway. "Gotta go! Talk to you Tuesday!"

Putting her phone in her pocket, Alex sighed, inhaling the dank, musty smell wafting up from the tunnel below. She felt disappointed, hoping, as she always hopelessly did, to hear those three words she so needed to hear.

I love you.

Alas, it was not to be.

Chapter Fifteen

NeueHouse Madison Square was not impressive from the outside, but the interior was another world altogether. In the elevator, clutching her cappuccino, Bee tried to look haughty and uncaring, as if participating in a fashion designer contest was something she did every day. But like the workspace rental building where the NYC Fashion Award Contest for Young Entrepreneurs was taking place, she felt quite different inside.

She was careful not to catch the eye of any of the fellow competitors, judging that the four other people who occupied the elevator were her rivals. In front of Bee stood a slender Black woman with dreadlocks carrying a patent leather sewing kit, with a plaid laptop case slung over one shoulder. Beside her was a short young Black man whose wavy hair was streaked with silver; Bee couldn't tell if this was premature *ombre* or a clever dye job. He wore a white-and-black polka-dot suit jacket and slacks, the jacket black on white, and the slacks white on black. To Bee's left, hunched against the back corner as if afraid to be touched, slouched a blonde in clear-rimmed glasses. She wore purple lipstick and a tailored gray top with a peplum detail around the hem, hung over a red ruched miniskirt. Between Bee and the blonde stood a buff-looking man, vaguely Asian in feature, maybe Filipino, in a black leather jacket and white cargo shorts. He had rings in both ears and a big portfolio tucked under one arm.

What a pretty picture we make, thought Bee as she surreptitiously sized up her competition. She had dressed for this first day with care in her ribbon miniskirt, tie-dyed silk-stretch top, red felt cloche, and fishnets. As she shifted her 1950's vintage makeup case to her other hand, she wished she hadn't tried to lug over so much stuff—messenger backpack stuffed with trims, ribbons, buttons, and samples. Over-the-shoulder home-made laptop bag for her iPad, extra sketch pads—she went through whole trees of pages—brands of pencils, charcoal, and markers that she preferred. She knew the show runners were supplying everything, but she liked to be as self-contained as possible.

The elevator doors opened on the top floor into a long corridor occupied by a table and a waving greeter in black—shirt, jacket, and trousers.

"Welcome, people, welcome!" the greeter called, waving them forward. "Let's see." He jutted out one hip as he fingered his chin. Then he pointed at the blonde. "You're Camille, and you—I know you are Plato." The greeter gave Plato, the wrestler type, a big smile. "And Elijah, so nice to see you." He and polka-dot man gave each other cheek kisses.

"Wow, the hair. You have to be Sasha. Welcome!" he told the Black woman, who gazed at him wordlessly.

Then he turned to Bee. "And you must be Bing—all that color!" he gushed. "I knew it had to be you."

Also because I'm the only Chinese American woman in the contest, Bee mused, taking his extended hand. In the roster of the lucky fifteen, she had seen two other Asian names, and they were both male.

"I'm Joseph," the young man purred, eyeing them all over. "I will be your go-to go-to. Everything and anything you need, bring it to me." He paused to throw them all a serious face. "Oh, and that's Joseph. Not Joe. Not Joey. Joseph. Good? . . . Good." Smile back in place, he gestured through the opening behind him. "Shall we?"

Bee was relieved he didn't go by Joe or Joey; the last thing she needed was to accidentally call him Jojo.

Bee's mouth dropped open when she saw the workspace for the first time. It covered the entire top floor. Arched windows along one wall had a view onto East Twenty-Fifth Street. Eight worktables stood in three rows, with two perpendicular to the others. At the far end from the doorway to her right was a stage set with a runway jutting out into the room, and along the interior wall was a row of makeup mirrors with lighting to suit. Several feet to her left were fabric bolts rising to the ceiling, flanked by cabinets of flat drawers—probably more trim and such than Bee would ever see her entire life.

Each worktable was set up to be shared by two contestants, with two sewing machines, four dress forms, grids, rulers, and tapes. Motioning them closer, Joseph pulled open one of the worktable drawers to reveal cutters, chalk, pattern paper, and drawing tools.

"We have a fabric printer," he told them, lips tight in a gleeful smile. "If you want to design your own fabric patterns, that is."

Bee's heart flipped. She couldn't wait to get her hands on that sewing machine. The funders had sprung for the best Juki sewing machines in the universe. Best of all, the room was filled with two of Bee's favorite fragrances: dark roast coffee and brand-new fabric.

It seemed that her little group of five were the last that the elevator had disgorged. Several people already milled around the room, opening drawers, fingering fabric. Joseph hopped onto the stage and clapped his hands.

"Okay, people! Hooks on the wall over there for your coats and things. Each work desk has an empty bottom drawer for personals. But first, come down to the stage to meet your eager staff and the brass who run this outfit. Come, come! Hurry now!"

I hope I can survive the next two weeks without committing murder, Joseph being my first victim, Bee thought as she hung her coat on one of the hooks.

There certainly were too many names to remember.

The two designers who ran the contest, however, were easy. They were Penelope Orton, a former model with a famous face and an adorable Australian accent, and her partner, Matt Parish, who styled for celebrities like Rihanna and Cardi B. Penelope was willowy tall and blonde, and Matt had flamboyant and weightless red hair.

Behind the runners stood a row of several staff members; they included seamstresses, colorists, and gofers. Bee winced at this news. She liked to do her own sewing and color decisions, but had to admit that, with the crazy timelines they were facing, it would be nice to have a little help.

"Everyone has an assigned place," Penelope announced loudly and handed a pile of papers to Joseph. "Joseph will be handing out a map of your locations. Find yours, pack away your stuff, and sit down. It's lecture time!"

Bee found her spot along the window wall. Her table mate was the sullen Camille. The lecture was not as bad as Bee feared. She and her fellow contestants were given slides of previous winners and what they were doing now, various trendy runway looks, Penelope's three-year-old. The music was good, too. This was followed by a reading of the rules. These were scary, but not impossible. Bee was relieved to hear that they could have the use of the room and all it had to offer all night, if they liked. Their security/participants' badges, handed out by Joseph and a handful of gofer people, were coded to unlock the door.

She raised her hand. "Can we bring our dogs?"

After a brief silence, Matt opened his mouth, but Penelope chimed in first.

"The building, unfortunately, has strict pet rules for the rental spaces." She smiled sadly, spread her hands. "So, no fur babies, I'm afraid."

Figures. Bee had stashed Wan Pi at the pet hotel in her building but winced at the price. And, for overnight boarding, the price skyrocketed. *But, maybe*, she thought, *if I work at night, Wan Pi can slip in with me in a shopping bag.*

"Now, your assignments for the first cut." Rubbing his hands, Matt, center stage, gestured behind him. Lighting grew, revealing a series of streetwear photographs taken in New York City locations. "You will create one for a woman and one for a man. You are free to design according to your individual style."

As Matt waved his hand again, the hanging streetwear photographs rotated to show office wear. "Consider that your street-wearing peeps have a Wall Street job, or public relations, or advertising. When they are not vamping around Manhattan on weekends, they are working on the Seventy-Seventh floor of One World Trade Center."

Sighs and whispered cursing filled the room. Bee slumped on her red plastic stool. Four outfits by Thursday. *Gah*!

Matt waited on the stage, hands folded before him. "All right, my lovelies. Let's have some lunch while you're making fabulous in your heads!"

No one wanted lunch. No one took the elevator down to the fourth-floor café where a buffet waited. Sketchbooks came out, patterns were drawn, fabric chalked out and cut. By the time Bee finally trudged out after nine p.m., she had pattern mock-ups of the street wear—cinch!—but decided to noodle over the suit designs while sitting on her living room floor, comforted by Noreetuh Musubi takeout and Wan Pi.

The next morning Bee's phone rang as she stumbled out of bed to the bathroom. It was her mother and, feeling bad that she had not answered several voice mails, Bee took her toothbrush out of her mouth.

"Hi, Mom. What's shakin'?"

"Ah Bing. My best girl. Did you call your father?"

"No, and I already told you why."

Xing's reply was drowned out by a passing siren. Bee didn't ask her to repeat it.

She asked, "Is Hao around? I tried to call him yesterday, but he never picked up."

"Your brother is MEA. I was hoping you would know where he is."

Probably trailing after the beautiful Becca, drooling like a puppy. "I think you mean MIA, don't you, Mom? Missing in America?"

Trying to straighten the bird's nest that was her hair, Bee left the bathroom for the kitchen. "Mom, does Dad know I was accepted to the designer contest?"

"He knows. He hasn't said, but I know he knows, and is proud."

"Has he told you that?"

"I know it, Bing. Because I know him."

Experience would prove otherwise, Bee knew. "If you hear from Hao, would you ask him to call me? I'm going to send you the link to the show's Instagram feed so you can follow along, okay?"

"Yes, yes. Send me the Instagram."

The rest of the conversation was a series of questions about the contest, one after the other. Bee gave answers to Xing's questions as she dressed, packed up, dropped Wan Pi at the dog hotel, and—carrying her scooter, because this March day had softened with spring weather—left her apartment. She buzzed to the café, bought a bagel and a cappuccino, and was standing in front of the Neue-House by the time her mother was ready to get off the phone.

After two late nights, little to no sleep, and a dwindling appetite, Bee's streetwear was ready, but her suits still felt like big zeros in her head. Elijah, who worked at a table opposite Bee's, had become something of a friend, especially after Bee, following a very long day, scootered home and brought Wan Pi back with her. Elijah went nuts over the dog, and a rather disturbed Bee watched Wan Pi spend most of the evening at Elijah's table. Sweet-tempered with a big basso laugh, he admired Bee's colorful, quirky appearance. Everyone seemed to like him and he made friends quickly, but he gravitated to Bee's table whenever he wanted to quietly complain about one of the contestants or the show runners.

Camille basically ignored Bee, having, for reasons known only to her, taken up a distinct distaste for the other woman. Worse, Bee was realizing with a growing sense of dread that she had not thought about the sort of clothing men might wear when they were not clubbing. Her day-to-day wear was "all Girrrl," and as she watched Elijah piecing together his man-suit, thought sincerely that she could never come up with this kind of idea.

Since she had helped Elijah with his streetwear designs, she crossed over to his worktable and watched him for a few moments.

She said, "I have no idea what I'm doing when it comes to the sort of thing a geezer might wear to work."

The older woman who was busily sewing up Elijah's tailored gray bomber jacket glanced over and smiled.

Elijah took a pin out of his mouth, cocked his head, and tilted his head slightly. "Okay. Think about this. Your 'geezer' is walking around on the weekends in a yellow and orange silk-screened tunic, braid-trimmed cargo shorts, and hand-painted ankle boots. So, what does he do for a living?"

He paused, and Bee figured out this was not a rhetorical question. "Graphic artist? Stage designer—no, he wouldn't need a suit for that. I know! Publicist for rappers!"

"Bingo. Bright, bright, bright. Even gaudy, but tasteful. Tailored."

"I'm so bad with tailored stuff." Bee had never liked the sleek styling of formal, upscale wear.

Elijah shook his head, eyebrows raised. "Don't worry about it. Just make sure your seams are straight and your ruffles are even."

She felt a glimmer of hope. Roping in her colorist, who was illustrating her own comic book while waiting for Bee's inspiration, Bee began sketching out designs.

I can do this, she told herself as she flipped to the next page of her sketchbook.

But doubt still nibbled around her edges. Without thinking twice, Bee picked up her phone and texted Alex.

Chapter Sixteen

s Jojo knocked on Raj's office door, her heart was racing. He'd casually asked her to come see him in five minutes, and she immediately felt her stomach loosen, as if everything inside had turned to jelly. Getting up, she ran to the bathroom, and when she got back to her desk, she had three minutes remaining.

Forgetting for a moment that Bee was on leave for her competition, Jojo darted around the wall of Bee's cubicle, but it was empty. She missed Bee being here more fiercely than she thought reasonable. If Bee were here, she could unload her shivering anxiety about why Raj wanted to see her. There wasn't time to call, so she sent a text: *Raj wants to see me. OMG!*

She wouldn't have to explain that the reason Raj wanted to see her was that he wanted to talk about her manuscript. Bee would know what she meant. She'd driven Bee crazy wondering what Raj was going to say about the pages she had submitted to him. Picking up her phone, she walked to Raj's office door when exactly five minutes had passed.

When Raj opened his door, he was wearing his *I give away nothing* face. Could mean anything, Jojo thought as she sat down opposite his desk. Her partial manuscript was lying on the desk before him as he took his seat.

"Jojo," he said and paused, leaned back in his chair, partially turning it to stare out the window, then came back to face her.

"Jojo, you are a good writer. Very good."

Jojo felt flash frozen in place, like a caught fish on a Pacific fishing vessel. All she could do was nod.

"I love the idea of female Chinese warriors, and from what I've read of it, the characters are deeply complex, and the background story is artfully done."

Unable to take her eyes off Raj's face, Jojo nodded again. It was as if she lost the ability to blink.

"That said—"

Uh-oh.

"We just can't take this on right now."

He leaned forward on his elbows, gazing at her with his head tilted to the left. As if his concern had pushed her backward, she sagged into her chair.

"How come?" she managed.

"Okay. For one, it's not finished. I know you mean to finish it, but I can't take it on spec. For two"—Raj was actually counting down on his fingers—"for two, we can't afford it. I mean, and don't take this wrongly, you're a new writer with no cred. I know that sounds terrible. I know you're working on that screenplay with Jackie's people, but for us to bank on a profit on a new writer no one's heard of, well, Gray Ghost just can't take the risk. Yes, you've had a couple of stories published in *Analog*, but those were science fiction, and there's not a lot of crossover between those two readerships."

Jojo knew that everything Raj was saying is true. *I don't blame him*, she told herself. Gray Ghost was a boutique press, with special limited runs and a small following of devoted fans—according to Cam, anyway.

I jumped the gun—I had made my vow to show it to Raj. Now I have, and he likes it. But I should have known . . .

Nodding and trying to smile, Jojo got to her feet. "Thanks for taking a look at it anyway. Thanks for the feedback."

Standing up, Raj saw her to the door. "Finish it. I mean it. And get busy with social media. A blog or something. And schmooze with other writers, the big ones, at your conventions."

Swallowing, Jojo nodded, thanked him again, and slouched back to her desk. Bee had answered her text. *Fantabulous. You must spill.*

Jojo couldn't answer. When it came time to go home, she couldn't remember what she had done. Talk to clients? Email the printer? She might have, but her mind was half in her work and half in the deep doldrums of disappointment.

When she got home, she told Jim about what Raj said as they dined on the pizza Jim had made.

"Maybe I should novelize the Jackie Chan script, peddle that around, or even self-publish," she told him as she licked up a string of mozzarella.

Jim shook his head. "I don't know. You don't want to end up in a literary ghetto. Remember how hard it was for Spielberg to crawl out of the SF slums after he made all those genre films? I mean, everybody else who worked on *The Color Purple* got Oscars but him. The movie won Best Picture and he didn't even get nominated for directing it!"

"Not helpful." Jojo put her pizza slice down and picked up her bottle of NA beer. "Raj's right, though. I need a media presence."

"He's right about another thing. Finish it! Keep writing and then start the next one." Jim held up his wine glass, and Jojo clinked it. "Here's to 'butt in chair.'"

Jojo knew a lot of folks in the science fiction community, but she needed to branch out, and Raj was right that she had to get more author party invites at the cons. Later, lying in bed next to the snoring Jim, she thought about starting a blog, but what kind? She used to have one—she might still have her old WordPress login. No one read it, though.

What would bring readers to her site? How could she get noticed? What did she really know right now that she could write about? Cam would have said a good place to start is to write about your occupation, lay the nuts and bolts down for readers, relate funny but non-libelous stories about work.

Nothing she had to say would interest readers. What did she really know, except that she had read every book Gray Ghost had published in the last three years.

Jojo sat up. *That's it!* She couldn't believe what a great idea this was. Sliding out of bed, she went into the living room and opened her laptop.

She had to change her login, but weirdly her old blog template was still up. She knew she needed a new design, but she could use her old domain, Jojowriter.com. For the next two hours she set up a new template, dug up a photo Jim had taken of her in her Black Widow con costume, and fumbled through her bookcase to find a recipe book Raj had rolled out last month that she had loved because the book included illustrations of the author working in the kitchen, created by a well-known graphic novel illustrator. Besides that, the dishes were de-lish.

She uploaded an image of the cover and one of the illustrations and wrote what she knew about the author's experiences. This made her wonder if she could include interviews with Gray Ghost authors on her blog—she probably needed to run that past Raj and get Cam's help.

By the time she dragged herself back to bed, she had a draft of her *The Ghost Speaks* blog by Jojo Zan. She knew Cam would hate her title, but he would come up with a far better one.

By the end of the week her first comments and shares began to trickle in. She had advertised the blog on Facebook, Twitter, and Instagram, and called in favors from con people she knew. This of course after Raj gave her his blessing, providing her with a set of guidelines and asking her to clear choices for her reviews with him beforehand. Also, Cam suggested she think about adding videos of her reading from and discussing the books, interspersed with photos. He promised to drop by the apartment to help her with the editing.

"No gaps, pauses, or stretches of black nothings," he told her as he leaned on her cubicle wall, a pencil in his ear and wearing blue eyeshadow. "Nothing topless, bottomless, or otherwise likely to draw the wrong readership."

Jim coached her through her videos. They set up a corner of the living room where there was a peekaboo view of the city through the floor-to-ceiling windows. Behind her beside the windows was a bookshelf—stocked with Gray Ghost publications, Jojo's flowering hoya, and a framed 8x11 color photograph of Jojo in front of the Eiffel Tower.

Cam wasn't happy with the backdrop, and he was right, of course. The light from the window behind her grayed out her face, and if she insisted on using it, she would have to get the proper lighting. They settled on the bookcase, with the visible shelves behind her stocked with Gray Ghost publications, and instead of the Paris photo, Cam asked why not the Black Widow Jojo one?

The first video garnered more comments than Jojo had ever gotten until now. She shared reader recommendations about the Gray Ghost books they read on a separate readers page. Jim asked Cam for advice about how to boost Jojo's internet presence, and he suggested that he could help her set up a running feed of fan comments on her site. When Jojo launched the live feed, advertising it in her newsletter and on Twitter and TikTok, her new blog site exploded with interest.

All this occurred over a two-week period. The popularity of the site was almost overwhelming; at first Jojo tried to answer each comment, but Jim finally talked her out of that impossible goal. The upside was that this was keeping her too busy to ruminate on her disappointment about Raj's turndown and worry about being a good mother. Even though she had less time to work on her novel, she vowed to add words to it every day at breakfast.

"I go in awe of you," Jim told her one morning as she was writing while eating a grapefruit. He was watching her latest video with his headphones on. Jojo felt a true glow inside. Stopping her work, she rose from her chair, circled around the table, and kissed him. Minutes later, they closed the bedroom door behind them.

Chapter Seventeen

Wednesday evening before the daywear runway show, Bee and Wan Pi waited for Alex at the front Neue-House entry. Famished, Bee had worked all day on her suit designs. With the help of her seamstress and colorist, who had agreed to cut patterns, she had gotten the jackets and trousers completed. But the shirts were a problem. Hao had left her a voice mail—after several missed calls and desperate texting—telling her he'd send over a couple bolts of Chinese silk with animal prints and some solids that the Lins had shipped over to a warehouse in New York while they were looking for floor space for the boutique they wanted to open in the US.

Relief flooded her when she saw Alex coming down the crowded sidewalk among rush hour walkers heading home. She carried a shopping bag that Bee prayed contained falafel pitas from Miznon in Chelsea.

Alex's cheeks were pleasingly flushed from her hurry to get there as quick as she could, but Bee's phone rang just as she kissed

Alex on the mouth. Seeing that it was Hao, Bee shrugged an apology to Alex as she let her through the entry door and answered the phone.

"Bing! I am going to Australia. With Becca. In three weeks!" He sounded so excited, he choked for a second. He breathed, "We're getting married."

Bee choked. "But you haven't even known her for a month!"

"Love isn't about how long you've known someone, Bing," Hao said. "It's about how *well* you know them. Becca and I . . . we just connected."

"Love at first sight, huh? Nothing to do with the fact that she's a novelty item."

"What do you mean?" Hao demanded.

"Red hair? Awfully *not* Chinese?"

"She's aboriginal. Or at least her dad is. Her mom is Irish."

"Like I said, a novelty."

"Jade," he called her.

"Naif," Bee retorted as she smiled at Alex's puzzled expression. Bee conversed in the lobby, because the call would drop if she got into the elevator. Deep down, she was happy for him, and at the same time mad about him planning to ditch and leave her behind.

"Wish me happy, Bing," he sang.

"I do, you dope. But I think you're a scumbag to bail and leave me holding the parental bag."

Hao said carefully, "Bing, if I'm gone, who is Father going to get to run the business when he retires? If I abdicate, you're the only person left to take the bloody throne."

Bee stopped pacing around the lobby. Hao was right. Her dream was for Zhen to come to her, hat in hand, begging her to come back to the fold, to take over his executive office in Hong Kong or, better yet, to run a new American division.

"Bing?" Hao's voice sounded in her ear. "You fall in?"

"I'll miss you, big brother. I may forgive you someday, too." Then Bee remembered why she wanted to talk to him so badly. "Hey, where's that silk you promised me?"

"It's not there yet? It's got to be. I got the confirmation."

Shit! If someone got the silk while her back was turned—

"Gotta go. Don't get run over by an emu. Love you, bro!"

Pulling Alex with her, she dashed into the elevator. When she reached the hallway outside of the workspace, she saw the silks leaning against the wall at the far end.

She knew someone had deliberately hid her order from her on purpose. And she would find out who it was if it killed her.

Sweeping the bolts into her arms, she led Alex to her desk. As she laid the fabrics out and started to pin her patterns to them, she couldn't stop thinking about her last few words with Hao.

I could tell Dad, when he comes to me about taking over Hao's work, that I've got too much on my plate already, running my own business.

"Dad, I'll buy you out, though."

"What are you so happy about?" Alex asked her. "We're going to be here all night!"

Shrugging, Bee handed a pair of scissors to Alex. Beside the table, as if he knew this would be a long haul, Wan Pi curled up on Bee's old fisherman's sweater with a deep sigh.

"I was just thinking about my dad."

Bee was still sewing the men's shirt when Camille came through the door in the morning, and Plato and Keitu soon followed. Everyone was twitchy and nervous. Their models would arrive soon, to be dressed and made up and taught each designer's choreography. The fifteen had previously turned in their chosen music for a producer to assemble. Another producer would cue the models with the music, and each designer had simple but specific moves they wanted their models to exhibit.

Alex had gone home to sleep, agreeing to drop off Wan Pi at Bee's apartment. She had a shift tonight, but she was coming in for Bee's runway show; Bee had put her on the guest list. Bee was pleased that Alex, although she had never done it before, quickly managed the button-sewing feature of Camille's Juki, which they had commandeered for the task. She was a good presser, too, because ironing silk was tricky.

Joseph and the assistant producer had determined the lineup, and Bee's show would come near the end, giving her a chance to tune up her designs.

Camille sat down at her sewing machine and folded her arms. "Did you use my machine last night?" she asked coldly, picking a red thread from the sewing machine's deck. Camille preferred earth tones. Red was anathema to her.

"No," Bee answered as she fitted the men's shirt onto a hanger. "Of course not." Which was true. *She* hadn't used the machine; Alex had.

After a few minutes of silence, Bee asked Camille, "Did you happen to accept my order of silk when it came?"

Camille, who was sewing the cuff of a white cotton blouse, shook her head. "Nope."

Joseph's voice rang out. "People! Fabulous Fifteen! Your models are here."

Bee burned her finger on the iron. Models were one thing; she could handle that. But a handful of fashion press and influencers had been invited to today's show. Thinking about this made Bee's jaw ache.

She was so busy adjusting the fit of Simon's jacket while

instructing the seamstress to shorten the hem of Halemé's silk spread collar shirt, she didn't notice the woman standing right behind her, peering over her shoulder. She only got the idea that someone was near by the vague aroma of tobacco, someone who only smoked outside and not often, and who had just puffed on one before entering the venue.

Bee's staging area, as for all the contestants, was the open zone around her workspace. That made eight models hanging around the workstations, along with makeup personnel and hairstylists. Bee actually liked the bustle, especially because she was in charge, but one thing she didn't like was smoking.

Turning to pick up the bow tie she had made, also of Chinese silk, her elbow collided with something soft.

"Oof, sorry. Could you give me a little space, please?"

"You're Bee Lin, aren't you?"

Bee glanced over her shoulder to see the tall Chinese woman who waited there. The woman stuck out her hand.

"Hi! I'm Cindi Koh." Pulling a cobalt blue business card case from her pocket, she whipped out a card and placed it on Bee's table. "I'm here to interview you, Bing Lin, rising star of kick-ass fashion."

Cindi Koh's smile was beautiful and, to Bee, seemed truly genuine. Her name was familiar, too. Bee's irritation at this interruption drained away. And she hadn't made the slightest remark about Bee's accent.

Holding her phone in one hand, Cindi smiled. She was tall, a little shorter than Tina, and her features were even, perfectly arranged. Her hair was pulled back in a French twist, with a sheen of deep indigo. She wore a fitted cream wool suit, flattering to her figure, and gave the impression of gracefulness.

"You spent several years in London, I read." Cindi seemed impressed. "St. Martin's, of all places."

Bee felt her face warm, and Cindi's words barely registered, for Cindi's eyes stunned Bee for a few seconds. They were green, betraying the genetics of rarity. *Bollocks*, thought Bee. *How come they all have to have such beautiful eyes?*

Interpreting Bee's silence for a go-ahead, Cindi held her phone between them. "Tell me, Bee, what is your inspiration for your unique designs? I've been following you on Instagram and Pinterest, and I am always surprised and intrigued by your inventiveness."

Being surrounded on all sides by tall people didn't intimidate Bee anymore. Short people had to have tall personalities. Jojo had told her this when they were in boarding school together, and Bee always thought of that conversation as the beginning of the "Bee Big Personality."

Pulling her gaze away from the scintillating Cindi, on tiptoe Bee tied the bow tie around the neck of Simon's pale yellow brocaded silk shirt.

"I never know what's going to 'inspire' me, as you put it. There really are no words for what I do with color." Stepping back to critically examine Simon, she made Cindi stand to one side, and Cindi deftly kept the phone close to Bee's face.

As she moved from Simon and Halemé in their suit wear and guided the colorist in how to accessorize Bettina and Felix's street wear, she gave every question a similar response.

Cindi leaned in close to hear, and when Bee glanced at her, she saw Cindi smile and nod, as if impressed by each and every word. A feeling of confidence grew inside her. Everyone in her little stable—seamstress, gofer, even the models, and now Cindi Koh, eagerly watched her, waited for her command or suggestion, and hung on every word she said.

Wow. Maybe I've really got something here.

Joseph's voice echoed through the workspace. "Five minutes to the start of the show. Is everybody ready?"

Of course no one was truly ready. Gasps, whispered curses, and nervous giggling filled the room. Elijah's bellowing laugh echoed everywhere.

"Influencers, press, photographers, everyone take your places." Wavering electronic musical sounds rolled out from the amps on either end of the stage. The workspace lights dimmed. Random spotlights swept across the runway surface. Bee made a mental note to bring a small flashlight for next time. Her seamstress held the flashlight of her phone over Bee's hands as she finished attaching beads to Bettina's cape.

"Good luck, Bee," Cindi breathed into her ear before she left to take her chair at the runway. Bee watched her glide away, typing into her phone and managing to gracefully weave her way through the crowd.

"Ooh," Bee muttered to herself. "That girl has some . . . something."

Crabby Camille's offering was first on the roster. Standing on a chair, Bee watched as the jazzy dance mix made the floor quiver. Camille's models were paired male and female, and the first two to march out wore her street wear. The woman wore a banded tube bra, bare midriff, cloudy gray distressed jeans, and over it all a herringbone bomber jacket with neon blue solid cuffs. The model's black hair flared as a fan blew air across the runway.

Bee thought the look was pretty boring, but she heard the applause and murmured oohs and aahs, which instantly crushed her comfortable self-esteem and trust in her work flatter than a tin can rolled over by a Cadillac. Camille's office wear got longer applause, especially, Bee thought jealously, because of the shiny jacquard jacket and trousers worn by the male model. The tailoring was flawless.

Every one of the twelve designers who went before her made her feel worse and worse. She felt like crawling under the work-table to hide if only there weren't so many drawers. When the gofer fetched her to line her models up in the stage wings, her stomach felt tight, like it was tied up in ropes.

When she scanned the audience, she saw a familiar figure leaning against the coat rack wall. Alex, wearing a blue pork pie–style hat Bee had made her, sent a little wave, and Bee's gut loosened a little.

The golden fox is here. Nothing can go wrong now.

The music shifted to Bee's mashup of eighties dance tunes. As Bettina and Halemé marched out to Simple Minds' "New Gold Dream," Bee could hear murmuring in the crowd. She'd deliberately paired the women, one in street wear, the other on the way to the office, and choreographed them to walk past each other, eyeing and admiring the other girl's outfit.

Halemé's patchwork collarless silk shirt was the centerpiece of her royal blue, finely brocaded double-breasted jacket. The slacks were tight and tapered, and she strutted in bright red heels. Halemé had brought a wig pulled into a tight, thick braid around pliable wire that hung vertically from the back of her head and gently curved downward.

Bettina's eyebrows rose up and down as she exchanged looks with the other model. In a red baker's boy cap, she ran her hand along the lapel of Bee's below-hip-length coat, continuing the double-breasted theme, made of cinnamon-colored gabardine and embroidered with scraps of lace, beads, chains, and braid trim. Under this she wore a pair of black velvet shorts barely visible below the jacket hem. Her long legs were bare, and on her feet she wore GANNI rubber–trimmed Chelsea boots with mismatched socks.

The sound of the applause shocked Bee. Elijah threw an arm

around her. "Those are fabulous," he breathed. "It's so original that you paired street with office like that. Wish I'd thought of it."

Bee knew it was daring, and she told herself she was being "Bad Bee," the rebel. Deeper than that, she hoped some of the audience caught her little innuendo about same-sex couples.

The boys, Simon in his office suit vest made from the same swatches of patchwork silk Halemé had worn, and Felix in a pork pie hat like Alex's and Chinese silk parachute pants, drew even more applause.

Bee sank into her chair as Simon and Felix exited the stage. There were three designers left, and Bee felt too exhausted to climb onto her chair to see them. Cindi appeared at her side; could this woman walk through walls? Teleport herself?

Squatting beside Bee, Cindi touched her forearm. "You rocked that look, Bee. Eye candy from start to finish. I'm already writing up my blog. Could you send me photos of some of your designs? But remember the competition doesn't want me to use anything you style for the contest."

"Sure." They exchanged phone numbers, and Bee sent four photos that she had used for her entry application.

"Oh, wow," Cindi breathed. "Amazing. I know my followers are going to eat this up."

She touched Bee's arm again. Her fingers were long, and her manicured nails painted pearl white. "I'll be in touch. I'm going to interview you again if—I mean, when—you're in the second round."

She stood up, and Bee gazed up at her. Cindi said, "Even if this competition doesn't work out, I want to keep tabs on you."

Smiling warmly, Cindi turned and walked back to her chair. While Cindi had meant to bolster her confidence, Bee felt ill. The winnowing of the fifteen would happen right after this show. As she glanced around, she saw the others biting their nails and glancing around nervously.

To distract herself, she reached for Cindi's card and her eyes widened. *Jeebus, THAT Cindi Koh?* She recognized Cindi's TikTok and Instagram handle: "Velvet Diva."

Oh my God, Bee wailed in her head. *I was so rude to her during the interview. She's only the hottest fashionista in New York—probably the world. I have cornered the market on stoopid.*

Chapter Eighteen

As Mei Tang pulled the last Diet Coke out of Doran and Cross's well-stocked staff refrigerator, she heard a familiar voice behind her.

"Hello, Mei. How's everything going?"

Straightening, Mei pulled the tab on her Coke. "Great, Dick. How are you doing?"

Dick was the "Doran" of the law office where she, also an executive lawyer, worked on contracts, real estate, and public offerings. He was a handsome man somewhere in his seventies, with a shock of white hair and a trim figure that announced he still worked out. Unlike his younger partner, Randall Cross, Dick did not mispronounce her name. He had other . . . habits she found annoying. So, she put on her bright and happy face as Dick stepped through the break room door. Russel, sitting at one of the tables occupied in his favorite habit of ice-chewing while studying his phone, straightened in his chair.

Unbuttoning his signature Brooks Brothers Regent-cut gray suit jacket, Dick leaned against the counter where Mei was standing. He gave her his signature lazy smile.

"I need help with something, and I know you'd be perfect for it." Dick glanced over at Russel, caught him watching, and nodded a hello.

"Hey, Dick," Russel replied, then went back to his phone. Mei raised her own phone and peeked at it before responding.

"Okay," she said. "What would that be?"

Dick ran his hand down his tie. If he was expecting her to purr, *Of course, Dick, I'd be happy to help you out,* he wasn't going to get his wish.

Dick asked, "You know Steve Chen?"

"Sure. Sure, I know Steve. Great guy." A partner. A male partner. And Chinese. It must have made Dick's teeth ache to name him partner.

Nodding, Dick said, "Yes, he is. Great guy. And his birthday is coming up."

"Oh, nice." Mei stopped herself from adding, *We should do something for him.*

Straightening a cuff, Dick added. "You're a knock-out organizer and you're supremely tech savvy."

Mei kept her eyes on him, nodding. *Damn straight*, she thought.

Giving her an exaggerated nod, and with a conspiratorial expression on his face, Dick said, "It's settled then. You'll organize his birthday party? Somewhere off site, good food. Did you know Steve loves to cook?"

Mei felt her stomach sink into her feet while Dick turned to leave. She hated that this blatantly sexist request—with racial overtones, to boot—stunned her a little. As he wove through the tables, she blurted, "Why don't you ask Steve's admin, um, Mary, to do it?"

Dick didn't bother to turn around as he answered. "Well, dear, I thought you could use a fun project to distract you from your disappointment at losing the Warner case to Sebastian Cole. Besides, Mary's gone on early maternity leave."

Mary is always on maternity leave, Mei spit to herself. And now this humiliation. Inside, by now, she was seething, but she kept silent.

To her distress, Mei heard herself saying, "Okay. When's the party?"

From the doorway, Dick turned. "Saturday."

"*This* Saturday?"

"I just found out about Mary," he said, as if that explained a damn thing, then added, before disappearing into the hallway, "I know you'll pull something off. Your organizational skills are the best. There's simply no one else to ask."

After he left, Mei felt frozen in space. She stared at her phone, seeing nothing and beating herself up for tacitly agreeing to Dick's obviously prejudiced ask. She had to make a good impression even to the self-privileged Dick, who shrugged off any hint he might be a bit misogynist and a bigot, but this was the stupidest thing she'd ever agreed to do.

After a few moments, Mei glanced at Russel, who was just lifting his ice water glass to his lips.

Oh no. He's going to chew the ice again. Mei wanted to knock the glass out of his hands.

"Try putting your water in the fridge, rather than on the rocks," she snapped, and stomped out. Grabbing her coat, she took the stairs up to the terrace, complete with a grill for employee use. The spring air was lovely; the breeze cooled her burning cheeks.

Now Dick could add this request to his roster of stereotyping. *Of course, I'm Chinese, so I would know how to arrange the appropriate party. Well, dang. I'll arrange a real bash.*

Her first call was to Tina.

When she explained the unreasonable timeline handed to her, Tina was quick to offer special Drive-by Dumpling catering from her parents' food truck operation.

"I'll visit the aunties tonight on my way to the truck. When I explain it's for my very best friend, who is a leading female law attorney, they will be so impressed that you actually completed an advanced degree, they will go overboard with dumplings."

The sting of Dick's request began to lessen as she listened to Tina. "You are saving my life, girlfriend. I get the best dumplings *jiaoxi* in all of New York for my sexist, racist ass of a boss."

Next, she dialed Bee for decoration ideas.

"What have you got on hand now, Bee best buddy, for last-minute birthday party table ornaments?"

"Oh, girl. Just wait. I've been making bows, and my seamstress —ha! my own seamstress!—is itching to do more." She laughed, and Mei could hear the buzz of a sewing machine through the phone. "I'm too much of a control freak. Listen, I'll get some shit together. Just let me know where to bring 'em."

"Bee, I love you. I love you. I love you."

"Whoa, babe. I may get ideas."

Mei stood for a moment, considering how to quickly find—and call in hopes there was availability—venues to rent for the Saturday afternoon party.

This is going to take me all afternoon and I have a case to get ready! Damn Dick. And Mary too. Why does she need so many children?

Tapping her phone on her chin, she thought about Jojo, wondering how she could help. A moment later she had it and called Jim Yuhan, Jojo's husband.

Her cheeks flamed a little when Jim answered his phone. She'd had a lot to drink the other night at Wilfie and Nell's, and she hoped she hadn't said anything offensive.

"Hey, Jim. It's Mei. I just wanted to—"

"Hey, Mei, how are you?" Jim interrupted her. He sounded like he was in a car. "Wow, the other night, when you were talking about the male privilege thing and how frustrating it is, I totally get it."

"Oh, that. Thanks, Jim. Listen." Mei told him quickly and precisely about the humiliating job Dick the dick had plopped into her lap.

"Saturday? That's kind of short notice, but there's always something. Give me an hour. I'll call you back."

After signing off with Jim, Mei lingered a few more minutes on the deck, appreciating the organized chaos of color and shade that was New York City. "God, I love living here," she breathed to herself, just as two colleagues came through the glass doors. Time to leave. People liked to sneak a vape out here.

Back in her office, Mei worked on her brief for a suit over a contract violation, feeling for the first time in a long while as if a great burden had been lifted from her shoulders.

Twenty minutes after she called him, Jim rang her back.

"A lot of places are booked, but I nabbed one that had a cancellation. But it might not be appropriate."

"Anything, as long as it's not a strip club."

"Okay. How do you feel about ping-pong?"

The place was called SPIN. Mei had played ping-pong as a kid but had never taken to it. While Jim was on the phone, Mei browsed their website. Nice decor—not over the top, lots of seating, and half a dozen ping-pong tables.

"They'll give you a break on the price, especially since you already have a caterer. Ping-pong clubs use it for meets, but they rent it out for all kinds of occasions—weddings, wakes, you name it." Jim sounded as if he'd like to throw a party there. Jim's talent was his ability to rouse his clients' excitement. "But it may not be a lawyer thing."

Mei thought about it for two seconds before responding.

"Perfect! Office staff can dine at a terrific dumpling buffet, drink champagne, admire colorful boxes wrapped in bronze wire and dotted with silk roses and bows, and best of all, play ping-pong for hours."

Jim promised to seal the deal for her, telling her they would call her about the billing. After he was gone, Mei smiled to herself and stretched her arms over her head.

She slipped on her headphones and relished in the thought of Dick Doran, who played squash in his private court and preferred Mozart to MIA, standing in the middle of the noisy party, assailed by the sounds of paddles and balls and champagne corks popping away.

Chapter Nineteen

After the FAYE fashion show guests had finally filed out, Penelope and Matt lined up all of the designer contestants on the runway. Bee's entire body tingled with dread. They were going to knock the fifteen of them down to ten.

Wondering what Cindi Koh had written about her on TikTok, Bee wished she hadn't eaten the *banh mi* sandwich Alex had left for her. It felt like a squatter setting up a home in her gut, who was never going to leave. On the stage in the same order as in the fashion show, Bee stood between Plato and Keitu.

One by one, each designer was called forward and heard feedback from Penelope and Matt about their designs and all the aspects of their runway show. Each one of them received complimentary comments as well as negative remarks, especially from Matt, such as: "I've seen that before"; "You overdid the leather trim"; "The fabric seemed wrong."

Then the condemned names were called out, one by one, each disappointed contestant given encouragement and praise and advice on improvement. Bee was left standing, and her stomach felt empty and light. Camille, Elijah, Keitu, and Plato were also among the ten survivors.

Sighs, prayers, and whoops filled the workspace as Joseph handed them their assignments for the next round. They hugged each other, even the disagreeable Camille, and wearily packed up their stuff to leave the building. Plato suggested they go out for celebratory drinks, but everyone, exhausted, simply wanted to go home to sleep.

It was almost midnight when Bee stuck her key in the lock, praying to her eclectic mix of natural gods and goddesses that Alex would be here waiting for her. She really needed a cuddle from the golden fox.

Her heart soared when she saw Alex's backpack on the sofa and her shoes lying on the living room floor. The other sign was that Wan Pi had not rocketed to the door. He was having a dog date with Alex in the bed. Dropping her cases and bags on the coffee table, Bee went straight to the bedroom, stripped off her clothes, and, without even brushing her teeth or soaking her contacts, fell into the bed beside Alex.

"How'd it go?" Alex asked sleepily, throwing her arm over Bee's.

"I'm still alive in the contest," Bee muttered, nuzzling her forehead against Alex's chin.

"I knew it! Fantastic." Turning over, Alex pressed her delicious lips on Bee's.

Bee snuggled close. "Ah baby, rock me to sleep, okay?"

"Who is Cindi Koh?"

Bee gaped at Alex, who was tying up her running shoes. "Only the most influential influencer in all of creation. I met her yesterday. She interviewed me for her blog."

"Oh. That was the one in the white suit who was hovering around you."

Leaning her elbows on the dining table, Bee gave Alex a quick once-over as Alex, sitting on the sofa, bent over her shoes.

"That's her," she said, searching for any hint of jealousy in Alex's face as she straightened and rose from the couch. Alex wouldn't meet her gaze.

Oh dear. Bad sign.

She said, "You need to see what she wrote about me. Listen: 'Pinky B's bold styles are breathtaking. At least my breath was taken as I saw, and later had the privilege to feel, her Chinese patchwork shirting. Casual versus decorative, elaborate versus easy sapphire blue brocaded suit wear. Embroidery, braiding, fringing: bygone styling bumped up into woke splendor.'"

Now Alex was listening. "Really. She wrote that?"

"Luv, if I get her to shine on me throughout the contest, I'm going to win."

"She seemed friendly, too." Alex laid her hand on the doorknob. Even though this act made no noise, Wan Pi shot from under the dining table and started dancing around the door. Leaning down, Alex apologized for not being able to take him on her run.

Getting up, Bee ran around the table, across the studio, and grabbed Alex's other hand. "Yes. I think she liked me. It's a big deposit in the fame bank account to have an influencer on your side."

Alex nodded. At least she was smiling now.

Relieved, Bee asked, "You're coming tomorrow night, right?"

"Miss a chance to dine at Chelsea's famous Fleur? Are you kidding me? Have you been inside that place? It's stunning."

Opening the door, Alex seemed surprised as Bee didn't let go of her arm. "You mean you've been there before?"

Shrugging, Alex leaned over and gave Bee a kiss. "Yeah, a long time ago. I'll be back in an hour."

Mei had scheduled the Fleur get-together weeks ago—that was the soonest she could reserve space for everyone and their pluses. She had just won a big contract case and invited them all out for drinks at one of the most popular upscale clubs in Manhattan. Bee had vowed to herself she would not drink too much, nor would she flirt with anyone or talk about Bumptious Bettie. In fact, she'd best stick to a single topic: her fashions.

Bee wasn't the only one who walked into the FAYE workspace in the late morning. She felt bad about the vacant tables, where the first-cut losers had worked. She understood how they must have felt. Once the final ten were all there, Joseph gathered them up beside the runway. Sitting on it, he looked down at them and blathered praise and kudos ad nauseam. Finally, to Bee's great relief, he got to the subject of the schedule—the next showdown would be on Monday.

Back at her worktable, Sheila the seamstress at her side, Bee pondered what the f**k she was going to do about this assignment: workout and sleepwear. Both terrifying and boring. She had never given a thought to workout clothes, and sleepwear was so blasé— she never wore it, so what did she care?

But Alex, seeing the assignment, spilled over with ideas. After all, she was a jock. Okay, not really, but she loved the outdoors and had an uncanny sense of both the practicality and necessity of the proper clothing for rock climbing and mountain biking. As for sleepwear, all Bee could think of was kid stuff—freakish cartoons and flannel. But she had all that silk . . . huh.

As she was spreading out her sketches, Elijah slid his stool over to see what she was doing.

"I see you are channeling Colorado there," he said, squinting down at her renderings, laying a finger on a design of cargo shorts and a ripped-style spaghetti-strap tee.

"You take care of the Bee-boy look, I'll do the ladies. The real ladies, mind you."

"I'm all about the men's nighties. Can't wait." Giving her an evil grin, Elijah rolled his stool back to his table.

Bee was deep into designing a pair of boy shorts to be fashioned from the Chinese silk when she felt a soft tap on her shoulder.

Startled, she gathered herself and turned to see Cindi gazing down at her. Today Cindi's hair hung straight to her shoulders, with bangs. In a pearl gray tunic, black miniskirt, and paisley heels, she looked cuter than hell. Bee felt her entire body smiling.

"Well, hello there," she breathed. "Thanks for the fab review— so complimentary!" Bee wrinkled her nose. "I thought I kinda botched our intro yesterday, though."

Before Cindi could answer, Camille pushed a stool forward for Cindi to sit on. "I love that tunic. Did you style that yourself?"

Looking proud, Cindi nodded. "I loved your suits—Camille, isn't it? The tailoring was awesome."

Bee had to put a stop to this, but before the snark came out, Cindi returned her attention to Bee, effectively shutting Camille out. The other woman returned to her own table, her facial expression even more sour than usual.

Cindi shook her head. "You were busy, I know—the level of stress in this room was so thick you could smell it. But you talked to me. I was thrilled that you did."

As Cindi ran a finger along the back of Bee's hand, Bee felt a little thrill of her own, and when the influencer asked about Bee's fabric choices for the activewear, Bee felt a definite vibe. Cindi sat very close to Bee, her phone lying on the table, recording their chat.

Bee fought to stay focused on her design goals, but she kept thinking how the coral shade of lipstick Cindi wore somehow gave her an undeniable "come hither" look. The tunic followed the shape of Cindi's breasts in a way velvet shouldn't even come close to.

After thirty minutes or so, Cindi said she had to move on and seemed disappointed about it. But she wanted to interview a few of the other ten survivors. She photographed Bee at her worktable, along with some of the chosen fabrics that she arranged in an attractive pattern, and the atelier in total. Cindi was not allowed to post images of the designs, even though she had captured tons of them, along with videos during last night's fashion show. She showed many of these to Bee, and Bee thought the photos of her own offerings gave the best impression.

Watching Cindi glide away, she suddenly remembered the club party tonight and wished she had invited Cindi, but at the same time remembered her Yoda vow. *No Cindi tonight. Nada.*

The Fleur Room, top of the Moxy Chelsea Hotel, was loud, packed, and beautiful. Through the floor-to-ceiling windows, New York City lay bejeweled and pristine, a magic city against a backdrop of royal blue velvet. Everyone was there by the time Bee and Alex arrived, arrayed on one edge of a long serpentine sofa as Bee, Alex beside her, threaded her way through the crowd.

Seeing her, Jojo applauded, and the others joined in. In a red brocaded silk miniskirt, a black silk shirt, and a pair of Paul Smith sneakers she had embellished with embroidery, Bee steepled her hands and bowed. Beside her, Alex was a soft soufflé of plaid puffy-sleeved midi-length grammy dress, ribbons braided through her golden hair, and wearing Bee's Chinese slippers appliquéd with tiny dogs.

Sitting on the sofa next to Raj and Tina, Bee mimed extravagant air kisses and sheepish shrugs. Mei, just beyond Tina and Raj, had a flushed and happy face. To see Mei having a great time, with a look of contentment on her face that Bee hadn't seen in a long time, pleased Bee. Picking up the bottle of red wine nearest him, Raj filled the glasses in front of Bee and Alex.

Picking up her glass, Bee called for a toast praising Mei's success with the case she had been working so hard on. Then came toasts for Bee's surviving the first cut, Tina's newest shoe bargain, Jojo adding two thousand words on her novel that very day, Jim landing a chic new client, and Alex's beautiful hair.

Bee held Alex's hand as they traded stories, finding out where Mei had gotten her handbag, Raj getting his pilot's license—another toast, and shrieking with laughter at Alex's story about the man who came to the emergency room to have a flash drive removed from his anus. The patient would not, no matter how often he was asked, reveal how and why it got there.

Glad she had stuck to wine rather than her Manhattans, Bee had to pee like crazy. But she didn't want to leave the sofa because five minutes earlier, just as she was going to slide past Alex, she had seen Cindi Koh . . . and Cindi Koh had also made eye contact with Bee.

How did she know I was here? Or is it some kind of ironic coincidence?

Bee felt flustered, not knowing whether to be glad or panicked. She didn't dare meet eyes with Alex beside her, in case Alex would read something in her face.

Cindi had nodded and smiled at Bee, then blithely turned to the group she had come in with. Fleur was a popular place and, Chelsea being right next door to the Garment District, the club naturally would be a fashionista watering hole. It had to be a coincidence, unless—Bee riffled through her memory. Had she somehow let it slip that she was coming here tonight? She didn't think so, but then, Cindi had rather bewitched her.

You could have said anything, Bingo.

Her bladder about to burst, Bee had to get to the bathroom or pee all over the plush seating. Busy with her friends, Cindi's back was to Bee, and the crowd between the Leftovers and Cindi's posse was thick.

"Gotta go." She shot Alex a desperate look, stood up, and wound through the crowd—several people deep at the bar. There was no way Cindi could see her.

After finding great relief in one of the stalls, Bee stood at the sink, washed her hands, adjusted the spikes in her hair, straightened her blouse, and reapplied her lipstick. As she turned to go back to her friends, the bathroom door opened, and Cindi Koh walked in.

She came straight up to Bee, stood beside her, and checked her hair. "I thought you'd never separate yourself from that rabble. The blonde is the girl I saw you with at the workspace, isn't she?"

"Yeah, that's my . . . that's Alex. She's helping me with the show. Support from friends is important. Especially when you're just starting out."

Cindi flashed a $1,000 smile and Bee couldn't take her eyes off her. "You're so right." Cindi moved one of her LBD straps. The black garment wound so tightly around her that every curve and crevasse was visible. "Support from friends—especially well-placed friends—is so very important. I'd like to think that I'm a well-placed friend, Bee."

She gave Bee a coy sidelong glance.

Sensing a moment here, as if life was calling on her to make a choice, Bee chose. "I'd like to think you're a well-placed friend, too."

Cindi's smile deepened. "I'm the queen of well-placed friends. My TikTok channel gets tens of thousands of views every day."

To Bee's utter astonishment, Cindi leaned in and kissed Bee full on the mouth. At the same time, she pressed another business card into her hand. "In case you lost the last one I gave you. Call me," she said softly. "Soon. I've already got your number."

Cindi checked her lipstick in the mirror, and Bee watched her runway-strut out of the bathroom, sultry laughter trailing behind.

Bee wanted to follow her but checked her own face for lipstick that wasn't her own.

"Bollocks!" She blotted Cindi's brick red from her lips and reapplied—again—her own deep plum before hurrying back to her party, but not before she tucked Cindi's card into her tiny crossbody bag. Alex was watching for her, she could tell. Bee smiled gaily— she hoped—and plopped on the seat beside her. Someone had refilled her glass.

"Must've had to wait, huh?"

"Oh, no." *Best to be honest.* "I ran into that fashionista gal, you know, Cindi whatshername, and we had a little chat."

"Whatshername is Koh." Frowning, Alex stared into the crowd.

"Right." Bee quickly sipped her wine. "Wish there weren't so many people here. We could dance. This music is so hot!"

Alex nodded, but she didn't seem enthusiastic about the thought of dancing.

They sat in silence for a short while. The rest of the group was lit now, laughing at Jojo's enthusiastic critique of *The Mandalorian.*

Bee felt sulky about Alex's sulkiness. *It's not like we're in some heavy, serious relationship, right? Alex knew what she was getting when she took up with me.*

When it came time to go, Bee stayed close to Alex, who led Tina and Raj, also leaving at the same time, to the elevator. When they got to the first floor, she grabbed Alex's arm.

"Your place busy tonight?" she asked.

Alex turned toward her, then shook her head, a soft smile on her lips. "Grammy is visiting her daughter in Florida. Lulu is doing a night shift."

Bee felt her spirits rising because Alex was talking to her again. Cindi's business card in her purse imprinted with the words "call me" felt like a heavy weight. Pushing that out of her mind as she and Alex walked through the soft New York night to Alex's flat, she held Alex's hand.

The two women couldn't be more different, Bee mused: Alex, a warm, soft, sweet teddy. Cindi, a hot, shiny diamond in a stunning gift box. No, very different, but no less interesting.

Chapter Twenty

Tina Lu knew her mom, Lian, was watching as she took two dumplings from the warmer, boxed them, and handed them to Web Martel, one of the Lus' favorite regulars. He was at her mom and dad's Drive-by-Dumpling food truck nearly every day and often lingered to talk to Tina's dad about subjects like Kant, Stan Getz, or the paucity of Asian characters on the TV series *The Boys*, which Tai secretly streamed on his phone when Mom wasn't looking.

Tina usually was amused by their conversations and occasionally offered her opinions, which always made her dad giggle. But today she felt distracted by her tiff with Raj over his rejecting Jojo's book, and even though they'd patched things up (and how), the memory still stuck in her throat.

It had been their first real fight. Tina hated fights; she often fought with Mei, her roomie and one of her best friends, and Mei could be irritating, but she also forgot her anger quickly and all would return to normal. Tina tended to nurse affronts, though lately she had tried taking a leaf from Mei's rule book.

After Web left, Lian told her husband she needed a break, and so he began doling out the orders. The truck was never lacking for customers, especially at lunchtime, which was when Tina tried to help out.

Tina knew something was on Mom's mind, and she had to leave soon anyway, so she gave her father a kiss, took off her apron, and set the folding table they kept roped off from the public near the front end of the truck. Lian brought tea in DbD-stamped paper cups.

"It must be that big school," Lian commented as she slid into the seat opposite Tina. Behind them, another line was forming, and every one of the other little folding tables had been declared by someone saving places while their friends picked up the order. "I see you looking like a ghost is following you."

Tina tried to tell herself she was prepared for this, because some variation on the "ghost" theme was always the prelude for "Why do you go to school? You would be happier working here with us."

To avoid this, Tina replied, "No, Mom, it's not that at all. I love school. Except—"

Lian was on her like a mongoose on a snake. "I know. I know it! You must quit school or that ghost will suck all the life out of you."

In her DbD ball cap, Lian did resemble a coach of some sport or another, and Tina was always the worst player.

"Well, no. The thing is, I think I have to change the focus of my thesis. I'm just not feeling that I'm on the right track, and I keep thinking that I need to blow up everything I've already done and go in another direction."

There. It was out. Better to bitch at Mom about school, not about Raj, whom Mom hadn't even met. Either tack was peppered with landmines, but it was easier to avoid them with the subject of

Tina's PhD program than the subject of men and potential husbands.

Tai's hearing was more acute than a bloodhound's. "Why he tell you that?" he asked from the truck's serving window. "What is wrong with it?"

Not having bothered to share the mysteries of her paper, "History vs. Archaeological Reconstruction: How Assumptions Steer Scholarship," Tina didn't elaborate. "Nothing, Dad. But I think *she* is lukewarm on it."

Lian said, "Then it's time to think of something else, like working here."

Before Dad could retort and the dialogue deteriorated into the perpetual argument about Tina's life, Tina got up from the table.

"I really have to go now." She pushed an unruly lock of hair from her eyes. "I have hundreds of undergrad papers to read and grade."

"Look," Lian said, getting up and rounding the table to face her. "You aren't happy. I see you hate this papers thing. Working here, you have fresh air and sunshine and us—"

Leaning down, Tina kissed her mother's cheek. "I'll call you tomorrow. Bye, Dad. Bye, Mom."

Trotting toward the subway, Tina glanced back and waved. Her mother stood beside the table with her arms folded. But Dad waved at her from the window.

At least he's on my side. Tai was her champion, just like her three best friends, Bing, Mei, and Jojo, encouraging her to stay in school when she despaired succeeding, helping her find money for tuition like the big grant her dad had found for her. Lian, on the other hand, had heart and mind set on Tina becoming part of the Drive-by-Dumpling team. An only daughter, Tina carried a heavy burden. *If there were two of us, or I could split myself in two, it would be so much easier.*

Raj shuffled uncomfortably in the doorway of Tina's cramped office in Steinhardt's Academic Resource Center. Here, PhD candidates who bore the burden of taking on first-year classes the tenured profs didn't want to teach were crammed into tiny offices. Tina, over Raj's shoulder, could see Maisie in her office across from Tina's, door open as all the doctoral students doors were supposed to be unless they were holding a student conference; eyebrows raised, Maisie fanned her hand as if she'd touched something hot.

Understandable, since Maisie was getting a clear view of Raj's well-toned butt. Wearing a pale blue shirt, yellow tie, and carrying his Hugo Boss jacket over one arm, he smiled coyly at Tina as he laid a box of Coffret Maison chocolates on her desk.

She smiled up at him, happier about his showing up out of the blue than she liked to admit. Now she could stop fretting about scholarly bias and think only about Raj.

"Oh, still contrite, are we?" Tina leaned back in her office chair. "I'm really not mad at you anymore."

"Never hurts to buy extra insurance."

Once Raj was safely inside her storage locker–sized office, Tina took one of several stickie notes off the inside wall, pasted it to the outer door surface, and closed it.

Raj, examining a fertility figure Tina used as a paperweight, gave her a puzzled glance. Tina grinned. "It says 'Student Conference—DO NOT DISTURB.' It's so someone doesn't just barge in."

Walking up to him, she took the points of his collar in her hands and turned him around to face her. Just looking at him, his wide shoulders, doe-like eyes, and rakish good looks, struck her with delight.

"Are you sure no one's going to barge in? What if someone left something in here and needed it for class?" He aimed a glance at the door, but Tina pulled his chin back toward her.

"Well," she breathed, nuzzling his neck, "I'm not sure, but isn't it exciting to think about it?"

"I'm glad you like the chocolate, but we really—"

Tina placed her lips on Raj's, drawing him close and turning so that she was leaning against the edge of her desk. His hands responded, roaming freely over her body and hair. She began to unbutton his shirt; he lifted her sweater.

This is more like it, she thought, relishing his touch and scent. She could feel him responding in other body parts as they kissed. He swept the chocolates out of the way, cupped her buttocks, and lifted her onto the desk.

The office door creaked as it opened. Jerking back, Raj nearly tripped over a waste can. Tina jumped off the desk, pulled down her sweater, and brushed her hair out of her eyes, while Raj turned his back to the door and tucked in his shirt.

Tina glared at the student who poked his head through the partly opened door. "Sorry, I—"

"Didn't you see the sign? This is a private meeting," she snapped. She recognized this kid with sandy hair, glasses, and a boyish face, but she felt too rattled to recall his name at the moment, and she made an effort to remember her student's names. She leaned against her desk and glared at him.

"Sorry, I didn't see a sign. I just wanted to drop off my paper," Unknown Student said with a nervous laugh. "Sorry I'm late with it, Ms. Lu. It was the toaster oven."

Now Tina remembered his name. John. An old-fashioned name for a Gen Z stoner. Toaster oven, huh? "Excuse me?"

John sidled through the door, holding a folder. He offered it to Tina, who took it and held it carefully in her hand. Raj retreated to look out the window, still keeping his back to the student.

"My paper fell into the kitchen sink, so I put it into the toaster oven to dry it out, and . . ."

Tina felt her mouth twist ever so slightly. Picking up the folder, she opened it. The papers were a little crisp around the edges.

"It sorta baked." Giving a nervous laugh, John turned and bolted through the door. Behind her at the window, Raj snickered.

Tina added John's paper to one of the stacks on her desk. "That's a new one. I guess 'my iguana ate it' is passé." For a moment her spirits drooped. She had more than one hundred to grade by the end of the week.

"Well." Raj walked over to her, leaned against the desk beside her, and nudged her with his elbow. "I guess our next makeup sex session will have to wait until tonight."

Tina poked him back. The near-miss of clueless John walking in on the sight of them fucking on top of her desk didn't douse the flame; on the contrary, it fed it.

"That's what you think," she told him. Returning to her door, she found the "do-not-disturb" stickie note on the floor. Grabbing a binder clip, she fastened it to her name plate, shut the door, and locked it.

Raj's eyes widened again. Grabbing his hand, she pulled him around the desk, sat in her chair, and pulled her sweater off. Gratified, she saw his worry melt into a crooked smile as he began to unbuckle his belt.

Thesis, schmesis, Tina thought as she leaned back. *This is a scholarly bias I can really relate to.*

Chapter Twenty-One

Over the weekend, while Bee was at the atelier frantically sewing then resewing her sleepwear, Cindi Koh fell into the habit of dropping by. Bee was a little surprised at the unexpected happiness she felt every time Cindi walked into the workspace.

Mostly they chatted about fashionistas, designers, and new Instagram posers trying to get big hits on their pages. But then, there was the time they walked up on the stage and Cindi kissed her again. Only a few contestants were in the workspace at the time, and they stood behind a stand of stage lights in the very back where no one could see them.

Cindi Koh tasted like coconuts and not of tobacco. If she was still smoking, she seemed to take care not to indulge before her visits with Bee. As they hid backstage, Bee felt as if she and Cindi were embarking on a caper. It felt dangerous, and Bee was flattered, because Cindi brought a whiff of upper crust culture into the room. She dropped names of designers she had met at the chic parties she got invited to, and she described outfits designers pressed on her to push on her Instagram account—which, naturally, made Bee wonder if Cindi thought she should give her a Pinky B look.

Bee loved that Cindi was snarkier than she. Cindi sat next to her at her worktable, scrolling through her phone, answering texts, and cleverly dissing people in the industry. Bee never, ever wanted to land on this woman's bad side. She had no doubt that a bad Koh review would be any aspiring designer's death sentence.

Cindi leaned close to show Bee a photo. "This one, she fucks all her photographers. They have to fuck her to get the gig."

Bee was astonished. She knew this house well—they dressed celebrities for the Oscars.

"And look here at this slime." Bee saw a familiar face with his arm around Cindi, beaming into the camera. "He was all over me that day, tried to pull me into the men's room for fuck's sake." Cindi wrinkled her nose as if at a putrid smell. "I'd been warned about him and was able to talk my way out of it. I told him I had herpes."

They giggled wildly. Bee loved seeing Cindi laugh. She always raised her chin and looked upward, as if she was replaying the ridiculous scene on the ceiling.

After this entertainment, Bee had to focus on her work, and her glee drained away.

"I just don't feel like I'm on top of those pajamas," she fretted.

"That plus-size model is going to rock your kimono. C'mon, girl. Stop fussing." Cindi massaged Bee's neck with one hand. She excelled at bolstering Bee's confidence, mostly by smiling patiently and shaking her head.

Tomorrow was the critical day. The fashion show for the semi-final cut to three contestants was to start Monday at ten a.m. Bee was happy enough with her silk screening for the active wear, but the silk kimono and boy shorts made her jaw ache.

"I want to see it one more time on the dress form," Bee said, getting up and sweeping up the kimono she'd been sewing. She wished she could but didn't dare kiss Cindi right here in front of everyone. Cindi's elegance dazzled her, but she felt antsy and tense. They weren't the only ones here this Sunday night. Several others, including Elijah and Keitu, were frantically—and literally—tying up loose ends.

Giving Bee's hand a squeeze, Cindi drifted over to Elijah. Part of Cindi's job, along with the journalists who were interviewing all of them, was to get the message out about who might be NYCFAYE's new knockout designer. Bee sighed, knowing that she wasn't the only contestant featured in Cindi's social media, but she felt a special closeness to Cindi, and she was pretty sure it was mutual.

Bee felt like her eyes were crossing as she examined the hemline of the kimono for the hundredth time. Worried about the length, she pinned it up, then undid the pins, ripped out the hem, and held a two-inch strip of gold-and-black trim along the edge.

That's it. Quickly basting the trim in place, she replaced it on the dress form. Bee tried to remember Dot's shape, the relationship of hips to bust. Which look would be flattering to the plus-size model? This item was more like a kimono-style jacket, and the beauty of a kimono is the vertical line of it. Maybe she shouldn't have pictured Dot in this one, but she wanted to show her best pieces on the figures of the majority of women, young and old, living in the United States and yearning to buy her clothes.

As she stared at the dress form, trying to call up a vision of Dot wearing the kimono, her brain refused to work. She'd lost count of how far into sleep deficit she had fallen. Maybe she should go home and try to actually sleep. Alex was working a night shift tonight, but she'd come over to Bee's apartment in the morning after her shift to escort the hot mess that was Bing Lin to NeueHouse.

In the morning, she could clear her head with caffeine, and better yet, Dot would be here for the adjustments. Smiling to herself at the thought of Alex coming with her tomorrow, Bee brushed her hand along Cindi's shoulders and said good night to Elijah.

As she grabbed her backpack and jacket, Bee thought about Alex and Cindi. *Merino wool and diamonds. Alex and Cindi.* Merino softness and wonderful feel or a diamond's hungry gleam. Bee felt strongly that she was attracted to both. Who wouldn't be? Somewhere deep down, she suspected Cindi might be using her come-on skills to gain Bee's confidence, but this played both ways. Even if this thing with Cindi was a short ride, it was fun.

The ten survivors stood in a row on the stage as Penelope and Matt, still arguing about the final choices as they traded pages from their ragged notebooks, scanned the contestants' faces. Bee caught Elijah's eye. He gave her an exhausted shrug.

It was impossible to judge anything from the reaction of today's audience. They applauded and whistled at every model. Dorothy did rock the yellow velvet boy shorts and Bee's red silk kimono; with Sheila and Alex's help, Bee had managed to build the perfect hemline over Dot's hips. In kitten heels and ribbons tied around her wrists and ankles, flowing behind her as she strutted, Dot earned raucous applause. Felix, with a hank of gold-tipped hair over his left eye, sashayed with his PJ top open. Bee had hand-covered every button and sewn the surfer-length shorts from ribbon and braid. For the activewear, Bettie, paired with Simon, wore St. Lewis sunglasses and showed her silk-screened black spaghetti tee and cargo shorts patched with Chinese silk; the pair had colorful climbing ropes hanging from their shoulders. Bee had made two hats, a bright green trilby for Bettie and a black stockman for Simon.

Nervous energy was Bee's food and drink today. She'd been unable to get anything down, even when the golden fox tempted her with a Caffe Roma cannoli. By now, waiting for the dreaded results, she wanted to scream, "Hurry the fuck up!" The fumbling around down there was making them all crazy. Stoic, stony Camille appeared like she might go to tears at any moment.

Finally, Penelope stepped forward, a piece of paper in her hand.

"This has been a brutal choice. You all are so talented, creative, the best group of designers we've ever had . . ."

How long is this crap going to go on? They probably say that every year. To distract herself, Bee stared through the arched windows at a group of gulls circling in the clear blue sky. She knew Penelope was speaking, but her voice receded in volume somehow. *Concentrate on the birds. They don't give a shit what is happening in here. No one in the world cares.*

Repeating this mantra to herself over and over, Bee felt like she was about to float through the window to join the birds, when someone grabbed her arm and jerked her forward.

Everyone was clapping. Bee found herself standing near the edge of the stage beside Elijah and Camille.

I'm out? I have to go home? Camille IS crying. How come I'm not crying?

Alex was jumping up and down, just behind Joseph, who was applauding madly.

Elijah grabbed Bee's hand, Camille's on his other side, and raised them.

"Congratulations, final three!" Matt's baritone voice boomed above the applause. Blinking, Bee finally came to, and it finally sank in that she had made the final cut when Halemé leaned down and kissed her on the cheek. Bountiful Bettie had a big smile on her face.

Cindi was on the stage now, and standing in front of the three, filmed them with her phone, throwing out questions like, "How does it feel to be this close to the prize? What is the first thing you will do if you win?"

Bee didn't remember answering any of these questions. When Cindi grabbed her into a big hug, Bee clung to her.

Before she knew it, she said into Cindi's ear, "Listen. Wednesday night. Are you busy? Dinner?"

"You bet. I'm totally free for you," Cindi breathed back. Bee wanted to kiss her right then and there, but she knew Alex would be watching, so as Cindi turned to Elijah, Bee made sure to beam down at Alex and wave. To Bee's relief, Alex grinned and blew her a kiss.

It wasn't until she walked to the subway with Alex, who needed to go home to sleep—she had another night shift tonight—that Bee remembered she and Alex had tickets to an off-Broadway play this Wednesday and had planned for a late dinner at a Village hangout. Alex had just disappeared down the subway stairs after saying good night, and Bee felt a little sick.

How am I going to wriggle out of this one? Bingo, you are a buffoon.

Chapter Twenty-Two

Bee's apartment always smelled like pears. Not that Bee was much into fresh fruit the way Alex was, but somehow it was true. Closing Bee's front door behind her, Alex flipped on the light. Wan Pi met her at the door, wiggling his chocolate-brown body and thrusting his squished little face up for a kiss.

"Hi, WannaPee. Did Bee walk you when she came home?" Kneeling down, she accepted several wet kisses. Scanning the living room, there was no sign of damage, signifying that Wan Pi had all his breaks while at the dog hotel. He always made his displeasure known to Bee if this did not occur—and on time.

Still, Alex felt disappointed about Bee breaking their theater date; Bee apologized like a maniac, explaining that NYCFAYE had called a Wednesday-night meeting and she had to be there, and she'd forgotten all about it. She begged Alex to go to the play anyway, and to find a friend for the extra ticket.

So Alex had gone to the play with an old girlfriend—their affair had ended amicably and they'd remained friends—had dinner with her, and then come alone back to Bee's apartment to wait for her, bringing dinner leftovers to surprise her.

Bee wasn't home yet. This wasn't unusual for Bee—the three finalists had probably stopped somewhere for drinks after their meeting, but that seemed unlikely, as Alex remembered Bee mentioning Camille's animosity toward her.

She'd laughed. "Maybe she hates dykes too, like that model's douchebag husband."

But Bee did like Elijah—so did Alex, for that matter—and maybe the two of them had gone to a gay bar somewhere. Alex felt a little sad that Bee didn't text her and ask her to join them, so to pass the time she decided to take a bath and get ready for bed. Going into Bee's bedroom, she began to take off her clothes and then noticed Bee's backpack propped in a corner. It was odd for Bee not to have taken her backpack to the meeting, especially if she had gone straight from work.

Shrugging, Alex slipped out of her shoes and skirt, looking forward to a late snack and cuddle with Bee. Surrounded by lit candles, Alex soaked in fragrant oils for as long as she could stand, Wan Pi napping beside her on the bathmat. She couldn't stop herself from fantasizing about living with Bee, together, maybe even married, enjoying a nightly joint bath. Of course, the tub would be bigger and deeper, with jacuzzi jets.

Just as Alex left the bathroom wrapped in only a towel, she heard a key in the lock. Wan Pi raced to the door, but instead of dashing into the bedroom to throw on her robe, Alex suppressed a silly giggle and decided to stand in the hallway in her towel and see how long it took for Bee to notice her.

But Alex heard two voices—one was Bee's, and the other she couldn't quite place. Alex stiffened. There was no doubt that the other voice was female. Maybe one of Bee's friends, Jojo or Mei? Realizing she was practically naked, she dashed silently to the bedroom, turned out the bedside light, then returned to the ajar door to listen.

Alex heard Bee's keys clatter to the floor, followed by a giggle. "That's it," Bee was saying. "All this stress has given me a stroke. And this is my needle hand, too."

The answering voice was contralto and very soft, but Alex heard the other woman plainly. "Where you're going, babe, you'll have a stable full of seamstresses. You won't have to pick up a needle again."

"You say the sweetest things."

There was a long silence, broken only by a faint rustling noise, Wan Pi's nails on the flooring, a few random steps, and then, Alex's heart froze as she heard a kiss, and another, and a third.

Her face grew warm, and everything began to melt, coalescing into a burning mess in her gut.

Cindi Koh.

Tearing off her towel, Alex began to dress as quietly as possible.

I don't believe it. How could Bee—?

Her fingers shook as she tried to zip up her skirt—one that Bee had made for her. Peering up at the bedroom window, she wondered if she could crawl out and get the hell away from here. But just as she was straightening her top, a firm resolve hit her and she turned back toward the door.

I'm going to just walk out there. Confront them. Throw this little clock at Cindi.

Alex picked up Bee's tiny travel alarm clock that had never once been used—it was an old wind-up kind that belonged to some long-dead relative. The thought of this particular action pleased her, but she knew she couldn't do it. To be truthful, she felt paralyzed. Their walking in and finding her skulking around the bedroom would be her chance at confrontation, but no, it would just get all vulgar and awkward.

"Your dog is so cute. What's his name again?" Cindi Koh was asking, with a hint of boredom.

Then there was a sudden intake of breath from the living room. "Shit. Shit," from Bee. "*Shit*, my girlfriend is here. That's her backpack on the sofa."

Cindi answered languidly, "Your *girlfriend*? Oh my." After a moment, Alex heard the sound of high heels clacking across the wooden floor. "Too bad. I guess I'll leave you two to it, then."

Bee said nothing.

Alex sat down on the bed to wait for the sound of the front door opening and closing. She'd so wanted to throw the little bedside clock at Cindi's head, but the influencer wasn't to blame here. Bee was. The realization of what Bee had just done to her hit hard. Quivering with hurt, she felt sick inside.

Bee called to her from the living room. "Hey, Alex, sweet girl, you here?"

Alex's skin felt was if it was on fire. *This is the last and final killing straw. No more, goddamn it.* Getting up, she flung open the bedroom door, stomped down the hall in her bare feet, and glared at a surprised Bee from the hallway entry.

"So," she said, making her voice as icy as she could. "You had this meeting with the producers and the other contestants, and Cindi Koh just happened to walk in?"

Bee shrugged and gave Alex a sheepish smile. "Yeah. I just invited her over for—"

"Why would they invite an influencer to a private meeting? I recall you said it was private."

Bee ran her right hand up the side of her head, burying her fingers in her hair. It was a tell that Alex knew well. "Oh, they do it all the time. Those folks are part of the family, sort of."

Still smiling, although moving a little stiffly, Bee strolled into the kitchen, and seeing the takeout bag, opened it and started to remove the cardboard boxes. "This smells heavenly. Where'd you go for dinner?"

"Tokyo. Hong Kong. Paris. Where else?"

Bee's smile vanished, and Alex felt gratified to see her worried expression, just like someone caught in a bare-boned lie. "Are you mad at me for inviting Cindi in for a nightcap?"

Now is the time for you to admit you kissed her. I heard you kissing. And it wasn't just a good-bye peck.

When Alex made no reply, Bee said, "I really did forget about that meeting when I got us those tickets." She came around the counter and approached Alex, who kept her arms folded. "And the meeting went on so late—"

"I heard you talking." Alex kept her gaze on Bee's and she saw a little flush at Bee's temples. "You sounded pretty chummy."

"Oh, sure." Bee tried to giggle again. "I have to schmooze with her, you know. Then she'll write great things about me."

Kissing like what Alex had heard wasn't just schmoozing. And there was something else Alex noted that gave credence to the lie.

Inhaling the odor of alcohol on Bee's breath, Alex turned her head away to stare at the floor. Anger at Bee's wheedling made her chest tight; she couldn't stand to hear another apology for not doing the "Yoda thing," knowing Bee would go ahead and pull the hurtful shit she always pulled.

"I'm going home." Alex retrieved her shoes from the bedroom and grabbed her backpack from the sofa. She should have skewered Bee, called her on her bullshit; more than anything she wanted to see Bee cry, just like she was going to go home and do. But she was too bone and heart weary, and she knew it wouldn't do any good anyway.

"No, wait, please stay. I'd rather sit here with you and—"

"Nope. I'm gone."

She closed the door carefully behind her, ignoring Bee's pleas that she stay the night. She felt like she was caving in as a landslide of pain and anger ate at her gut.

Imagine, stupid me, dreaming about settling down with her, even a wedding. I'm a damned idiot.

There hadn't been any meeting. Alex could smell the alcohol on Bee's breath. She could smell the whiff of coconut lotion, too, a cosmetic that Bee would never use. Bee had been with Cindi all evening. She had broken her date with Alex to go out with Cindi.

By the time Alex got to the subway station, she was still wiping tears from her cheeks. Inside her brain she heard the voice of reason lecturing her in an endless loop: *You'll never be able to trust Bee ever again.*

The tears kept flowing and flowing; Alex thought they would never stop.

Chapter Twenty-Three

Bee stared at the drawing of the evening gown she'd just finished, tore out the page, crumpled it up, and threw it on the floor. Camille, now working three sewing machines away from her, as only the three of them were using the workspace now, glanced over.

Eyeing her, Bee saw a tiny sneer come and go on Camille's face. Getting to her feet, Bee strolled toward Camille, passed her, and glanced at the pattern Camille was laying out on two yards of pearl-gray sateen. She stood behind Camille for a count of ten until she saw Camille throw a quick glance over her shoulder. Then she strolled on, hands behind her back, as if pacing to clear her mind for the design of this gala wear.

A ball gown was the last thing on Bee's mind. She couldn't stop thinking about last night, how Cindi's lips had felt and tasted. But the pleasant heat of that memory was chilled when she saw Alex's anger and realized that Alex had heard everything, knew she was lying, and was fighting back tears as she left. She knew she needed to send out a conciliatory text, and she'd tried to compose one several times, but they all sounded trite and disingenuous.

I'm such a fuck-up. What is wrong with me? Is it pathological?

She'd had a long early phone call with Jojo about it. Jojo had said, "You do it to yourself. Cock gun. Shoot foot. Don't you see that Alex is the best thing that's ever happened to you?"

"But I've never had a steady. I don't think I've ever even missed not having one."

"You've been with her for more than six months, idjit. Count it out. I've known you since you got your first period and you've never, ever been with the same girl for this long."

Bee stared out the workspace windows. She could see, between the clutter of Chelsea, a sliver of the Hudson. What Jojo said stunned Bee. She hadn't even thought about it like that. Usually, she got tired of the girl, or fucked up with infidelity, like she'd just done. But with Alex, until Cindi Koh, Bee hadn't stepped over the flirting line with anyone else.

And she wasn't tired of Alex. She felt great with Alex; they meshed; they were comfortable. Content.

This inner turmoil was maddening, Bee thought. It was interfering with her creative process. *Lovers! Always complicating things, throwing my brain into the blender.*

Bee marched back to her table. Sheila glanced up from her machine and nodded. Sheila was a good soul, quiet, reliable, really skilled, and had Bee's back.

The cocktail look for both men and women was nearly done. Sheila was sewing gold mesh ruffles onto the black satin. The men's Chinese silk Nehru jacket-style shirt hung on one of the dress forms, and the slim-fit red trouser was suspended from easy-clips on the rack.

The men's gala outfit was almost done too but needed more work. Bee wanted the shirt to be fitted and the jacket slouchy, and she'd fussed with it so much, she had to take a break and work on the women's gown.

She had finished drawing several images to silk-screen onto the butter yellow organza, but she was stumped about the style of the dress. She wanted big and fluttery, a look that floated. Strapless, fitted waist, but she was having difficulty with where each image should go. She laid out her images: black swans, demoiselle cranes, harlequin ducks, great blue herons and ospreys, all birds of water, and the organza had to swell like waves on the sea.

Bee was running behind. How would any of these be ready by Saturday if she printed each in a repeating pattern on the gown skirting? It was too ambitious. She'd never pull it off. She could use the fabric printer, but she wanted this one dress to be hand printed.

"There's too many. I'll never get the fabric done in time," she muttered.

The sewing machine hum stopped as Sheila glanced up at her. "You have five designs, right? What about a five-panel skirt, each printed with a large version on each one, or ten prints, two of each bird?"

Bee stared at the prints, then at Sheila. "Yes. That would work." Bee's mind began to race. "Sheila, you're a genius!"

Smiling, Sheila raised her eyebrows and shrugged. "My genius is to help other geniuses."

Rubbing her chin, Bee realized she would need help. While she was cutting out patterns in the vinyl plates, she could save time by having someone running the press.

Picking up her phone, she went back to the silk-screen table she had set up at the back of the workspace, where the presses and vinyl plates were waiting to be used, and searched for the red ink she had pulled out of one of the drawers. It was gone, and as she dug through the ink drawers, she couldn't find it. A minor annoyance, really, and Bee decided that the red mark on the crane's neck would be pink. A better choice for Pinky B, anyway.

She stopped herself before dialing Alex. It would be awkward to call her now, only to ask for a favor. She thought, not for the first time, that she should send Alex a gift, something really special, but she was having a hard time figuring out what it should be. First, she should call her and apologize for lying about her date with Cindi. She should have been up front about it, but when she learned that she had picked the worst possible evening, she was too chicken to back out by then.

Feeling glum, Bee dialed Tina next, hoping she could spare a few hours to drop by to work the press. Tina'd had a lot of fun last weekend helping Bee by pinning the patchwork blocks for the kimono and wandering around the shop drooling over the others' designs. Also, she could get Tina's take, and advice on what to do about Alex. She left a desperate-sounding message on Tina's voice mail, hoping she would call back immediately.

Who else?

Bee hit Hao's number. She hadn't spoken with him in nearly a week; he was quite busy, seemingly, planning his elopement with Becca. Finally getting introduced to Becca when she ran into them at the library, Bee found out that she liked the Ozzie. Glib and funny, Becca peppered Bee with questions about the contest, and showered her with congratulations for her progress into the finals. Hao, standing quietly next to them, couldn't take his eyes off his girlfriend. They were truly in love.

"Hao. Where are you?" she asked when he answered.

"I'm home—I mean the hotel. Where else would I be?"

"Sidney? Perth? The Outback?"

"Not yet, sis. We're not leaving until week after next."

"Did you tell Mom and Dad yet?" Bee's voice rose to a squeak. She swallowed. "Wait, I know the answer. No, right?"

She heard Hao breathe in deeply. "I just can't. You tell them. You can do it."

"So, they can explode all over me, not you." *Hao is such a freaking coward when it comes to dealing with Dad.* Granted it was no picnic for Bee, either.

"Sis—"

"I don't talk to Dad," she said.

"But you talk to Mom, don't you?"

"Don't make me lay this on Mom, either. She always has to run interference with Dad. It's not fair."

"I'll email them from Sydney."

"That's crass. Anyway, I need some help over here." She told him about her silk-screening idea, and he sounded impressed. He was busy, he claimed, but he could give her a whole day tomorrow, if he moved some appointments around.

"Thanks, you are my hero." Bee hesitated for a moment, then asked, "How is Dad, anyway? Mom tells me he's just fine, happy, and busy and all that."

"He is, as far as I can tell."

After Hao signed off, Bee called Xing, who had several questions about "the big girl in the fancy robe." Bee had sent Mom the link to the Instagram photos of the finalists' outfits.

"We need to make great clothes for larger people. It's a thing in America."

"Yes, but why only a large woman? Where were the large man's clothes?"

Bee couldn't think of an answer, but she thought Mom had a point.

Xing asked, "Have you talked to your brother? He never calls me. Your father is worried. We're supposed to go home in a month —he bought Hao's ticket."

Oh, shit. Changing the subject was in order. "How is the search for a shop? You find anything yet?"

This diversion worked for a while. Mom told her about several in Manhattan, Flushing, even Brooklyn. "It has to be Manhattan, I tell your father. But he's cheap. Doesn't want to spend the money." Xing sounded like she was sipping tea. "To make money you have to spend money."

Hearing her mother quote an American tycoon, Bee stifled a giggle. "You're right, Mom. You should open the store in Manhattan. I could ask some of the fashionistas I met about locations. And there are lots of new hotels going up that might rent a space to Lin Fashions."

"Thank you, good daughter." There was a pause. Mom's voice sounded a little sad, Bee thought. "Bing, you haven't talked to your father in weeks. If your brother won't—if he chooses not to take the weight off your father, then." She stopped.

Bee's heart did a flip under her ribs. Did Mom suspect something about Hao and Becca? Xing Lin was a darker horse than Bee thought, if this were true. "Will Dad talk to me?"

"Yes-yes! He will. I will make sure that he will."

Bee wavered. She still couldn't forgive Dad for all his snubs of her talents, and this silence between them was only making it worse. As Mom would say, Bee had gotten her stubborn streak straight from her unbendable *ba*.

She told Mom that Hao was coming to help her tomorrow.

A big sigh filled the phone. "Oh, good. Very good. It's good that you asked and he agreed. You tell him to call me. Right away, okay?"

Xing was happiest when her family was in harmony, which didn't happen often enough. Bee said she would tell him, and she wished she could confide in Mom about Hao's insane plan to ditch them all and run off to Australia, of all places, with his tall, creamy-skinned redhead.

But before she could betray her brother, something she knew she shouldn't do, a shriek echoed through the workshop behind her. Ducking, Bee whirled around to see Elijah, arms shaking, holding up a section of his ball gown. She could see from across the room the dazzling splotch of red paint marring the golden velvet skirting panel stretched between his hands.

Elijah bellowed, "Who did this? *Who?*"

"Mom, gotta go."

"Who is yelling? Bing! Don't—"

Mom's voice faded as Bee lowered the phone and ended the call. Sickened, she quickly guessed that the "paint" on the velvet had come from the missing jar of ink. A rancid mixture of anger and fear swirled inside her gut.

Moving quickly, Bee found herself standing behind Camille, who was pinning a silk blouse together on a dress form, looking over her shoulder at Elijah.

"I know it was you," she muttered, seething.

Camille hates me. Camille knew I was silk-screening, and she'd seen me handling that red ink.

"What?" Camille swirled around, blonde hair floating into her face. She batted it out of the way. "What the fuck are you talking about?"

By this time Elijah strode toward them, the velvet swath bunched in one hand. His eyes, rimmed with tears, burned from his stricken face. Bee cringed inside at the deranged face Elijah gave her.

"Which one of you bitches did this to me? Was it you?" He thrust the velvet toward Bee's face.

"Jesus, Eli, why would I do that? I wouldn't think of doing such a thing to you."

Nostrils flaring, a tear tracking down his face, Elijah turned to Camille, who said quickly, "It wasn't me. I wouldn't go so low as to sabotage someone's work. Never. Never occurred to me." Her chin jutting out, Camille's voice was high-pitched and quivering.

Sheila and the other seamstresses huddled close by, watching this drama unfold, concern etched on their faces. Behind them, the cutters and colorists appeared frankly terrified. Elijah's seamstress, Monica, took a few steps forward and tried to touch the fabric, as if to remove it from Elijah's hysterical grasp, but he pulled away from her.

Bee stared at Camille, while hatred and ire filled her brain. "You fucking liar. I know it was you. You took that jar of ink from the drawer. You knew I was going to use it. You're sabotaging both of us."

Camille's lips whitened. She moved close to Bee, standing tall over her, and poked her finger into Bee's chest. "You little shit. You've got more jealousy of me and Elijah in that skinny body of yours than there is in all of Hollywood."

Slapping Camille's finger away, Bee raised her hand, but to her surprise Sheila quickly put her arm around her and started to march her away. Bee knew what the phrase "seeing red" meant, because she couldn't see anything but that red wound on the velvet as Sheila gently steered her toward her workstation.

"I know it wasn't you," Sheila breathed in Bee's ear.

Me too, Bee thought as she placed her hands on the table and leaned forward, briefly feeling short of breath. *Me too.*

Chapter Twenty-Four

Bee shouldn't have been surprised that she, Camille, and Elijah would be called into a meeting with the three show runners the next morning. In the tiny conference room that was the leadership team's current office, they listened, contrite, as Penelope chided them for their "childish antics."

Penelope shook her head like a disappointed mother. "I know you're all stressed out. Scenes like this do happen, as unprofessional as they may be, in the back rooms of runway shoes and in designer ateliers. But the ones who keep their heads, who are calm and professional in their work, are the ones who truly succeed."

Bee had not been able to lay aside the thought that Elijah believed she'd splashed that ink on his fabric, and the belief that Camille had done it to frame her. She half listened to Matt as he echoed Penelope's lecture; this lay heavily on her along with her failures with Alex, the rift with Dad, the thought of Hao abandoning her, and how much, how truly much, she wanted to win this contest.

Camille is right. I am a little shit.

She and Camille got off with a warning: Don't let this happen again, or . . . The "or" loomed like Godzilla in the room. Someone would be booted out. And Bee feared mightily that it would be her.

When the trio, avoiding each other's glances, paraded out of the conference room and back to their places, Cindi was waiting at Bee's station.

She said, stretching out one long leg, "Hey, girl, a little bird told me there was a bit of a spat in here yesterday."

"Maybe," Bee told her, not wanting to go into details of her suspicions about Camille because that little item might show up on Cindi's blog. "We got our hands slapped. And some sympathy for the bloody stress we're under. Ya think?"

Cindi flashed her million-dollar smile. Her eyes lit up a little. "So that cute chick Alex is more than a friend, huh?"

Nodding, Bee sank into her chair. "She's pissed at me."

"Well." Cindi rubbed Bee's back. "Maybe I can help with that."

Before Bee could think of a reply—her feelings about Cindi being unsettled and cloudy—a familiar voice floated from the entry.

Tina breezed in, walking quickly like she always did, and aimed straight for Bee. "I finally found you. There's no help in this building, signage or anything to tell a person where anything is happening."

Seeing Tina just now filled Bee with joy. Rising, she grabbed Tina into a tight hug. Neatening her wind-blown hair, Tina appeared puzzled. She was wearing tight jeans, a loose, filmy blue cotton blouse, and of course her signature Louboutins.

"Okay, here's the cavalry. Put me to work. I have to be back at school by one."

Because Hao was nowhere in sight, Bee was ecstatic to have one of her besties here. She was relieved, too, as she might be able to unload some of her worries while they worked.

Because Bee's bird images required multiple color layers, she set Tina to cutting out transparencies. Tina had confident, delicate fingers—mostly from helping her parents to fashion dumplings, but also honed from her archaeological field work, where precision and gentleness was essential when uncovering fragile artifacts. She could easily follow Bee's color-numbering system. Measurements would be tricky, but Bee told Tina not to fret over it. Lack of time required quick work.

Cindi hovered nearby, videotaping Bee's work while Sheila cut and readied the skirt panels. Bee almost wished Cindi would leave so that she could talk to Tina about Alex. But she needed Cindi, and she liked Cindi. More than she should.

So, they continued their flirting game. Cindi rested her hand on Bee's shoulder as she poured the ink into the bottom of the framed screen; Bee gently bumped into Cindi as she shared her ear pod music, one ear pod in each other's ear.

At one point she saw Tina eyeing her curiously, as if to ask, *Is this your new girlfriend? Is it over with Alex?* Bee caught Tina's eye a few minutes later, after Cindi moved away to answer a call.

"It's complicated," she whispered.

Tina's eyes narrowed. "Does Alex know?"

Bee picked up her squeegee. "Yeah. You could say that."

"Poor Bee. Love is hard sometimes." Tina offered her sympathy. Then she leaned closer. "Sometimes I think Raj is pulling away; the next minute I think he's too attentive. It makes no sense!"

"Alex has pulled away big time. I don't think she's ever going to speak to me again."

Tina's attention was distracted by someone coming in, and as Bee turned to follow her gaze, she saw Hao in the entry.

Right behind him was Becca. Bee gave Hao a mock sneer. Rolling his eyes, Hao took Becca's hand and guided her to the silk-screening tables.

"Jeez, Bee, these are beautiful." Hao picked up the sketch of the demoiselle crane and showed it to Becca.

"You drew these?" Becca asked, gaping at the drawing.

Bee gave her an exaggerated nod. "All by my little self."

"Tricky silk-screening," Hao said as he brought the sketch close. "All this subtlety. Didn't they let you have a digital fabric printer?"

"Yeah, but I wanted to hand print these. Later"—Bee handed the screen she had just used to the colorist, who ran to the sink to wash it—"later, when I'm famous, I'll use the robot."

"When is your fashion show?" Hao asked, incredulous. "This is a lot of work!"

Picking up the osprey sketch, Bee handed it and a vinyl sheet to Hao. "Get busy then. In a bit I'll need you for the printing."

Tina nudged Bee, and grimacing, Bee realized that she rudely hadn't introduced her brother and his fiancée to her best friend, so she remedied this immediately.

The group became quiet as they began to work. Bee saw Becca approach Cindi after waving at her. Of course they would know each other. They chatted for a few moments, then Cindi drifted over and told Bee she had to get photos of Camille and Elijah, too.

"Want to meet tonight?" Cindi murmured into Bee's ear.

Bee did want to meet tonight, but the thought of Alex stopped her. "I think I'm going to be here all night."

Cindi smiled. "Well, then, I may just drop by later."

This sounded safe enough. Alex was unlikely to waltz in here to surprise her, kiss, and make up. This realization made her feel a little sad.

Becca came over as Cindi sashayed away, and Bee gave her the assignment of blow-drying the skirt panels between each color layering.

"You know Cindi Koh, huh?" Bee asked her.

Becca tied on the apron Bee gave her. "Yes, don't I though. It's very good that she's profiling you guys. The best publicity. Just never get on her bad side." She winked as she said this.

"Yeah. Right." *This is why I'm making nice with Cindi. I wish Alex understood that I have to stay on Cindi's good side.*

"Say, might I take a peek at your other sketches?" Becca asked. "In between drying, that is. I'd love to see more of your work."

"It is fantastic," Tina added. "Go on, Bee. Get your little sketch-book out."

Bee ran back to her workstation and grabbed her backpack. Opening it as she returned to the silk-screening table, she slipped her hand into the spot where she always kept the idea book.

It wasn't there. She stopped. *I must have taken it out.*

"Hey, Sheila, is my sketchbook over there?" Sheila got up from the sewing machine and began to sort through bits of fabric and pattern paper littering the tabletop. Catching Bee's eye, she shook her head.

Bee ran back to the worktable and started riffling through the drawers while Sheila checked the floor. Bee upended the backpack on the table, but the sketchbook was nowhere to be found.

Feeling physically ill, Bee leaned against the table. *What if it fell out of my backpack? While I was on the scooter?* This was a disaster. If that had happened, she would never see it again.

"It has to be somewhere."

Tina was beside her. "Let's look everywhere. Maybe someone borrowed it."

Bee's breath quickened, and she felt her cheeks grow hot. *Camille, the bitch.*

As if she read Bee's mind, Sheila said she would ask Camille if she had seen the book. Bee followed Tina around as they walked the entire workshop, checked all over the staging area, and even went into the hallway and searched the now empty conference room.

Nothing. Nowhere. The sketchbook, the physical papers Bee was required to keep to show Penelope and Matt on demand, were gone. She had replications of most of them on her iPad, but paper copies were essential. Bee sat heaving in a folding chair beside the entry. Tina sat beside her and put her arm around Bee's shoulder. Becca stood before them, sympathetic, and Hao shook his head.

"Big suck, sis. Big, big suck." He stuck his hands in his jeans pocket. "But we better get back to work, huh?" He tapped his Apple watch. "Deadline coming up."

His watch started singing "Baby Shark." His eyes widened in embarrassment as he tried to turn it off while Tina and Becca giggled.

Bee felt the tears come, burning into her eyes, and she angrily rubbed them away as she rose from her chair. She was sure Camille had stolen the sketchbook. She would, once she learned the truth, wreak revenge big time.

Chapter Twenty-Five

"Yeah, shocking, isn't it?" Sebastian Cole, Mei's opponent in her pro bono case, had called her at work, in the middle of the day.

Recognizing Seb's name from her contacts, Mei gathered her composure before she answered. Shocking, yeah, that Cole would call her at all, but to learn that the antebellum building she was hired to defend from an encroaching developer had been irreparably damaged by a fire sprinkler malfunction took her breath away.

"*What?* How?"

"The insurance company is investigating today. Their agent called me this morning."

Mei wanted a moment to mourn this beautiful building. Yes, it was a pro bono case assigned to her—one of the many Doran and Cross handed out to their staff to handle for the purpose of adding to the firm's prestige—but she had grown to like and respect the handful of neighbors fighting to preserve it.

"We were set to win," she said out loud before she realized it.

Seb laughed. "Yes, you were, Ms. Tang. I would have crawled home with my tail between my legs."

This was a side of Seb Cole he kept hidden during the negotiation sessions, but Mei knew better. Before she'd worked with him on the Warner case, she had been warned about his wily ways, his ability to change persona depending on what he wanted. Relentless, he interrupted, badgered, and did not hesitate to voice his frustration with the stupidity of his adversaries. She'd personally overheard the way he disrespected his opponents, calling them "head-up-the-ass NIMBYs" and worse.

Then out of nowhere, he asked, "What say we meet for drinks later this afternoon, to pick over the ruins?"

"I really don't think—"

"Yes, but I'd like to talk to you about your case. It was remarkably sound. Like when you dug up that statute about a certain kind of granite—"

"Okay. I'll bite. Where?" Mei was intrigued. She could use this cocktail meet to find out more about how Seb Cole ticked. The Warner case would, she knew, not be the last time she had to face him down.

In the back of her Uber to the Marquis Marriott after work, Mei scrolled through her messages. She'd gotten scores of thank yous from staff about Steve Chen's birthday party at SPIN, the ping-pong night spot. Especially the food. Mei reminded herself to tell Tina about all the kudos, and to ask if more people were showing up at the food truck, because Mei had liberally dropped the Drive-by Dumpling name and whereabouts. The problem was that now everyone kept asking about fun places to have parties, like she had somehow become the event planner for the entire office.

For the tenth time this afternoon, she ran over every detail in her case, and she could find no errors. Seb Cole had even admitted that her clients were going to win in their bid to ensure that the building be qualified for heritage status and could not be touched. Two inspections—one by the contractor and one by Mei's clients—disagreed on the shape the sprinklers were in. Mei had picked apart each area of dispute, proved that the building's infrastructure was sound, and that the cost of restoration would be reasonable.

Such bad luck.

She thought about her father, who would have said, *there is no such thing as luck.* As difficult as it was, Mei had to agree with him.

Seb had secured a cozy table right next to The View's floor-to-ceiling windows, through which Midtown Manhattan sparkled. He lounged with one arm on the back of the booth, smiling at her as she approached him. In his tailored black suit jacket, tieless dress shirt, and Rolex glinting on his upraised arm, he was the picture of privilege, even down to his boyishly friendly smile. She wondered, not for the first time, if the boyish smile was real or just another mask from his box of fake charms.

"Everyone, and I mean e-ver-y-one, is looking at you right now, Ms. Tang."

Seb got up to help her out of her coat. It was a nice, if slightly corny act. His comment about the attention of the busy New York spot rotating on the top floor of the Marquis Marriott in midtown, was pure bullshit. In her gold twill Theory blazer and pencil skirt, she looked exactly like every other woman at the bar's happy hour.

She didn't reply but slipped into the booth and settled her brief beside her.

Putting his hand around his glass of something smoky-looking on ice but not raising it, Seb said, "My first time at this place. Yours?"

Mei nodded. She was saved from saying something trite like "beautiful view"—which it was—by the waiter approaching. Smiling up at him, she picked up the drinks menu and opened it to the cocktails. "What's the bartender's best drink tonight?"

Raising his eyebrows in a friendly manner, the waiter quickly pointed to the gin and tonic. "You must try his gin and tonic. The best I've ever tasted, and that's no lie."

"All right." With Tanqueray No. 10 gin and Elderflower liquor, it had to be good. Seb was looking at her in admiration.

"I'd say he's in love with you now. We'll get great service."

"You want to win the waiters over to your side, kind of like you would a judge."

He laughed and politely waited until her drink came before he sipped his scotch. After they toasted, he said, "I liked you in the negotiations. You had the better case, by dumb luck, really. You would have wiped the floor with me."

By dumb luck. Mei did not for a moment believe this statement. She was quite accurate, after all her years dealing with clients, at knowing when someone was lying. But still, Seb managed to look chagrined, as if the subtext was that he'd never been up against a better counselor.

Before coming here, Mei had spent a significant portion of her afternoon listening to Claire Wright, one of her angry preservation clients. The woman wasted no time in invoking foul play at work in the incident of the errant sprinkler. Mei couldn't deny that this thought had crossed her mind, but in the end, she had to conclude that accidents like this could happen anytime in an old building with systems that had been left to rust.

Seb began to ask her questions about where she was from, but, as she always did when people asked about her past, she glossed over her unhappy childhood in China and managed to ease the conversation around to funny law school stories.

Seb burst out with a guffaw, as if he had truly been amused by her tales. When she told him one of her female professors had actually told her class that the three branches of power in the US were like incestuous brothers and sisters, always screwing each other, he almost spit his second scotch onto his plate.

By the time she'd finished her second gin and tonic, Mei was feeling pleased with her impression that Seb was viewing her with new, and respectful, eyes.

As he helped her on with her coat, she told him, "It's not easy, trying to break into the old boys' club that is the law. Women are still, even now, disrespected. I told you some old law school jokes, but it wasn't easy finding anything to laugh about back then."

After giving her a friendly nod, Seb followed her to the restaurant door. At the top of the stairs, he stopped her.

"Which way are you going? Share my car?"

His blue eyes gazed straight into hers. "Sure," she said, wary. "Tribeca. I can get an Uber, though."

He smiled in his crooked, charming manner. "I have a car waiting. I'm going that way too."

Why not? The more time I spend with this guy, the more chances I have to figure out his weaknesses.

The car was a legit limo, from a service, Mei was pretty sure. Sebastian opened the door for her when it glided forward to a stop at the hotel entry, then slid in beside her. He'd become, for these last two hours anyway, easier to like than she'd expected; she felt comfortable—he paid attention to her and actually listened. She'd ended most of the dates she'd been on lately with knowing everything about the men, including the location of their tattoos, while they were still trying to remember how to pronounce her first name.

When she felt Seb's hand on her arm, she glanced at him. "What?"

He was gazing at her, eyebrows raised as if to ask, *Is this okay*? To be polite, she didn't move away, but she felt a little wary. She gave him a questioning smile. *Seriously, dude, what's up?*

When he slid closer to her, Mei's heart ticked up a beat. Not wanting to have to fight him off, she shifted away. He refused to let her; reaching around with his free hand, he pulled her head around and planted his lips on hers. Then, his hand wrapped around the back of her neck, he leaned away, winding his legs around hers, and brought her down onto his chest.

"God you are so beautiful," he whispered.

This all happened with quick, practiced speed. For a few seconds, Mei was frozen—unable to stop his advances or even defend herself. Glancing at the driver, she saw him staring straight ahead, his eyes never flicking to the rearview mirror.

Then she understood, with a flush of terror that swiftly merged with anger: his car, his driver, his rules.

He breathed, "You don't know how crazy you made me in those meetings. I've been so . . ." Seb felt for one of her breasts, still holding her in an iron embrace.

With wrenching strength, Mei got one of her legs free. Bending her knee, she flung one hand behind her, trying to snag her shoe.

"Look, Seb," she gasped, "I don't . . ."

Sinking his paw into her hair, Seb pulled her head back and ran his tongue up her neck. Disgusted, Mei wished she could vomit on him, but nothing came up. His other hand began to pull up her dress.

There was no way to reason with him. She felt her shoe, but Seb's movement pulled her foot away from her. Reaching with her other hand, she gripped his thigh and squeezed as hard as she could. This made him jerk away his dress-seeking hand and seize her wrist. This gave her time enough to reach down and, with extreme effort, wrest the shoe, with its three-and-a-half inches of stiletto heel, from her foot.

The toe of the shoe firmly in her hand, she brought it over her head and slammed the heel into Seb's cheek. He made a sound that was equal parts roar and yelp, and his hands went to his face.

"You son-of-a-bitch!" Mai spat as she flung her knee into his groin. He doubled over with a strangled scream. Finally free of Seb-ranging-monkey-hands-Cole, Mei made a hunching lunge toward the driver and rapped the barrier between them.

"Pull over. *Now.*"

Without hesitation, amid a cacophony of honking cabs, the driver expertly got the car to the sidewalk. Grabbing her brief, Mei reached for the door.

Behind her, Seb snarled curses into the car seat. She heard *bitch cunt fuck* mixed in with French and Spanish, of all things. She didn't dare turn around to inspect the damage, but she sincerely hoped there would be blood.

Once she slammed the door behind her, the limo burst from the curb like a rocket, setting off another shrieking of horns.

Now that she was free, Mei started to shiver, almost violently. It was then that she realized she had left her beautiful Gucci shoe in the cab. Leaning on a lamppost, catching her breath, she saw a raw scrape along her ankle where she'd broken the strap as she pulled off the shoe. She hadn't felt anything but rage when she'd pulled off that wonderful savior of a shoe. It was a worthy sacrifice.

Now that she had a moment to see around her, and found that she was still miles from home, she raised her hand for a cab, then lowered it. She needed to walk. She needed the crisp New York City air to cleanse her.

Her ankle burning, she started south on Seventh, carrying her remaining shoe. As if Seb was getting his revenge for the jab to his cojones, Mei eventually had to give up her cleansing walk and call an Uber. Manhattan sidewalks were no fun to walk barefoot.

Once inside the car, to get her mind off the pain in her ankle, she occupied herself with the pleasing task of conjuring up ways to wreak further revenge on Sebastian Cole, pound of flesh by pound-of-satisfying flesh.

Chapter Twenty-Six

The only good thing this morning was that the gown's silk-screened panels were finally done. Bee hadn't bothered to go home and woke up on a couch in one of the small conference rooms with Wan Pi on her feet. After peeing and trying to unflatten her bed head, she scootered Wan Pi back to the dog hotel and bagged a quadruple cappuccino and a breakfast sandwich on the way back.

The workshop was still empty when she got back, except for one of the gofers who was cleaning up the monstrous mess of the silk-screening table. The panels were dry, and Bee stared at them, drinking in their gauzy mystery and dreaminess. Not waiting for Sheila, she began ironing them to set the colors more deeply into the fabric.

All that was left for this morning was to finish the bodice and the underskirting. This afternoon her models would arrive for fittings.

As she ironed, she waited to hear Penelope and Matt arrive. She had to report the theft of the sketchbook. Even though the evil

Camille had been her first suspect, she realized that it could have been Elijah. As sweet as he was, a hurt like his could drive him to seek revenge if he suspected Bee of the crime.

Both stunts were unforgivable. Bee mourned the loss of her beloved sketchbook as much as she might mourn the loss of her right arm. *Her sewing arm.*

Penelope and Matt, along with Joseph, were shocked and pissed at the same time when Bee told them of the theft. First the ink, and now this. They expressed sympathy and promised to investigate.

Joseph walked Bee back to the atelier. "This shit happens every time we get close to the finish line. I'm just glad it stops with thievery and other mischief. So far, no maiming or murder."

They were laughing together as they came through the door. Joseph's silly observations comforted Bee. But that comfort vanished when Bee caught sight of Camille bending over the table where Bee had laid out her panels.

"Get away from those," she snapped, striding across the floor. Joseph followed her, whispering fiercely, "Bee. Don't."

Camille's cheeks flamed. She marched around the table toward Bee. "What's your problem? I was just looking at your kooky designs."

"If I had my way, you wouldn't even be in the same room with them."

Camille seemed to tower over Bee. They stood face-to-face; Camille's haughty, down-the-nose gaze made Bee burn.

Joseph, behind her, said, "Ladies. Please. Time to back off."

"I know you took it." Bee growled, pointing her finger at Camille's chest.

"Took what? Your ratty little drawings? I think you did it yourself, like the ink thing. To get attention." Camille wrinkled her nose. "Your shit is, like, like rags, clashing ugly colors, half-baked embroidery—"

"And yours is so drab it looks like prison wear. That's it, we should have had a prison wear assignment. Camille would win every time!"

It wasn't really a slap, but it felt like one. Camille's hand snaked out and boxed Bee's ear as she seized a purple hunk of hair above Bee's temple.

Bee felt like she was about to explode with the shock of that pain. Cursing roundly, she pounded Camille's forearm until the fellow contestant let go, then she pushed Camille so hard that Camille lost her balance and almost fell.

She thought wildly, *I want to see you on the floor. I want to see you groveling.*

Someone was yelling. Someone else stepped in between them. Bee realized she was the one yelling, and the one between them solidified into Elijah.

"Bee," he said firmly, giving her a steady gaze. "Let it go. It's not worth it."

Tears stung Bee's eyes. *What a crap show to cry when you're angry.* Turning away, she inhaled deeply, trying to clear her vision, empty her mind of all the shit that had piled up in it this week.

Empty the trash. Empty the trash. Are you sure you want to delete everything?

When she saw a security guard standing beside Camille, Bee's attention sharpened. Thanking Elijah, Matt spoke to both of them.

"This is unacceptable. Other than separating you two until we have a winner, I see no other choice but to ask security to search the venue for Bee's sketchbook. And while they do this, you all sit quietly along the wall, and"—glancing first at Bee and then Camille —"you do not say a word. Not one word."

Elijah sat between them and gave Bee a helpful hand squeeze, while Bee kicked herself for losing her temper. Leaning back in her chair, she closed her eyes, wondering painfully whether the debacle with Cindi Koh meant that Alex would never want to see her again. This thought made her ache inside, and she wanted to wish this ache away. It was weird and novel and so not a "Bee thing."

Is that why I blew up just now? Is it more than Camille being a class-A bitch?

It seemed like hours for the two security staff to complete their search, but in reality only twenty minutes elapsed. Hearing footsteps, Bee opened her eyes and sat up to see Penelope and Matt approaching. Seeing that neither of them had her sketchbook, Bee slumped back into her chair.

Penelope approached rapidly, Matt trailing behind her. Penelope's lips were set in a hard, thin line, and Matt appeared a bit shell-shocked. Stopping before them, Penelope met eyes with Bee, then Elijah, and finally with Camille.

"Camille, please come with me."

Letting out a quiet gasp, Camille got to her feet, and without a glance at either Bee or Elijah, followed Penelope and Matt out of the room.

Bee caught Elijah's glance as they shrugged at each other. Bee whispered, "Are they going to interrogate us privately, do you think?"

"Harsh light in our faces? Hard chair in a soundproof room?" Elijah seemed as if he was trying to stifle a laugh. "Good fashionista/bad fashionista?"

"Thumb screws. Water boarding."

"Listening to twenty-four-hour Britney Spears songs."

Bee wanted to laugh, but she felt like screaming instead. At that moment Penelope and Matt reentered, without Camille.

Penelope was smiling now. "This is not exactly what we expected, but now, instead of three finalists, we have two!"

Bee's mouth dropped open, then she shut it quickly. She stood up the same time Elijah did. "What happened?"

Now Matt spoke—and appeared vastly relieved. "It seems that Ms. Camille was the culprit behind the ink stain on your gown, Elijah. We found drops of the ink in her hallway locker."

Opening her mouth, Bee couldn't figure out what to say. Grabbing her, Elijah squeezed her into a breathtaking hug. "I knew it wasn't you. I knew it," he told her.

Hugging him back, Bee barely felt the relief she should have felt about being exonerated of the ink crime. "My sketchbook?"

Matt shook his head. "They're still looking for that. Haven't found it yet."

An hour later, the sketchbook was still missing. So was Camille, who had left as soon as she was removed from the contest, leaving her patterns, outfits, and threads behind.

Chapter Twenty-Seven

onner Maxwell closed the door of the private lounge the hedge funders used when they visited the contest workspace. Bee watched him approach the couch in his flower-patterned Kato shirt and perfectly fitted jeans. He indicated that she should sit in the chair angled next to the couch, and she obeyed as a roiling sickness welled up inside her.

She had never met the man before, and vaguely remembered his name from the Partners Research and Management materials. She and Elijah had been told that today, the Saturday before the BIG day, the fucking BIG day of the finalist round runway show, they would be called in to chat with the honcho. Oh, well.

As an act of rebellion for this taking up her prep time, Bee had brought Wan Pi with her into the building. She was too tired to care about repercussions. At least, she thought as she settled into the buttery leather and gave Conner a smile in return for the one he was giving her, she wasn't here for a lecture about belligerent behavior or getting along with über-competitive witches.

Mostly, she was annoyed by this act of mandated ass-kissing. The models would be here by now, and although Sheila could handle the measurements, Bee wanted to be there to make sure the right model was fitted for each look; Sheila never made a mistake, but Bee was a control freak of the highest order.

Conner could have been somewhere between thirty and fifty; he seemed to have had work done: skin faintly tanned and wrinkle-free, fitted to his skull as carefully as his Kato shirt was fitted to his trim but muscular torso. His hair was flecked attractively with silver, and he was clean shaven, not dusted with the not-quite beards that so many men seemed to think made them look smoldering. He was relatively short, too, not towering over Bee like a building crane.

She found herself liking him, especially when he petted and complimented Wan Pi, saying nothing about the dog not being allowed in the hallowed halls, blah-dee-blah. But Wan Pi appeared lukewarm toward Conner, as he always did with people who didn't really like dogs.

At Conner's request, Penelope had coffee brought up from the lobby espresso bar. He'd made sure that Bee got her favorite coffee drink.

Picking up his cup, he took a sip, gazing at her over the rim. "You know, your talent is huge. Your stuff flies along the runway; it's young and old at the same time, you know what I mean? Artistic but fun."

"Thanks. I've learned so much during the last two weeks." Bee winced inside to hear her schmoozing words, but she wanted Conner to like her. "Having to meet deadlines, deal with models, and even orchestrating the entire show, as if it was mine at some big venue."

"When did you begin to love sewing?"

"My dad, actually. He owns Lin Designs, a Hong Kong fashion

line." Bee swirled her quadruple espresso. It felt strange for her to admit to this, but Conner seemed genuinely interested. "He taught me to sew, and I'd take scraps and leftovers and make little outfits."

Nodding, Conner leaned forward, elbows on his knees. "Fashion is in your blood, then. I like that. I like good clothes, well-made clothes. Yeah, I'm a Wall Streeter, but making fashion and making money are very much alike, don't you think?"

He smiled a little sheepishly, and Bee laughed. He was quite disarming, not at all the button-down suit she'd expected.

"It feels good to make money. And it feels even better when a look comes together with every stitch, bead, and button exactly where it's supposed to be."

"Yes, yes!" Leaning on the arm of the couch, Conner brought his face close to hers, resting his chin in his hand. Bee fought an urge to slide back into her chair. "I meant it when I said your talent is huge. You are going to be big, big, and bigger. Your color choices, the Chinese silks—fabulous!"

To her relief, he leaned back, his face seeming to glow with expectation. Bee wondered if he'd said these same words—except about the Chinese silks—to Elijah.

"You know, Bing—"

"Please, call me Bee. You know, I'm the B in Pinky B, my brand."

"Pinky B. Love it." He sat forward again and managed, some-how, to shift even closer to her. "I want to fund you. Whether you win or not, today—and you deserve to win—I want to back your line. There's good money in talent and ingenuity. It's not easy to make money backing designers, or even for the designers to meet their bottom lines. But you . . ." He shook his head then, reaching toward her, and ran his hand along her upper arm.

Unable to move, Bee watched him, trying to read what he meant by touching her like this. Touchy-feely was not okay anymore, right? Boundaries, barriers, safety zones. Not to be exploited. Me too?

Conner removed his hand. "You are going to be hot. And I can see durability in your work. Timelessness, like Chanel."

Relieved that he was no longer touching her, Bee gave him her brightest smile. She warmed all over, feeling her face flush. *Timelessness, like Chanel. I got me a sponsor!*

As if he could read her mind, Conner nodded. "Partners?" He held out his hand.

"Partners," Bee replied, her heart dancing in her throat. *Like Chanel.* Bee actually hated the Chanel look, but she understood Conner's meaning exactly. She took his hand.

When he didn't let go as she tried to pull away, her dancing heart skipped a beat. He was closer now, his breath scented with coffee. "You know, partners help each other out. I give you something, you give me something back."

Conner slid his other hand along the inside of her arm and gently grazed one of her breasts.

Stiffening, Bee yanked her hand away and jumped to her feet. Grinning up at her, Conner laced his hands behind his head. "It's easy, and sensible. You want what I have to give. And I want to give it to you, but the good things are never free. I'm letting you know my price."

Fury built a fire in Bee's chest, and the heat of it climbed into her cheeks. She fisted one hand. "Uh-uh. No. It doesn't work like that with me. You don't get to buy me this way."

Still grinning insanely, Conner shrugged. "You'd be crazy to turn me down."

"I'd be crazy to take a fucked-up deal like this. I don't do sex for money."

Standing up, Conner moved close. Bee tried to spin away, but he gripped her arms. "Listen, Bee, listen. This is simple, a transaction. You can't afford to not take this offer."

At her side, Wan Pi gave a soft growl. "Yes, I can." Tears of rage burned into her eyes. Elbowing Conner fiercely, she broke free and made for the door.

Goddamn it! It'd better not be locked, the swine.

She jerked the door open, turned, and stared at him. His smarmy smile was gone, and, his eyes narrowing, he opened his mouth to speak.

Bee interrupted him. "Dude. I think this is where I'm supposed to say, 'This is why I only like girls.' I also think you should hope I don't report this to the contest producers."

Conner gave her a smirk. "I'd suggest that you not."

"Maybe I'll leave you guessing about that."

Swinging the door open with all her strength so that it banged into the wall, Bee took off down the hall, walking stiffly and rapidly, Wan Pi at her heels, until she got to the stairs, raced down, and out the lobby doors.

She had to calm down before she went back upstairs. Standing to one side of the entry in the mild March weather, Wan Pi's leash in her hands, Bee faced the building wall, wiping her eyes with the back of her hand.

Douchebag. Scumbag. Self-satisfied dick. Her mind raced. She vowed to keep quiet about what happened until after the evening show. Especially since, if the bastard found out she'd squealed, he could destroy her.

What did he say to Elijah? Did he hit on him, too?

Quickly she dialed Jojo; she had to talk to someone sane, because everyone upstairs was nuts. Except Elijah. But she got Jojo's voice mail and didn't leave a message, not trusting her voice. The pounding dread filled her all over again as she tried Alex's number, with not a little trepidation.

Did this shit happen all the time? Does this Maxwell sleaze-bag —ah another 'bag'!—always pull this stunt?

Alex didn't answer either.

I wish I knew what to do. And then it came to her. Taking out her phone, she punched Cindi's number.

"Hey, Bee darling. How's the big day going?"

Bee tried to control her shaking voice, but she was too rattled. "Not too well." Her throat seemed to tighten; she coughed. "That Conner guy, the hedge guy, he—" Just as she was getting started, the words coming fast, she heard the dreaded double beep of the call being dropped.

"Shit!" she blurted, getting a surprised look from two men walking past. She redialed but got no answer. Sighing deeply, Bee wished she could throw her phone to the concrete, but it was too expensive to get another. She and Wan Pi walked inside and took the elevator back up to the workspace.

From the entry, she saw her models, all five of them, standing around her worktable laughing at something Sheila had said. Elijah strode past her, saw her, and raised his eyebrows in mock fear. Bee nodded and tried to smile. They would be toe-to-toe up there, each one doing their best to paste the other.

Using staple guns and drills, hired stagehands were building the runway set; in the scaffolding, lighting technicians aimed and tested the spots. At intervals, music pounded from the speakers as the sound tech judged the levels. Bee felt a headache coming on, and the cacophony around her didn't help. Going out into the hallway, she leaned against the wall and googled Cindi's Instagram site.

She'd done this before, admiring the juicy language of Cindi's posts and her excellent imagery and videos. Cindi had a real knack for social media. Scrolling to the most recent one, a photograph caught her eye and she froze, gaping.

In a post from only one minute ago was a selfie of Cindi and

Conner Maxwell, heads together, smiling wildly. And as Bee watched, another photo appeared, of the two in a full-on kiss, eyes closed, at a wonky angle captured by Cindi's phone.

"What the—" Bee stared at this in sickened shock. Of course, Cindi would know Maxwell. Of course, he would go straight to her after Bee turned him down, to tell her the entire sordid story but spiked with lies. Instead of being appalled by what Maxwell had done to her, here was the bitch flouting her relationship with him.

Angrily she dialed Cindi again, listening to it ring and go to voice mail. "You—you—I saw your post, Cindi. Do you know what the dirtbag *('bag' number four!)* you're drooling over tried to do to me? He hit on me. For sex, in exchange for backing me. He—"

Bee was getting a call. She saw Jojo's number and hung up on Cindi to take Jojo's.

Because Bee felt like spitting, it was hard to get her words out. Stumbling around the events of this terrible day, Jojo interrupted.

"So, who is this Cindi person that you care she's kissing some guy?"

"She's an influencer. A big one. We were getting along so well, and I did flirt with her a lot, and I got this extreme vibe from her that she really liked me. But—"

"So, she can't influence for more than one person?"

"Well, yeah, but with this geezer . . . he's not even a designer, he's one of the funders, and—"

"That's her job, right. Influencing? So some influencers are dirtbags, obviously, but they are necessary, sadly—"

"She made me think it was more than that. She certainly didn't act like a dirtbag around me, and the stuff she's posted about me has been fabulous." Bee sighed heavily. "She seemed very real about me."

Jojo cleared her throat. "Bee, think about it. You flirt all the time. You are, like, the queen of flirt. Sounds like this girl really got to you. Wow." Jojo paused for several seconds. "I guess this means you broke up with Alex, huh."

Jojo's assessment stunned Bee. "No . . . at least, I didn't mean to. But she doesn't seem to be talking to me right now."

Silent for a beat, Jojo said, "Maybe you should think about why that is."

Chapter Twenty-Eight

Before she could even think about Alex, Bee found herself back out on the sidewalk with Wan Pi sitting beside her, tilting his little head curiously. She began walking north along Park Avenue. The mild March air on this early afternoon cooled her cheeks. She didn't know where she was going, but only that movement could unwind the tightness in her gut.

Memories of the last several weeks paraded through her thoughts, starting with her first misstep of many: using Alex to punish her father when she kissed her right in front of him. There appeared the first crack in their relationship, a hairline one that used to be shallow but had since deepened and widened by more thoughtlessness on her part.

Goddess, how I love New York.

Waiting for a light beside a venerable five-star Manhattan hotel, she knew why she loved the city. Misbehavior was tolerated; at least most denizens pretended not to care. For all this time she'd used the city energy as a shield, hiding her own misbehavior. Until the last few months, she realized with a heavy heart, she'd blazed a careless trail through life, playing the rebel, and even, she feared, using her preference for women as a key to heartless play.

Along the garden meridian separating the lanes of Park Avenue, early buds clung to the cherry trees. Soon the tulips would blaze into color like a carnival carpet. Bee wondered if Alex had seen them. Alex had often talked of her desire for a garden; Alex claimed she too loved the city, but Bee thought at times she missed her grandmother's rural home in Pennsylvania where she stole strawberries out of Nanna's strawberry patch.

Bee felt her chest tighten as she thought about Alex. *Why did I fuck everything up? Oh, golden fox, how I miss you.*

The Chrysler Building seemed to pierce the sky above her. She decided to cut over to Lexington before it emptied into Rat Central, her latest nickname for Penn Station after trying to take a train up to Long Island during rush hour. Another of Bing Lin's not-so-great ideas.

Too many of those lately. Like getting lit and entertaining Mei and Tina with dumb-ass stories about her models. Like maybe taking the flirting a bit too far on audition day with the models.

The warm spring air brushed her face. She wished she had brought water for Wan Pi, who, though spunkily keeping up, was panting.

Like Cindi Koh.

Bee didn't even want to think about the little make-out sessions backstage at the contest venue, tucked behind a black scrim. And the worst thing—an aid car blared past, sirens at ear-piercing volume—the worst thing she'd ever done, so stupid, so stupid, was to bring Cindi home.

No, that's not it, you loser. Lying to Alex, that was the worst thing I've ever done.

This thought almost doubled her over. She walked straight into two elderly ladies laden with Victoria's Secret shopping bags. The ladies were also in possession of an astonishing vocabulary of foul language and, tone-deaf to her apologies, heaped it on her.

For a time after that, she just ran. She didn't like to run. Wan Pi enjoyed this, galloping on his little legs ahead of her. That was another thing she teased Alex about. *Madame Jock. Rock Cat Lady.* Just now, though, for a while she realized how it felt to be moving through air with little thought to what was being left behind.

After two blocks she slowed down. Checking her environment, she had the disoriented feeling of not being sure where she was. Trying to catch her breath, she stared up at the street sign like a dumb tourist. She was headed east on East Sixty-Fourth. Lenox Hill. She'd just walked all the way to Lenox Hill from Kips Bay.

Lenox Hill. There was a reason she had ended up here.

It took only twenty minutes to walk the rest of the way to New York Presbyterian. Entering the emergency department, Wan Pi at her side, Bee waited impatiently at the desk until she caught the charge nurse's eyes and asked for Alex Ingles. The woman's eyes narrowed; she definitely was not happy about tracking down a hospital employee. Beside Bee a man had muscled in, angry, begging to be allowed to see his wife.

Ignoring him, the nurse tapped into her computer. "And who should I say is looking for her?"

"Tell her it's Bee."

She tapped a final few keys. "Wait here," she said. "It might be a while." She gestured at the man beside Bee. "We're really swamped right now."

Bee settled in to wait, shifting position several times and trying to keep Wan Pi hidden underneath the seat. A full hour later, after watching countless doctors and nurses hustle past her, stretchers loaded with sick or injured people coming and going, she saw Alex marching quickly down the hall in blue scrubs, her gorgeous hair looped into a bouncing pony tail, a stethoscope hanging off her neck, and a sort of walkie-talkie clipped to the neckline of her scrubs.

Bee's heart melted, seeing her. Then it began to race. *What if she sees me and turns around? What if she slaps me? That would be something, anyway.*

Neither of these things occurred. Her mouth parted with uncertainty as she approached Bee and tilted her head, saying nothing.

"Hi," Bee said softly. "I need to talk to you."

Alex inhaled. Her face seemed oddly impassive—maybe this was her "work face." She said, "I can't take the time now. I have to get one patient ready for the OR and another sent up to ICU."

"Sure. Sure. I understand. Totally." Bee wanted to reach for one of Alex's hands, but Alex had folded her arms tightly around herself. "Later, then? When do you get off?"

"Seven thirty, eight—depending."

"I'll wait for you at your apartment. Maybe we can do dinner somewhere?"

Alex gave her head a little shake. "Okay, but listen." She leaned in close, unsmiling, tense. "Don't make promises you can't keep."

It was after nine p.m. by the time Alex got home. Bee was waiting for her in the vestibule, cold, shivering, and hungry, cuddling Wan Pi beside her. Punishment, she thought. She needed to suffer, but it sucked. Her feet were throbbing, her throat sore, and her head felt like a balloon.

I should have waited in Molly's, staying warm over a scotch.

When Bee saw Alex step out of the subway station across the street, she sagged against the vestibule wall; every muscle in her body refused to support her. She laughed, feeling the cold concrete through her jacket, grateful that the police hadn't been called about the woman sitting on the steps and that the young, hairy, smelly homeless man didn't stay to chat after he tried to bum a cigarette.

She knew when Alex saw her sitting there as she jay-walked to her building, because she stopped dead in the middle of the street.

Bee forced herself to her feet, which felt like they were encased in shoes of flame. "That's right," she called. "I'm here, just like I said I would be. After waiting for hours, now I have to stand here and watch you get flattened by a bus?"

Chapter Twenty-Nine

When the huddled human blob on the building's steps spoke, Alex couldn't quite make out the words. Wearing her earbuds, she was listening to Fleet Foxes, trying not to feel anything about whether Bee would actually show up or not. Then she got mad.

That's all I need, some creepy lowlife having a meltdown in my entry when I'm depressed as hell and feel like I've been run over by a bus, and that bus coming at me is about to do it again.

She darted between two parked cars, determined to bolt past the homeless person; keys were in her hand, even though the outer door had a key code pad. She was two steps up the stairway when the douchebag reached out and seized her arm.

"Oh no you don't," Alex snapped, bringing up her fist, keys poking between her clenched fingers. A little shapeless dog in the shadows began to bark shrilly.

The blob said, "Hey, what, are you bonkers? Or are you just that pissed at me?"

Gulping, Alex watched as the shape transformed itself into Bing.

"JEEzuz. You scared the shit out of me." Alex swallowed. It felt like her heart had jumped into her throat and was slowly oozing its way back into her chest.

"Sorry, luv." Bee gazed at her through bruised-looking eyes. "I'm here, though."

"So you are." Alex had to laugh. She reached out and hugged Bee. "And Wan Pi, too. Thank God."

Then Alex remembered, and the memories brought on first regret, then anger. Pulling free of Bee, she turned and opened the door. Just now she couldn't speak, because to speak would be to allow all the crap roiling in her head to spew all over Bee. Who thoroughly deserved it. But still . . .

"Okay," Bee said behind her as she pushed through the door. "We're going upstairs now."

Grammy's bedroom door was closed. Alex grimaced, remembering that Grammy was working tonight and that Lulu was probably in there with her boyfriend, a surgical resident who, if he wasn't sleeping at the hospital, couch-surfed with other staff if Grammy's bedroom wasn't available.

Alex left Bee standing in the middle of the great room, went into the kitchen, and opened the refrigerator door.

"Wait, wait," Bee said quietly. "I brought some takeout."

"Thank God." *I'm thanking God a lot tonight.*

She sized up Bee, who stood forlornly in the middle of the room, only one rung up from a street person with her spiky hair, coat falling off one shoulder, and a plastic bag hanging from one hand. Alex didn't like that her first impulse was to go over and hug her, but the memory of what she had done—what they both had done—helped in her resolve to wait for Bee to start the conversation. *And it better not be with the word "sorry," because you're not sorry. Not really. It's just a word you say to make people stop being angry.*

Pulling her last two favorite beers from the refrigerator, Alex picked up her coat and motioned toward the door. "C'mon," she said as Bee stared at her quizzically.

To Alex's relief, the twelfth-floor terrace gas fire was burning. On days when the weather was too awful for running, she climbed the stairs to the terrace, back down, and on good days, up them again. But this time, for Bee's sake, she hopped the elevator.

New York muttered and murmured and growled below them. The strongest stars glowed in the silky black sky. Alex remembered the sky at Nanna's looked like salt granules spilled everywhere, amid a streak of spilled milk. The air was chilly, maybe fifty degrees, but near the fire—no one was here yet, which surprised her —the heat was comfy.

Sitting carefully beside Alex, with Wan Pi on the bricks between them waiting eagerly for the food boxes, Bee set the bag on the low table in which the fire was centered, removed a box, opened it, and handed it to Alex, along with a pair of disposable chopsticks.

"They're not as good as Tina's mom and dad, but they're close," Bee said quietly as Alex inhaled the wonderfulness that was *jiaoxi.*

Bee added, "I tried to keep them warm under my coat, but they got a little cold."

"I don't care. I could eat worms, I'm so hungry." Bee's trying to keep the dumplings warm under her coat amused Alex, but she turned her face away. She glanced at Bee, who was looking into her *jiaoxi* box but not touching anything. "Thanks."

They ate in silence for a few minutes. Alex struggled not to speak first, because the lectures kept lining up, waiting to be given. This is Bee's show, she told herself.

Setting her box on the bench after giving Wan Pi little bites of what was left, Bee sighed. *Here it comes*, Alex thought, stabbing her last dumpling with a chopstick.

Finally she spoke. "I don't know how to say how sorry I am, Alex."

Alex bit off a reply. *Damn. That's not what I wanted to hear—next she's going to promise to do better.*

Bee let out a sharp breath. "About Cindi, I mean. I let things get stupid, um, I kind of lost control with her." She lifted a hand as if she knew Alex was about to speak, even though Bee's gaze was fixed on the flames.

"There's no excuse for lying to you. It was childish and selfish to break our date just for a chance to—"

"I heard you kissing her. I heard it, Bee." The words were out before Alex could stop them. Now the dumplings felt like lead in her stomach.

"Shit."

Alex could barely hear Bee. She felt her throat tighten. *Take it slow. Don't yell.* "You could have told me. You didn't have to lie about ditching me, either—if you'd said it was the only time Cindi could meet with you—"

"But it wasn't that, Alex," Bee interrupted. "This wasn't like an appointment to talk strategies or anything. It was a date. I wanted to have dinner with her, and then, I got the idea to bring her home—"

Alex saw it, then—what she'd been too love-blind to see before: Bee saw their relationship, arrangement, whatever it was, completely differently than she did. They'd probably never been on the same page. She'd expected the wrong things of the wrong woman.

She sighed. "And I was there to fuck everything up for you."

"No. No." Bee turned to her, laying a hand on Alex's arm. Alex wanted to shrug it off, but she felt frozen in place like a salmon hauled onto an Alaskan fishing vessel.

Bee said, her voice shaking as if she were about to cry, "Like you saved me. I know, wait, I know. It's crazy, but you being there sort of shocked me, in a way like a thunderbolt. A near-death experience."

Alex couldn't stop herself from staring at the woman next to her. The firelight dappled Bee's face, and there Alex could see the real pain Bee was feeling. She had never seen Bee this vulnerable before.

"I didn't sign up to be your savior, Bee," she said. Seeing Bee's face fall and feeling a bit regretful, Alex added, "I signed up because I'm in love with you, as stupid and inconvenient as that is."

Bee's mouth actually dropped open.

Feeling her throat tightening, Alex decided to go further. She'd blurted *I love you.* What else did she have to lose? "I'm not like you, Bee. I'm not a player. And I can't see myself in a casual relationship with a player. I want a life with someone, and if this isn't that, then I don't want it."

Bee was staring at her hands. "I've never felt this terrible in my life."

Shaking, Alex swallowed again and again, trying not to cry, trying to be stone, but it wasn't working. She saw Bee shoot her a nervous glance.

Bee murmured, "I've never felt this way about anyone in my life, either."

"Who? Me or Cindi Koh?" Alex was on her feet. She didn't remember getting up.

Bee scrambled up. "Cindi Koh is a flying bitch. I know that now. I was too stupid and selfish to see it. Alex, it's always been you. I don't understand it, exactly, but I don't want to keep hurting you and I don't want to lose you."

Alex stared into the fire. That was something. *Bee can't say I love you any more than I can tell a patient to go off and die. But she did say she didn't want to lose me.*

She turned toward Bee, who stared up at her, hands balled together before her chest. "Maybe you won't want to keep me after I tell you what I did."

Her chest hollow, Alex moved past her and picked up her coat. Bee's sketchbook fell out of the folds before Alex could catch it. One of the loose papers floated toward the fire, and Alex grabbed it before Wan Pi could, feeling the sting of one of the flames on the back of her hand.

"You? *You took it?*" Bee squeaked, kneeled, gathered up the precious papers, and stuffed them between the covers. "How could you? I don't believe it!"

Alex felt sick. Bee would never be able to forgive her for this, and when she did it, she knew it was "stupid and selfish," to use Bee's favorite descriptors. But she'd been so angry. So wounded.

"I was so fucking mad at you, Bee. You broke my heart when you kissed that woman, and I wanted to hurt you too."

She felt a sob in her throat and couldn't stop a soft hiccup.

Bee, sitting back down in her chair, held the sketchbook to her breasts. She was almost doubled over. "I deserved it. I did. I totally deserved it."

Alex saw one of the terrace doors opening. A couple she had seen in the elevator a few times, an older man and woman, came through. She liked them, but they loved to talk, and right now the last thing Alex wanted was company.

She sat down next to Bee. "Let's get out of here. We could go to the Cubby Hole, if you want."

"How about my place?" Bee said quickly, running the back of her hand over her eyes.

Alex wrapped her arms around Bee. Hugging Bee was like hugging a warm, wriggling bear cub. They rose together, Bee clinging to Alex's hand, and as a mild spring breeze cooled Alex's face, they walked past the couple, who nodded and smiled. Alex felt like she was gliding, as if the terrace was on a river sparkling with jewels and flowing through a soft Manhattan night.

Chapter Thirty

ee and Alex arrived at NeueHouse early, Wan Pi in tow, pretending to be Alex's dog; they could work out some kind of excuse if anyone noticed. Worker bees had been busy all night, because all the worktables had vanished, twenty more feet had been added to the runway, and the number of chairs for guests had multiplied.

"Where's my sewing machine?" Bee shouted, her voice echoing off the walls. Then in a lower tone to Alex, "I hate it when they mess with my stuff."

"They're on the stage behind the scrim," someone in the stage area that they couldn't see replied.

Joseph appeared from behind a curtain and waved at them. "How gauche of you to arrive at this hour! Come on up and see your new show space!"

The entire stage had been redesigned. A new pale blue opaque scrim had been strung across midstage, and behind it were two stations, one for Bee and one for Elijah. Each had a worktable with sewing machine and prepping tools, and behind them were racks where all of Bee's outfits—the silk-screened ball gown/wedding gown, her two cocktail dresses, and the men's evening suit and tux —were hung. Under the rack was a cupboard for shoes and accessories. A makeup table that could seat four models stood against the back wall.

Bee's heart had been skipping beats all morning. *I'm going to need a pacemaker after this is over.*

Last night with Alex had been low-key and rejuvenating, at first, until Bee couldn't sleep, even after they bathed together and gave each other massages. While Alex slept soundly, Bee got up, made a cup of tea, and turned on the light over her worktable. She'd spent the next few hours until daylight sketching out designs for silk screens and doodling outlandish, alien outfits as if she were dressing an E.T. from one of Jojo's favorite science fiction shows.

Coffee and over-the-top adrenaline kept her going now. Rousting Alex out of bed early, Bee had hustled her out of the house, disallowing Alex's morning run and stopping only for more espresso. Alex was grumpy but compliant.

"There's no way I'm letting you go to your big finale alone," she said as they headed for the subway. "My rock-climbing skills will be handy when someone needs to peel you off the ceiling."

Now, Bee was really glad Alex had come along and was prepared to stay to the bitter end. Carrying Bee's basket of trims, Sheila came striding toward them. She said breathlessly, "Thank God you're here. When I was pushing the rack up the ramp in the back, one of the bozos working on the lighting appeared out of nowhere and snagged the—" Breaking off, Sheila held up a broken beaded strand. This was classic Sheila, never finishing a sentence except with a demonstration.

"Okay," Bee said calmly, even though she was jangled to the point of dizziness. "We have to double up on the threads and oversew where they're fastened on."

Sheila nodded quickly, then peered over her sewing glasses at Bee. "You're okay, right? You disappeared last night."

Bee wrinkled up her face. "Yesterday was a hard day. I took a walk to, um, rejuvenate." She spread her arms. "You know, renew."

Glancing slyly at Alex, Sheila said, "Yup. There's something of the renewed about—" She pointed at Bee. "Hi, Alex. Hi, Wan Pi!" She knelt to pet the wriggling bulldog. He was decked out today in his finest tux.

Alex said, "Hi, Sheila. That's Bee's companion dog. For anxiety, you know. Can I help you with anything?"

Sheila opened her mouth, but Bee took the basket from her and handed it to Alex. "You can find stuff in here for me. I'll tell you which. And Sheila, if Alex helps me with the beading, you can start dressing the models as soon as they arrive. Will we have a makeup artist?"

"Yes, two of them. And hairstylists." This came from Joseph, who poked his head around the scrim. "Do you have your heads ready?"

"Yes," Bee answered and heard Elijah's deep voice answering at the same time. Turning, Bee made straight for Elijah as he came up the ramp, followed by his seamstress Ted and his boyfriend Deon. They hugged each other deeply.

Bee looked straight into Elijah's chocolate-brown eyes. "Good luck, mate."

"You too, you darling. You too."

Then they got to work.

While Bee and Alex repaired the beading on the skirt of the cocktail dress, Sheila herded the models. Felix dragged himself in as if hungover, and Bettie was rosy, as if they'd both had great nights but had been occupied in very different ways.

As Sheila fitted Dot into the ball gown, she clucked. "You've lost weight, dear. Watch out, you won't make those plus-size salaries for long."

Sighing, Dot brushed her luscious hair out of her eyes. "I broke up with my boyfriend."

"Oh, my, I'm sorry, sweetie. Here, give me a moment to take this in here and there." Sheila whipped her measuring tape off her neck.

By the time the music started, indicating the guests would be arriving, the models were nearly ready. The makeup artist working on Bee's team was an athlete, applying the blue and purple eyeshadow, dyeing eyebrows white and inking a high and thin curving line over them, then painting on deep mauve lip coloring. For hair, Bee wanted the best look for each model: Bettie's black bangs and chin-length pageboy highlighted with violet; Dot's gorgeous mane frizzed with gold spray; Felix's black mop stiffened full and swirled with silver.

Gold and red swirls decorated Halemé's sheared head. Simon had showed up with a boxed-up, curved temple buzz cut, and Bee was so impressed—Simon had hoped she would like it—that she didn't touch it.

Nails sported no polish, and the makeup stylists buffed them to a shine.

The intensely swirling and happy energy fed Bee. She thrived on this, the expectation and chaos, little panicky moments, like Halemé's period starting or Felix stubbing his toe on a cord.

"This is why you wear shoes here, Felix," Bee scolded him. The first thing he'd done when he arrived was kick off his shoes.

Bee was on her knees, fussing with Bettie's hem, when the faint smell of tobacco wafted past her nose.

"Hey, girl. I hope you're feeling better—your call got dropped and I—"

Getting to her feet, Bee turned to face Cindi Koh. In a white jacket brocaded in gold, a very-low-neckline black top, and creased trousers, she looked as striking as only Cindi Koh could.

Bee had planned to ignore Cindi as long as she could, but there was no time like the present for ripping Cindi's head off.

"No," Bee told her, feeling her nostrils flare. "The call didn't drop. You hung up on me."

Shrugging, Cindi ran her hand along her neck as she eyed the models getting readied. "Yes, well, I've never been into all that emo drama. Just can't take it, you know? I'm just a casual, fun-loving kind of girl. But you're better now, right? We can pick up where we left off?"

"I am better." Bee kept her gaze on Cindi's face and her hands at her sides. *She's not even worth a slap.* "And no, we can't pick up where we left off. I have a girlfriend, thanks, and I'm not looking for a casual anything."

Cindi's smile tightened. "That's too bad. Wish you felt differently." Cindi looked over Bee's shoulder to where Alex was introducing Wan Pi to Halemé. "Girlfriend, huh? I knew it."

"And you know what else?" Bee folded her arms, thinking this was going to feel real good. "I saw your Instagram with Maxwell. The dick propositioned me. And stupid me, I was so angry and calling peeps to vent, and you, pretty far down on the list, hung up on me."

Cindi's eyes narrowed and her upper lip curled slightly. "You turned him down, huh? Do you even know who he is?"

"I know enough to not want to know. You fuck him all you want. I've got better things to do."

Turning away, Bee grabbed Sheila as she flew past with a pair of shoes. "Who are those for?"

"Dot. These are the ones—" Sheila waved the shoes in the air.

"Yeah, you're right. I picked those, but now I have another idea. C'mon."

When she glanced back, Bee saw that Cindi Koh had moved across the stage and was laughing at something Joseph had said. Bee felt like Mothra had lifted off from her shoulders.

Check that box on my self-improvement list.

"Show time, ten minutes," Joseph's voice bellowed over the music.

Frantic last touches were made to hair, jewelry, seams, and lips. Bee's heart was pounding. Alex was inhaling to prevent herself from weeping with excitement. As Bee lined the models up, she was full of pride. The models, everyone, smiled down at her, and she basked in the loveliness of her creations.

I did it, she told herself. *I made this happen.*

Halemé and Simon were first, Halemé wearing the black velvet pouf-skirted minidress with sleeveless, fitted quilted top, sinking to a deep V below the waist, the skirt trimmed with gold ruffles. Simon wore the red silk Nehru-style long shirt over slim red velvet trousers. Bettie shined in the embellished long-sleeved fitted minidress, embroidered with braid, beads, fringes, and metallic spangles.

And last, Felix was dapper in a deep purple silk suit jacket with tails, white vest trimmed with golden lace, and shiny black gabardine trousers. On his arm was Dot in the ball gown/wedding gown: strapless, with a fitted waist, butter yellow organza, silk-screened birds on each of six panels cut to points, and full underskirting.

Even through her nervously spiking brain, Bee had the pleasing impression that they looked like a row of elaborate Belgian chocolates or a display of crazy overwrought tulips.

Exactly what I was going for, she told herself, smiling at them proudly.

The next moment, applause filled their ears as Joseph took the stage and gave the usual rundown of the competition's benefactors, goals, blah, blah, including slime bag Conner Maxwell. The smiling, laughing models immediately snapped to attention, acquiring the pouty faces Bee wanted them to stride out with, and instructed that, striding back, to turn their heads and flash a dazzling smile.

"Now, from finalist Bing Lin, her line of evening wear from Pinky B!"

Bee's opening music was a K-Pop girl band, upbeat and fun. Her first two models waited as instructed for the first two measures, then strutted out when the chorus began.

The show runners had set up a laptop on which designers and staff could watch the runway show from backstage. Bee rocketed over to the crowd already gathered there, and they parted like the Red Sea for her. Alex trailed behind, and Bee picked up Wan Pi and grabbed Alex's hand as Halemé and Simon danced down the runway, twirling, then stopping and walking to the music, turning, showing every angle to the reporters, funders, producers, and hangers-on. Right on cue, they turned at the very end, after stepping to the wings to get close to the watchers and flashed those thousand-dollar smiles.

Bee had so wished that her Leftovers buds, Jojo, Tina, and Mei, could see this, but this show was invite-only. She felt a little sad about that.

The applause was deafening. Alex gently said, "Ow," as Bee's hand tightened around hers.

The K-Pop tune looped for Bettie now; the spangles of her dress caught the lights and dazzled. She twirled, strutted, closed in on each runway edge, and her smile at the end got whistles as well as applause.

As soon as Bettie was backstage, the lights came down and the music faded then rose in a dreamy deep lounge instrumental with soft beats. Dot and Felix appeared at either end on the scrim and into a single spot, taking hands as the music swelled and picked up in tempo. They sashayed to the end of the walk. Bee was certain she heard breaths being caught at the sight of her ball gown. She stiffened, staring at the screen.

Dot was fabulous, graceful. Her updo shone under the lights. She swirled the skirt, head held high, then she and Felix joined hands again to head back up the runway and flashed their beautiful smiles, first to each other and then to the audience. A sea of phones rose as the watchers snapped photos and videographed the models. There was only one thing to mar the rising excitement in Bee's chest. She clearly caught a glimpse of Cindi's white jacket as she sat in a chair in the front row stage right, and she wasn't photographing anything. Her head down, she was tapping away at her phone in a frenzy of typing.

Bee felt her chin jut out. *The bitch. Couldn't even be professional enough to do her fucking job.*

The camera moved, following the models, and Cindi Koh vanished from the screen. Turning, Bee ran to greet Dot and Felix as they returned. Everyone was hugging each other.

"I know you're going to win. You have to. They loved us out there!" Dot gushed, stroking the organza fabric as if it were the finest thing she had ever handled.

Now it was Elijah's turn. Bee felt chuffed about her success, but she loved Elijah, so she went over, kissed his cheek, and whispered, "Good luck."

Elijah's eyes were round with fear. "How do I follow that, Bee? You killed it."

Shaking her head, Bee rolled her eyes. "Eli, get real. They're going to love it. You know that."

He seemed so distressed, Bee gave him a hug. Then Joseph was announcing him and he pulled away as his models lined up, running from one to the next, tucking in, straightening, patting down.

Bee had to admit to Alex that she had mixed feelings about the reception of Elijah's edgy tailoring, mixing styles for men and women in a lovely "queer" mode. Elijah's ball gown, an off-the shoulder, single-sleeved dress sewn of pale pink satin with a wrap train that could be tucked up forward or back, took Bee's breath away, and for a crazy moment, she envisioned Alex wearing it as a wedding dress.

She felt her heart racing. *That was a weird thought. Oh, so weird. Why would I come up with this idea?*

Standing to one side, Bee watched Elijah's show and saw how professional and beautifully choreographed it was. She bit her lip. For the final, Penelope and Matt were going to pool together all the comments from journalists, influencers, and other industry experts, plus their own impressions, and the result would be in as soon as they were done. It might take all night.

While Bee was thinking about how terrible the long, cold night was going to be, she saw everyone setting up the finale. The models would line up across the stage, and then Bee and Elijah would step out for their bow.

"How do I look?" Bee asked Alex and Sheila.

"You look like you've been up for thirty-six hours, which is probably true, right?" Sheila said, fluffing Bee's hair.

"And that's why you look so great." Alex leaned over and kissed her, and there was no time for a lipstick check. The models were starting to walk on stage, and the applause and music was rising, and Bee had to get into place in line.

When she joined Elijah at center stage, they grasped hands and raised them in the air, then walked out onto the runway, their models trailing behind them.

Bee remembered walking out there, blinking in the flashes of phones, waving and smiling, and the next thing she knew she was backstage and mobbed with people congratulating her and asking about the fabrics and the quilting and the astonishing silk-screened bird panels.

Relieved when Joseph shooed everyone away so that the models could get out of the clothes and each garment could be hung safely on a rack, Bee sank into one of the worktable chairs.

"Proverbial truck?" Alex asked as she sat beside her. Wan Pi put his paws on Bee's knees.

Bee nodded. Except instead of a truck, this was a bullet train.

Someone proposed meeting for a post-show drink at a local bar. As weary as they were, just about everyone, even Sheila, who usually was in a hurry to get back home to Brooklyn and her husband, agreed to come.

Fifteen people, including most of the models, Bee, Alex, Elijah, Sheila, and other hangers-on added themselves into the early Sunday evening crowd at SPIN, the ping-pong club where Bee and the Leftovers had helped Mei throw the last-minute birthday party ordered by her boss. Pushing tables together, they terrified the waitresses with calls for drinks and Hop Pop chicken.

Alex, Bee, Elijah, and Deon, Elijah's boyfriend, squished around the head of the table. Bettie and one of Elijah's models started a ping-pong game. A couple pitchers of India pale ale appeared, and Bee glanced slyly at Alex, who shrugged.

Elijah leaned over to Bee. "Let's make a pact. Whatever happens, we are going to be friends forever, right?"

Bee felt warmed all over; the alcohol and all this camaraderie had soothed her jangled nerves. "Right," she said, raising her pinky finger.

Elijah gave out his bellowing laugh, turning heads, and gripped her finger with his own.

"Friends forever," they said at the same time.

Dot, sitting nearby, was staring into her phone. Noticing, Bee caught her eye.

"What's up?" she asked.

Seeming worried and almost to the point of pity, Dot shifted closer and leaned over Alex to show Bee.

Bee felt her stomach fall through the floor as she read Cindi Koh's comments on the contest finale.

"The lack of artistic vision in the designer of the wannabe Pinky B collection couldn't be more obvious. Bee Lin's 'poser' efforts blatantly fail with a hint of forced quirkiness, lame-ass rebellion, and a freakish pairing of models."

"What the fuck?" Alex said beside her.

Bee couldn't stop reading. Under Cindi Koh's sultry portrait, she saw phrases like "the sort of music they play in child care"; "a beautiful plus-size model poured into a confusing bundle of yellow —get this, YELLOW—gauzy rags"; "the hats were trying for cute and head turning, and they almost worked"; "breaking the prescript of the runway is not always smart—it's the conceit of a selfish designer who has no regard for her audience."

Cindi, against contest rules, had even posted photos on her site. Nothing was to be posted by any observer except by the competition itself until the winner was announced.

"I'm going to kill her," Bee heard herself say in a low, gritty voice. She was so angry that even speaking was painful.

"It's only Cindi, Bee. She's just one person. You killed it out there, you know it." Alex put her arm around her.

"But she's got power. You don't even know how much she means to the fashion industry." Bee felt tears sting her face, blinking them furiously away.

Elijah had caught on and was reading the blog on his phone. He sighed, "Oh, man, Bee. None of this is true. Does she have it in for you or something?"

"Apparently," Bee said through clenched teeth. She allowed Alex to pry Dot's phone from her hands.

"But she seemed so nice."

"A sleeping rattlesnake is nice, until you step on it." Bee sagged in her chair. She found the strength to meet Alex's eyes. "Babe, I need to go home. And I'm sorry, but I just have to be alone right now."

Disappointment floated across Alex's face, then she smiled and nodded. "I get it. I need to get home too, anyway. Laundry, makeup, grocery shopping. Gotta work tomorrow night."

Bee fell gently against her. "You're so good to me. I don't deserve it."

"Truer words," Alex said, getting up. "C'mon. I'll walk with you to the subway."

Chapter Thirty-One

While Bee was in the shower—not really washing but just standing under the steamy water—someone had called. The evening of the final show was still early —only seven p.m., and the sun had only now faded from the sky. She'd turned down Alex's offer of having a meal before they parted, and now she had the scraping feeling of hunger.

Her phone was perched on the sink. She reached for it as she was toweling off, and with a skipped beat recognized the number. Lifting his head from the bath mat, Wan Pi inspected her curiously.

Penelope. *I missed a call from Penelope!* Fumbling, nearly dropping the phone, Bee listened to the voice mail Penelope had left.

"Hi, Bee. We have our results. We'd like you to buzz back over to NeueHouse so we can give the news to you and Elijah in person."

The call had come in twenty minutes earlier. Heart racing now, still skipping beats, Bee threw on the leggings she'd worn earlier today, grabbed one of her silk-screened tees, and laced up her green canvas sneakers. She kissed and hugged Wan Pi, telling him he couldn't come with her this time. His ears dropped back as if he understood her words.

She raced into the sub-basement. Thank God the scooter was fully charged. Pulling on a thrift store bomber jacket that she'd restyled with patchwork, she buzzed onto the sidewalk and zig-zagged the streets northeast to NeueHouse. The night was nicely mild and clear, and as it was Sunday, crowds were thin enough on the sidewalks that she made good time.

Bee barely remembered her ride through the city. She was aware of zooming through intersections without her usual care, and didn't someone yell at her as she whizzed past? But she couldn't remember what they'd yelled. The evening air cooled her, she'd forgotten her gloves, and her hands ached with tension by the time she got to NeueHouse. She almost flew past it, because Penelope's call had changed the city somehow, making it a confusing maze of anxiety and dread.

Joseph met Bee in the lobby. He gave her a long, deep hug, and she tried to read his face but saw only friendliness and respect. He gave no clue to what the decision of the bosses had been, but maybe he didn't know yet. He led her into the elevator.

"This has all been so exhausting, hasn't it?" Joseph remarked, pushing up the skin below his eyes after examining his face in the chrome walls.

"Ya think?" Bee didn't want to see her reflection. She'd glanced at the mirror before she left in a minor state of shock about her appearance.

The door slid aside on the floor below the workspace, and Joseph waited for Bee to exit first.

"Am I late?" Bee asked as she followed Joseph down the hall. "I was in the shower when the call came."

Joseph laughed. "Yes, you are, but we're all here now, and

everyone was sort of on call, you know." He lowered his voice. "I was taking a nap in the lounge."

Penelope, Matt, and Elijah were waiting in the same private lounge where Bee had confronted Conner Maxwell. To her vast relief, he wasn't present.

Trying to slow her breathing, Bee realized that she hadn't grasped how her body had been running on empty; every single stress hormone that had kicked in was swiftly draining away. She sank onto the sofa next to Elijah.

Penelope and Matt sat in two armchairs that they had drawn together facing the couch. On a table to Bee's left, against the wall, she noticed an array of drinks and food, but right now even the aroma of fresh French roast made her feel a little nauseous. Joseph sweetly brought her a glass of water. Elijah held a mug of something steaming, and he set it down on a side table.

He grimaced at her, and she smiled bleakly. She was certain her face had the same rigor of anxiety as his. Without thinking, she grabbed his hand.

After Joseph had seen to their comfort, Penelope crossed her legs, then uncrossed them; Matt sat like a stone, both hands gripping the arms of his chair.

It seemed like hours ticked past before Penelope spoke, but in reality, was probably less than a minute.

"This was not an easy choice," Penelope said, shaking her head. She looked fresh and beautiful as always, with not a hint of exhaustion under her makeup. "You two didn't make it easy for us," she added with a short laugh that Matt and Joseph also joined.

Bee didn't feel like laughing, but when Elijah made a lame show of it, she tried to chuckle, but she sounded more like a frightened chicken.

Penelope fingered the stack of papers on her lap. "We heard from everyone, so much praise, kudos, excitement. I don't think we've ever had this much interest in our NYC Fashion Award contest for Young Entrepreneurs, do you, Matt?"

Matt jumped slightly. "No, never. And I've been doing contests like this for ten years. I've never seen anything like this."

Bee examined his face, looking for signs that Cindi Koh's devastating reviews had accounted for what he'd just said. But Matt smiled at them both with steady eye contact, giving no indication of anything other than nervous amazement.

Facing down, Penelope pressed her palms together. Here it comes, Bee thought, every organ in her body seeming to seize up while waiting for the verdict. Elijah's grip tightened.

When Penelope looked up, her gaze fell on Bee. Bee's mind began to whirl; for a frightening moment she thought she was going to faint.

"Bing. Your work is fabulous, cutting edge, brilliantly constructed. The looks you created for the show are inventive and new." Penelope paused; her solemn gaze never wavered from Bee.

"One issue every designer needs to consider is how far over the line to go, in terms of marketability. Who will the buyer be? What will the buyer be wanting to say about themselves via what they wear and where they wear it? And how does the designer get their message out to the public in a way that makes them need to snatch the clothes off the rack as quickly as they appear?"

Penelope stopped. Bee tried to hide her shaking, but she wasn't sure she succeeded.

The rest was Matt's turn. When he spoke, Bee's head snapped in his direction.

"The runway show audience is the toughest bunch on earth," he said, his eyebrows drawn down. His look of abject fear had vanished. "Bee, your edgy look is going to kick people in the ass, but I think you broke a few rules of the runway there. Pairing street with office, the dancing in the final show, and even the smiles—"

He raised his hand as Bee opened her mouth; she could feel a stirring of rebellious anger at his words. "People want to see the clothes; the models are mannequins. The clothes hang well on them, and they need to disappear inside the clothes."

Bee felt her face grow warm. She could see where this was going. And she knew who was behind it. Turning to Penelope, she saw nothing on Penelope's face except a tiny worry wrinkle above her right eye.

Feeling like she was sinking into the couch, Bee barely heard the next phrase. It was as if Matt's voice had been dialed down to one on the volume scale.

"This is why we made the choice to award first prize to you, Elijah, and let me elaborate on . . ."

Later, Bee could not, no matter how hard she tried, remember hearing the feedback they gave Elijah. At some point she no longer felt his hand. She had vague impressions of hugging him, offering congratulations and a big kiss, and a notion that he was trying to give her soothing words.

Shake hands with Matt, take hugs from Penelope and Joseph, walk without stumbling as you leave.

Finding herself outside the NeueHouse building, not sure how she got there, Bee started to walk before she realized she had left her scooter in the lobby. Humiliated, abashed, she waited until someone came down to let her back in; the first one down was Elijah.

Well, it could have been worse.

As they embraced each other, Elijah murmured in her ear. "You won't give up. You can't give up. Just because that little prick Matt bought into Koh's BS, you need to kick them all in the balls—get back on the horse—or the scooter, if you prefer."

Nodding, Bee listened to Elijah's beautiful laugh and drank in his beautiful smile.

"Keep in touch," he said. "Right? Keep in touch."

"Right." At least these nightmarish last two weeks had a couple of bright sides—meeting Elijah and becoming comfortable with the idea of Alex.

Scootering over to the Cubby Hole, Bee ordered a Manhattan and called Alex, who, hearing what had happened—Bee struggling not to cry—said she would come straight over to the bar. But Bee talked her down, promising to go home after one drink. Wan Pi needed a walk, and she reminded Alex that they both had to get some sleep.

Then she called Jojo.

Chapter Thirty-Two

When the light through the bedroom blinds began to lighten in a fluffy-cloud sky, Bee got up. She didn't remember sleeping, and she thought she might have between fits of fury and abject sorrow, but she felt cloudy and disoriented. She'd already left a message on Raj's cell that she was calling in sick—she was expected back at work today, Monday, the day after the show.

Jojo had gotten the word out. Bee's phone rang while she was reading shocked condolence texts from Tina, Mei, Cam, Jim, Elijah, and even Raj. She didn't answer the call, but a moment later she realized it had been Alex.

"How are you doing? Do you want me to come over?" Alex's voice was rushed but so sweet. Bee felt her eyes filling up again.

"I'm alive. It's me talking, right?"

"Poor baby. I can get over there in an hour. You're not going to work today, right?"

"You read my mind."

By the time Alex got to Bee's apartment, Bee had managed to

get dressed. Bee felt too depressed to shower because she would have to redo her hair, and the idea of having to fuss with it irked her.

I should just shave my head. Like a nun. Or a prisoner.

Matt had left a message that sometime today her fashions would be delivered. Thinking about that made her feel like vomiting. She really hadn't given a thought to losing. Everyone considers the chances of winning or losing, as a way to try to prepare themselves for disappointment. Bee had tried to do that once or twice, telling herself there would be other contests—what Jojo said to her over and over on the phone last night—and she could continue to develop her line and maybe do a pop-up somewhere. Jojo would love to help advertise it on her blog, blah, blah. But Bee couldn't shut out the voice that kept telling her, *You are the best designer here. You are going to win that money.*

She'd listed all the ways she was going to spend the prize money. First, a down payment on her own studio to live and sew in, her own storefront in the East Village: Pinky B Salon. Then it would be travel and shows and interviews and *Harper's Bazaar.* And then her own cable show: *Pinky B and Me.*

Bee reflected that Jojo's perpetual good cheer hadn't done her any good, but she didn't say that to Jojo. She mostly just bitched about Cindi. Jojo listened and heartily agreed that Cindi Koh deserved to be flayed by House Bolton, forced to watch orcs eat her fingers and toes, then be encased in a plexiglass capsule and shot into earth orbit for the rest of her life.

When Alex breezed in, she smelled of spring, summer, and fall all rolled into one. In one of Bee's silk-screened T-shirts and black jeans, she was more beautiful than anything in the entire universe, Bee thought as Alex flopped down on the couch next to her.

As they snuggled together, Wan Pi inserting himself next to Bee, the clouds that had been building up released their load of rain. It pattered against the front windows, forming rivulets that slithered down the panes like silver snakes. The sound was soothing to Bee's ears.

"I can't believe what that bitch did to you," Alex said, stretching her feet and settling them on the coffee table. She had already kicked off her Crocs. "Do you know where she lives? How about we hire an actor to put on a big overcoat and fedora and pay her a visit?"

"Make sure he has a fake gun in his pocket."

"How about we report her to Instagram for posting porn, or tell everyone that she's working for the Russians, stealing designs and selling counterfeits overseas—give the scoop to one of the conspiracy websites. Or better yet, tell everyone that she's faking all the great tweets she's getting on her Twitter feed."

Bee managed to laugh. She kissed Alex on the cheek. "I just want to break into her apartment, rip up all her clothes, pour pig's blood over them, and set them on fire."

"Like in the movie, we could rig a bucket of pig blood over-head, on a stage where she's doing a show." Alex had brought two venti cappuccinos. She picked one up and handed it to Bee. "What happened, anyway? Why did she sabotage you like that?"

Sighing, Bee didn't want to think about any of it: the repulsive Conner Maxwell or Cindi Koh's hypocrisy and pettiness as she flaunted a relationship with a sexual predator.

Jeebus, Bee realized, *Cindi is a sexual predator too, targeting me.* And with a sickening feeling of shame, Bee wondered if she herself was one; maybe what she viewed as harmless flirting was seen as inappropriate come-ons.

"What is it, Beetle? What's wrong?" Alex's voice was gentle in her ear.

"I'm such a terrible person. I don't deserve you." Bee said the words she was thinking aloud. It was a mistake. Now she just sounded whiney.

Alex snorted. "Yeah, you're pretty terrible. I came over here this morning because you're a terrible person. Your friends are calling you every twenty minutes because you're a terrible person."

At that moment, a text from Jojo came over Bee's phone: *Saturday. 2 pm. Rain or Shine. More details later.*

What was Jojo cooking up now?

When the buzzer rang, Alex got up to open the door and wait in the hallway. Deciding she had to look at least a quarter-way presentable, Bee sat up to see Joseph come through, carrying a score of garments on hangers in zipped plastic, followed by Sheila with the rest. Wan Pi bulleted off the couch to greet his new guests.

"Hello, darling," Joseph said as he scanned Bee's cavernous basement flat for somewhere to offload. Sheila saw the garment rack behind Bee's worktable and began to carefully hang Bee's creations: silk-screened tees, brocade tux, gabardine coat, and the ball gown. Alex helped her, straightening, fluffing, and shaking free. From somewhere Bee felt a slow build of energy and got her butt off the sofa, zipped open the bag holding the kimono, and breathed in the scents of fresh fabric.

Sheila walked out the door without a word before Bee could thank her and get a big hug, but she reappeared instantly carrying a stack of foil trays. The delicious odor of curry overwhelmed the crisp hints of silk, and Bee realized how hungry she was.

Her phone buzzed. Pulling it out of her pocket to see who the caller was, her mouth dropped open. It was Dad. He hadn't called her in weeks, not since the Fashion Week fiasco. She froze for a few seconds before she silenced the phone. *I'll listen to his message, if he left one, and call him back, depending.* Alex gave her a curious glance, but she shook her head and shrugged—*I'll tell you later.*

"Ah, I've been waiting for this for more than an hour." Joseph trailed after Sheila as she plunked the trays onto the table and peeled back the tops.

Alex brought plates, napkins, and silverware from the kitchen while Bee stood beside the rack, watching them, fighting back tears. *I am such a terrible person that Joseph and mistress Sheila have brought over Punjabi.*

"Come now, Miss Bee, get some food into you." A stern look on her face, Sheila waved her over. "You look like a wraith. After lunch we'll leave and you can take a nap. Looks like you need one."

"Mama Sheila has spoken." Joseph set down his plate and pressed his palms together.

Bee obediently sat in one of the wooden chairs, and Alex took the one beside her. Wan Pi stationed himself under the table, prepping for dropped food retrieval.

"Oh, terrible person, see what your friends who hate you have done," Alex said, reaching for the chicken vindaloo.

Joseph gave her a mock scowl as he stabbed his fork into his tikka masala. "Have you been holding a private pity party?"

Bee answered, "Who, me? And miss an opportunity to plan my revenge?"

Joseph's eyes grew wide—he slapped his hand to his chest. "On me?"

Shaking her head, Bee chuckled. "On a certain fashionista whom I could describe with a certain four-letter word, but as we are in refined company"—she gave Sheila a nod—"I will not even tell you what letter it begins with."

She felt Alex looking at her, but she didn't want to acknowledge the reproach that would be clear on the golden fox's face.

Sheila spoke after she gulped down some of her lassi. The mushroom matar was easily four-chiles hot. "I might agree with you about the four-letter word, but I don't think revenge is . . . I mean, you don't need it getting around that you're—you know, unhappy about losing."

Bee felt a little stung by this. "You mean a sore loser.'"

Wiping her eyes with her napkin, Sheila shrugged.

"Damn right, Sheila," Joseph added. "Don't mess with Cindi Koh." He scrunched up his lips. "What happened between you two, anyway? You were über chummy during the competition."

Squeezing Alex's hand under the table, Bee said, "That doesn't matter now. She pissed me off, and I pissed back."

"And good riddance," Alex added, nodding emphatically.

Joseph affected a dramatic shiver. "Mamma mia. I hope I never piss you off."

After snorting in agreement, Sheila, across the table from Alex, leaned in close. "What are your plans now? You've got these fabulous designs. What are you going to do with them?"

"Yeah, great question," Joseph put in as he tore a naan in half. "You still have gobs of good press out there. Personally, I think Matt-nelope had their heads up their butts, really, being influenced by that barrage of gar*bage*." He produced the word "garbage" with a French emphasis, rhyming it with "barrage."

"Cindi Koh is an influencer," Bee said drily, but hearing Joseph say this made her glow inside.

"Yes, but you're selling your fans short if you think they're all going to jump your ship. Have you checked Instagram lately?"

Bee shook her head. "I can't. Not yet."

"Okay, well," Joseph raised one shoulder. "Torture yourself."

"He's right, Bee," Sheila said, picking up the other half of the naan. "But you're also wise to just stay chill. I mean, don't get on the internet until you collect your thoughts. Like, count to ten, lay low, take a—that is, be cool."

"Yeah," Alex chimed in. "Plan for a pop-up. You said you

wanted to have one during the contest—a fashion show at your old digs with Mei and Tina and Jojo."

None of this sounded good to Bee right now. She just wanted to listen to Joseph chomp on Matt-nelope and plan even more elaborate revenge plots with Alex. Sheila was too good a soul to diss anybody, thus her cheerleading could get boring.

But she nodded, pretending to listen. And more than anything, as much as she loved Joseph and Sheila, she wished she and Alex could be sitting around a table with Jojo, Tina, and Mei right now.

The chance came on Saturday, when, about midmorning, she got another cryptic text from Jo. When Bee had gone back to work on Tuesday, she'd endured the condolences and hugs, especially from Cam, who had some choice words about Cindi Koh. Jojo wouldn't enlighten her about the Saturday date—where they were going, who would be there, what to wear. She was on her phone a lot too, answering it and then getting up to walk to the storage closet or bathroom or lounge to talk. Once Bee followed her and listened outside the door, but Jojo seemed only to be talking to Mei.

But what about me? Are they planning an intervention?

Jojo didn't even bring up the topic of Bee's contest loss. It was as if Bee had just been accused of murder or had been diagnosed with a terminal illness.

Bee dove into work, proofing, copy editing, answering emails. Partly this burst of activity was a way to stop herself thinking about what her parents were thinking about it all. She had talked to her mother, who shared all the platitudes regarding getting back on the horse, making more clothes, and calling her father.

Dad hadn't left a message the day he'd called. Bee found

comfort in telling herself that he wanted to apologize in person and was hoping she'd call him back. Alex urged her to do just that.

"It doesn't mean you're giving in. Not for a minute," she told Bee drowsily as they lay on the sofa together. "But it gives him a chance to do it. If he doesn't, well, you're no worse off than you were before."

They both fell asleep before Bee could pick up the phone to dial him.

On Saturday, when Bee got Jojo's message, she was sitting at her sewing machine idly sewing decorative circles in a piece of muslin. Alex had gone home to change her clothes.

Breathless, Jojo said. "Oh, good. You're home. We're coming over."

"Wait—who's we?" But Jojo had already ended the call.

Bee's apartment was a mess. Dirty dishes and half-eaten takeout cartons littered the counter. Today was a beautifully fine March day, and the sun illuminated the fine layer of dust coating every surface except her worktable. She had run out of toilet paper and had resorted to posting a box of tissues next to the toilet.

She picked up loose clothing, loaded the dishwasher, wiped down the coffee and side tables, shut the bedroom door on her unmade bed, and borrowed TP from a neighbor. Wan Pi followed her around as if worried she had gone insane. The buzzer rang an hour later; Bee opened her apartment door and walked back to her worktable.

Mei, Tina, and Jojo marched in, Mei wearing black jeans, embroidered sneakers—Jacks, Bee thought—and the T-shirt with the silk-screened origami cranes that Bee had made for her. She carried what looked like a food basket. In stressed jeans, Tina also wore one of Bee's creations, a shirt quilted from silk fragments. She wore a battered pair of Merrells that she had bought for one of her digs ages ago and carried a slotted bag holding three bottles of wine and three bottles of sparkling water.

Mei cried, "Wan Pi, my little man! The only guy in my life that is so happy to see me!" She snatched him up, and after one too many kisses, handed him off to Tina.

Jojo came last. She'd pulled her hair up into a Pinky B ball cap and wore a saffron yellow big shirt that Bee had sewn last year.

"The Leftovers Personal Rescue Squad has arrived," she said, setting a reusable shopping bag on Bee's table. "And we are taking you out. And I mean OUT."

They each gave her a deep, round hug, and Bee couldn't stop laughing. "What is this? What are you guys doing?"

Mei took a step back and surveyed Bee. "You can't wear that. Not where we're going."

Bee looked down at her tatty yoga pants and Goodwill sweatshirt. "You guys look like you're ready for a safari. I don't have a pith helmet."

"You need jeans, or sensible slacks—and your green sneakers would be perfect. Also a Pinky B Tee. I know you made some; where are they, your bedroom?" Mei started to walk away, but Bee stopped her before she walked into that chaos.

"They're here, in one of these drawers." She pointed at the dressers she'd lined up along one wall.

Tina had drifted over to Bee's clothing racks. She pulled out the sleepwear kimono. "Oh, this is luscious." Holding the hanger in one hand, she gently pushed the garments on the rack. "And this—oh my God, Bee, this is fantastic."

She was holding the brocade women's suit jacket. "Mei, this is perfect for you."

Bee started to walk around the table toward her. "Wait a minute—"

Jojo had been at the drawers and brought a black tee silk-screened with the Pinky B gamine. "You must put this on. And grab a coat—might be windy."

"Where are you taking me?" Bee put the kimono back on the rack. She took the T-shirt from Jojo.

"Go get dressed," Mei ordered, and Tina chimed in, "Yes. Hurry. I'm starving."

Exasperated, Bee dressed, grabbing a pair of jeans from her bedroom and digging deep into her closet to find her green sneakers. She was wary of her besties' outsized enthusiasm, but she mutely obeyed. Jojo had probably organized some kind of ride on the SpaceX Dragon.

Where they did go was not entirely unexpected. Getting on the subway, they took the N line to the Fifth Avenue Station. The train was crowded, and they, along with most of the passengers, debarked at this southeast corner of Central Park. The sunny day warmed quickly; all of New York was headed to the park. Plum blossoms fragranced the air along the Pond path.

Bee carried one of the shopping bags for Jojo, and peeking inside, saw boxes of expensive crackers, little packets of cheese, clear containers of cherries, grapes, and sliced kiwi. *A picnic.* Beside her, Wan Pi trotted primly, wearing a bright green Pinky B dog shirt and one of his tiny hats, a hipster trilby.

While she wished she felt more enthusiasm for what her besties were doing for her, planning all week, organizing the food, even ordering a beautiful spring afternoon, she couldn't summon up much. She'd not been in the mood for an outing. At least this wasn't a big dinner at a fancy joint that she would have to turn down.

As the girls walked, they talked and laughed; it was good to hear their voices and listen to Jojo relating some of the typos she saw in posts to her site, Tina telling the story of a singed paper a student had turned in, and Mei imitating her boss trying to play ping-pong. It was easier to stay quiet, and if they noticed her solemn mood, they didn't bother her about it.

"Almost there!" Jojo sang out. Bee could hear the music of the carousel; the air smelled fresh and green. Everywhere people were laughing, including a homeless guy laughing at something he was telling himself. Bee didn't feel like laughing. The blow of losing the contest was a burden weighing heavily on her, worsened by the worry that she would never get her brash Bing confidence back again.

And Alex. Even though she'd apologized and monitored herself and stifled stupid remarks that might hurt her, Alex had been there for her. A lot. Lassie was back, and Bee loved having her in her life. Still, there was that gaping wound that would take awhile to close up.

Jojo was waving at someone in the crowd around the carousel. The music blared maniacally from inside the carousel barn. A long line of riders waiting for their turn tracked along the walkway leading up to it.

Bee saw Jim appear from the sea of people, and with him was Raj, and even better, standing between them, was Alex.

Stopping dead, Bee set down her shopping bag. *I don't deserve this*, she scolded herself.

Mei turned around to see Bee standing behind her, jostled by folks wandering around the plaza. Marching back to her, Mei picked up the grocery bag. "C'mon. We're getting in line for tickets."

"What?"

"Everyone should have a carousel ride when things get shitty. I know I need one."

Mei took Bee by the arm and drove her to the ticket window, where she bought a whole slew of tickets, way more than was needed, while Bee had an epiphany—her friends, all of them, had things going on in their lives that hurt or angered or stopped them in their tracks, but here they were tending to *her* wounds. Mei clearly had something bothering her—Bee could see it behind the careful, wry composure. And she knew Jojo had just sustained a pretty big disappointment. Yet . . .

"Someone has to wait out the ride with our stuff. This way we all get to be on the ponies at least once."

Alex was beside Bee, leaned over, and kissed her ear. "Crazy idea of Jojo's. Mei wanted to go back to Le Bernadin, but Jojo said no—we needed to do something unexpected and fun."

Leaning against Alex, they took their tickets to the end of the line. Jojo and Jim joined them, and Tina and Mei; Raj agreed to watch the picnic supplies and Wan Pi, who was in love with Raj anyway.

Turning around to glare at them, Bee said, "You all are insane. Every last man jack among you."

Nobody said a word but just stood there grinning at her. Alex whispered, "They've hatched some kind of surprise for you."

Crap. How much more surprise can I take?

Chapter Thirty-Three

Bee was seated on a red horse with its nose raised in an air of triumph. When the big Ruth & Sohn Band Organ in the center of the painted herd blared and jangled a happy tune, and the horse leapt up and away, she began to feel a little better. Behind her, she could hear Jojo and Jim singing along with whatever the organ was playing; Bee had no clue what song this was. Beside her, Alex smiled crazily when her own red horse rose up as Bee's came down. A cool breeze brushed Bee's face. For a few minutes, she could forget it all, feel the cold steel of the pole, and consider a merry-go-round–themed silk-screen graphic for a children's line.

Nah, a line for all ages. Why should kids get all the fun?

The ride was over all too soon. Raj demurred riding again; the line was long, and the sun was tipping west. The picnic must start soon or they would be huddled around their basket in the rapidly cooling March evening. After crossing East Sixty-Sixth to Sheep's Meadow, Mei and Alex spread two old Indian bedspreads on the grass. Fruit, cheese, a charcuterie of meats, salads, and of course barely warm *jiaoxi*, were laid out and paper plates passed around. Wan Pi looked as if he thought he was in canine Nirvana, and each newly opened packet of food presented wonders so rich as to boggle his little doggy brain.

Mei's basket contained real wine glasses, and she poured generous portions of the merlot. Jojo, apparently still on her no-alcohol purge, drank Pellegrino.

Mei raised her glass. "To Pinky B. The new fashion line all of New York is talking about!"

Reaching forward, they clinked each and every glass. Bee clinked, and drank, and fingered a grape. Who would be talking about Pinky B now? Cindi Koh's knockdown was all over Insta-gram and Twitter, and probably a *New York Times* headline by now.

Shielding her eyes from the lowering sun, Tina watched her. "Hey, girl. You look like your favorite rat died."

"Which one?" Bee asked, wishing no one had noticed that she felt more unhappy than she ever had been, and it was worse because her besties were trying to help her. Maybe the unhappiness was because they were trying to help, and she didn't deserve it. "My place has so many, I haven't managed to name them all yet."

"I know how disappointing something like this is," Jojo added as she pasted cream cheese on a cracker. "I felt pretty bad when Raj had to turn my book down."

Tina poked Raj in the ribs; he winced and had the smarts to look sorry.

"Oh, I understand the reasons, completely," Jojo told him, earnestly. "It didn't lessen the disappointment, but like they say, when someone closes a door, God opens a window. Something else really great happened because of it. I started a blog, and as of this morning, I've got more than a hundred followers!"

"Hooray for literary critic Jojo Zan!" Mei raised her glass again. Everyone clinked.

Jojo turned back to Bee. "Look what you did. I mean, you were on television, for Pete's sake. Everyone saw the Pinky B new spring line. And, jeez, you were in the finals."

All were nodding, including Alex, who brushed her shoulder. This was pure silver-lining Jojo, and Bee loved her for it, but she couldn't summon any enthusiasm about her future in fashion.

It struck her, as she listened to her friends talk about her clothes, describe them, tell her which one they would wear to work or to an inauguration ball if they were ever invited to one—or the Oscars, added Jo—that what she wanted more than anything right now was her father's approval. Mom kept telling her that Zhen read and watched every interview and had started an Instagram account so that he could see her designs.

"He loves you, Bing. He is very excited whenever he sees one of your pictures," Mom had told her yesterday. "He said to me, 'Look here, Xing. This is my daughter Bing!' He crows like a rooster."

Bee didn't believe any of it.

After they finished the third bottle of wine (and Jo was on her second bottle of Pellegrino), the sun was hugging the Lenox Hill skyline to the west. Jojo put on her hat, and Mei pulled on her gloves. Raj started to stuff used plates into a garbage bag.

"I think we need to go somewhere to warm up," Tina declared as she stood up. "I vote for a visit to P. J. Clarke's."

"What about Café Fiorello?" Jim asked.

Mei gathered up her wine glasses. "We need somewhere with a view. To watch the sunset."

While they were discussing where to go next, Bee caught Alex's eye and shrugged. Alex nodded. Bee didn't want to extend the evening. She was rotten company anyway, and her epiphany about not being the only one here with disappointments and problems hadn't helped. As they folded up the bedspreads, Bee murmured to Jojo that she just didn't feel up to it; she and Alex were going back to Bee's studio.

"Wait, Bee, listen," Jojo said, grabbing her arm.

Bee shook her head. "It won't do any good. I'm bringing you all down anyway."

"No, it's okay, I mean—come here." Jojo handed the bedspreads to Mei and directed Bee a few steps away.

Bee glanced at Alex, who shot her a smile that said, *I told you they've got a caper in mind for you.*

"Will you have lunch with me tomorrow? I'm meeting with my Dragon Mother about something, and I need the support. You'd be doing me a huge favor, bestie." Hunching up her shoulders and clasping her hands together, Jojo shot her a pleading smile.

Damn it, Jo was every bit as winsome as Pinky B. Bee knew she was stuck. She could hardly decline the invitation, even though tomorrow she'd planned to stream every episode of *Bridgerton.* Twice.

"Okay. I'll take on Lady Dragon. Where, at TORS?"

"Oh, God, thank you! Yes, at TORS. One p.m. Atrium restaurant. Hey," Jojo added, "could you bring your portfolio with you? There was that red brocade power suit you designed that I thought would look great on Mom. It might help me butter her up."

Bee wished she could believe Jojo was asking for a sketch for her mother and not just to make Bee feel better. "Sure, I can bring the sketch."

"No, bring the whole portfolio. I wanted to see if there was something in your lingerie line I ought to get for Jim. I mean, get for *me* to *wear* for Jim. He hasn't, like, taken up cross-dressing or anything."

Imagining the handsome Jim Yuhan in boudoir drag, Bee laughed for the first time in days; only Jojo—and Alex—could amuse her like that. "Yeah, I know what you mean."

Leaving Jojo to explain Bee's absence to the others—she was tired, or Alex had to work or any old excuse; Bee didn't care—she and Alex and Wan Pi walked along the pathways as dusk laid a coat of indigo over the sky. Around them the city murmured and growled and wailed, and they walked close, side by side, holding hands. On the subway, lucky enough to squeeze into a seat together, they drowsed with Wan Pi on Bee's lap, rocked by the train's speed.

Bee thought how nice it would be if they could just stay on the train all the way to the tip of Long Island, walk to a cabin overlooking the sea, and go down to the water to skinny dip. Of course, it was only March, and setting one foot in the ocean risked hypothermia, but the thought of it soothed Bee, and in her head she began to design a gown of deep sapphire velvet with long, puffy sleeves, a V-neck, and with a long, flowing train. Alex would look great in that color.

Chapter Thirty-Four

ee tried her hardest to be on time, knowing how Wendy Zan felt about punctuality, but she was six minutes late to the table at Steam, the artsy atrium restaurant on the ground floor of the Towers on Rivington Street. The venerable hotel was Zan Enterprises' flagship and was currently undergoing expansion and a facelift.

Jojo was already there, at a large table in the back corner. Mirrors in elaborate frames of all sizes, shapes, and materials were hung all along the far wall; Bee caught multiple images of herself in the mirrors as she approached. She had dressed carefully for this meeting, in her ribbon miniskirt with white big-collared button-down, silky semi-opaque black tights, and actual heels—two-toned peep-toes she'd found on one of her thrift store junkets.

Wendy glanced at her watch as Bee rushed into her chair, fumbling with her travel portfolio, phone, and purse.

Leaning over to give Bee a kiss on the cheek, Jojo told her, "You look fantastic, Bee. Heels, huh? *Très chic.*"

In a wine-colored wool sheath and jacket, a multiple-strand fine gold chain around her neck, Wendy smiled at Bee. It was a beautifully tailored look, but Bee thought a brighter red would be more complimentary to the woman's complexion. "Nice to see you again, Bee. I was glad that Jojo invited you. I am very curious as to why my daughter wanted so badly to lunch with me here today."

Jojo, in a long baggy blue sweater and black leggings, her hair pulled back from her face in a ponytail, smiled demurely. "Maybe I just want to have a meal with my mom and also some girl time."

A waitress marched up and took their drink orders. Wine for Wendy and Bee, and a coconut water for Jojo. "I've read it's good for the hair," she explained.

Across the atrium, workmen in coveralls strode to the elevators, carrying toolboxes and lunch pails. Bee asked Wendy, "How's the renovation going?"

Wendy glowered at the workmen. "They're supposed to use the freight elevators," she said crisply. When she turned to look at Bee, though, the sharp look was quickly replaced by a smile. "It's really going very well. We're expanding the ground floor and lobby, redoing all the public spaces and shops, plus the business suites and restaurants." She waved her hand at the restaurant furnishings—sleek chrome and glass tables, centerpieces of fresh tulips and lilies, bright and airy. "I've been reviewing plans for this one, and a new name. Maybe I'll call it Joan's."

Bee shot a glance at Jojo, who looked appalled.

Wendy laughed. "Maybe we'll do the decor in orange and black—a Halloween theme."

Wendy's sense of humor came out often at the expense of others, but to Bee's surprise, Jojo laughed too. "I can't wait until we can have our first science fiction con here."

Amused, Bee snorted as she watched mother and daughter trade jabs at each other. Jojo and Jim's wedding had famously, at least to the Leftovers, been on Halloween, and decor, fashions, and even food had featured jack-o'-lanterns and scarecrows, Jojo being a rabid horror and sci-fi fan. The only thing white had been the ghosts Bee had designed from gauze and georgette.

Jojo turned to Bee. "Mom's buying a property in Flushing."

Thank goddess the snark is over for now. "Wow, Flushing?" Bee had been out there a few times, visiting Tina's parents' dumpling truck. She had not been impressed by the city but was very impressed by the *jiaoxi.*

Wendy's eyes lit up. "I'm very excited about this one site, right on Main Street. There's an old theater there, but my lawyer, Mr. Cole, tells me we shouldn't run into snags about tearing it down, even though there's a preservation group trying to save it." She frowned. "It's a fire hazard and falling apart; how these people think they can renew it into any kind of usable shape is beyond comprehension."

Bee had a vague memory of Mr. Cole. She'd heard Mei mention him as well. She'd met him once in the lobby of the Leftovers' condo. He was in his mid-thirties, tall, with lots of thick, wavy, over-styled hair. Handsome, if you were into that sort of thing. She'd forgotten about him as soon as he was out of sight.

Jojo leaned forward. "It's a beautiful building. An old movie theater, all Spanish Baroque and more. Arched doorways, tiling everywhere, heavy dark, carved plaster—really ornate and made by Italian women. Reminds me a little of Hogwarts School." She passed Bee her phone. "It's a shame it has to come down. Here's the link."

Bee had to agree with Jojo that it was a shame to destroy the grand old lady; Bee made it a habit, when she walked around the city, to keep an eye out for unique buildings. "Oh, that looks so cool, like a Persian palace or something. What a great place to build a catwalk and have a fashion show—or a wedding even."

Tilting her head, Jojo shot Bee a curious face.

Where did that come from? Bee shrugged. "I mean, for someone who likes that sort of thing."

"The cost of restoring a building like this," Wendy said, just as the waitress reappeared to take their orders, "is prohibitive to any entity that wants to preserve it. To get it declared a historical site is one thing, but what do you do with it after that?"

Bee ordered the Tuna niçoise, Wendy a kale salad, and Jojo stuck with the sweet pea soup, served with grapefruit and a side of roasted quinoa. Bee was surprised that Jojo declined to order the Gotham burger. In response to Bee's curious glance, Jojo just smiled.

Wendy added, "Teamar, my architectural firm, agreed with both of you, but Mr. Teamar had to admit that in terms of financing, the best option is to tear the thing down."

Bee could imagine *that* conversation, knowing that Wendy was the pit bull in any deal. Snatching a glance at Jojo, she could see a slight smile on Jojo's lips as she picked up a fork to examine.

Wendy turned toward Bee. "Speaking of fashion shows, I heard what happened to you and it's unbelievable. That little girl who calls herself an influencer needs to grow up."

Wendy's commiserating with her about it warmed Bee inside. "Thanks. It was rough."

"If that was the reason you lost the contest, then I don't have much respect for the judges."

"Too right, huh, Bee?" Jojo said. "I guess they had to consider every angle, but they obviously didn't consider all the great comments I saw on Instagram."

Maybe I just wasn't good enough, Bee thought, but there was no reason to talk about how sourly she viewed herself these days.

"Yeah," Bee answered. "Those contest people weren't very nice. The only good folks were the workers, seamstresses, and gofers, and Joseph, who coordinated the entire thing—I don't think he slept the entire two weeks." She paused as the waitress refilled her wine glass, then picked it up and sipped. "And Elijah, the winner. He's a sweetie. I could see that he felt really bad for me. But you know," she added as Wendy started to protest, "he deserved to win. Have you looked at his line? Not Pinky B style, of course, but so tailored, sophisticated yet startling. Crikey, I'm beginning to sound like Cindi Koh. I'll need to burn sage and incense for days."

Feeling comfortable for the first time in a long while, it seemed, here in this wide space filled with light, with Jojo and her mom, Bee told the story of Conner Maxwell. Having enough distance from it now, she added what humor she could find, with embellishments about hair plugs and how she used an umbrella to fight him off.

At first Jojo was appalled—this was the first time she'd heard the story. "What a dick," Jojo blurted, garnering a quick scowl from her mother. "And Cindi posted a photo of kissing him, just a little bit later?"

"What *cojones*, huh?"

Wendy squinted at Bee. "Co-ho-nays?"

Jojo leaped in with an answer before Bee could give the literal description. "Means arrogance, Mom, a guy who's all entitled."

Bee didn't think Wendy believed Jojo, but she let the subject drop. Wendy said, "You turned him down, and look what happened." She fingered her chin with an expensively manicured finger. "You should sue."

"Mom," Jojo pleaded and deftly changed the subject. "You remember Alexis, the nurse Bee brought to our Christmas party? She's still with Bee. Isn't that adorable?"

Wendy nodded approvingly. "I like Alexis," she told Bee. "She's a sweet girl. I guess opposites really do attract."

Bee felt a little stung, but found that, because of Alex, she could accept the sharp observation. Laughing, she said, "I totally had that coming."

"Self-awareness," mused Wendy, slanting a knowing glance at her daughter, Jojo, "is a virtue worth achieving."

The meals arrived, and the women spent a few moments oohing and aahing over the presentation and aromas, while Wendy watched Jojo pick at her food.

"It's the quinoa, right?" Bee asked. "You should have gotten the hamburger."

Jojo laughed. "It's just not the same, is it?" She took a tentative bite and raised her eyebrows. "You know, it's actually pretty good."

After two more forkfuls, Jojo put down her fork and slid Bee's portfolio closer to herself. "Mom, I have a proposal for you."

Blinking, Wendy, who had just stuffed a wad of kale in her mouth, gazed at Jojo and waved her hand, indicating she had something to say. Swallowing, she scooted back in her chair.

"My daughter who cosplays black widow spiders and daydreams about vampire slayers and endless five-year missions in outer space has a business proposition for me? I can't wait to hear this."

With an impish smile, Jojo lifted up the portfolio, pushed aside her plate, and laid it out. Bee felt her heartbeat tick up a beat, and she resisted the urge to snatch the portfolio away.

What Is Jojo up to? Another crazy scheme—a "caper" like Alex warned me?

"Okay." Opening the portfolio, Jojo slid out one of Bee's designs, which happened to be the silk-screened ball gown, on top of the pile because Alex loved to look at it. "Mom, you're a smart developer. You pay attention to the neighborhood, the clientele you expect. You ask around, get with the local boards—I've seen you quizzing shop owners and complete strangers about what they want to see in the neighborhood."

Wendy nodded, clearly baffled. Bee couldn't touch her food as she listened.

Jojo continued while she laid more drawings out, one after the other, next to Wendy's plate. "This renovation—I know you are going for a young crowd, the hipsters. I've heard you arguing with the designers about how the looks they're bringing you are too stale, am I right?"

"I didn't realize you were paying attention," Wendy said with a slight smile.

"I've picked up more than you think. Sitting right here, you have one of the most talented fashion designers whose inventive designs are adored by so many of the young and hip." Jojo rose, stood over the drawings, and handed her mother a sketch of Bee's office wear. Bee watched in wonder as Wendy raised her eyebrows.

Does she like it or loathe it?

"This is an unbeatable opportunity." Jojo sat down in the chair next to Wendy. "You've got all this space, and you've always told me how tedious it can be finding merchants who fit in with your vision. If you were to underwrite Bee's fashion empire, beginning with a trendy, upscale boutique in the galleria you're adding to the bridge between the original lobby and the new construction, people would flock here."

Wendy started to nod, thoughtfully, Bee hoped. Then she made eye contact with Bee and cocked her head. Bee was sure she saw a speculative gleam in Wendy's eyes.

A rush of eagerness hit Bee from out of nowhere. Before she could put a cork in it she blurted to Jojo, "We could stage a grand opening, a launch party! With live music, and—"

"A fashion show, of course," Jojo chimed in. "Bee's designs— very professionally done. She's worked with a really great seam-stress and can hire real models."

Her stomach swirling with excitement, Bee offered, "And if you have music every weekend in the main atrium, a DJ or some cool jazz or a string quartet—you could make this hotel lobby the 'it' place to be on Saturday and Sunday."

Pursing her lips, Wendy nodded solemnly.

"And I can write all about it," JoJo said in a rush. "Who's who that's here, the music, the food, the fashions, all of it."

"You? You write science fiction and fantasy," Wendy observed. "You live in an entirely different universe."

"Yes," replied Jojo. Bee caught uncertainty on her face. A second later she added, "But I'll have Cam to help me. He writes all the ad copy for Gray Ghost. And, to tie everything together, Raj's newest nonfiction author is Bucky Gerardo. He's so hot right now in the fashion scene that his new book is gonna have to ship in a refrigerator truck. We could have his book release event here, livestream it, and record it for the podcasts I've been doing."

Bee felt her mouth drop open. *Gerardo at my shop, standing before the front, streaming his live book launch in front of Pinky B.* "What a boost for me—I mean us, Mrs. Zan. The hotel and me. Bucky Gerardo here would be giant."

Wendy's smile appeared frozen and her gaze unfocused as if she was doing calculus in her head. Bee held her breath. Someone in the kitchen dropped a pot and she almost jumped out of her chair.

Jojo moved her chair closer to her mother. "Mom . . . are you . . . okay?"

Astonished, Bee watched Wendy reach up to her cheek to swipe away a tear. Laying her hand on Jojo's hand, she whispered, "I'm so proud of you, Jojo. I see a glimmer of the empire builder in you."

Turning to Bee, she announced, "Yes. I will invest in your fashion line, Bee. And I will offer you the largest retail store in the hotel. It's a good size now for a curio shop, but will double in size during the remodel. Now, as to terms, this expansion of space is also expanding the hotel's . . . usage, I suppose you could say, so . . ." She turned to Jojo. "I'm going to need a full-time event manager. Your husband has already coordinated several events here quite successfully—beginning with his own wedding. I was impressed. Jim is a natural-born problem solver. Do you think this is a position he'd accept?"

Jojo blinked. "Uh . . . I-I don't think it would hurt to ask. I'm sure he'd love to get a proposal from you."

"And of course," Wendy steamed on, "I will take you up on your offer to write articles and blogs about the hotel, its events and attendees. Do you know a good videographer?"

Jojo nodded mutely.

"Well, then," Wendy said, and took a sip of her wine.

Falling back in her chair, Bee noticed movement in one of the wall mirrors. Turning, she saw Mei and Tina threading their way through the tables toward them.

Here comes the rest of the coven of conspirators.

Mei took the chair opposite Wendy, giving Jojo a knowing glance. Taking a chair from an adjoining table, Tina crowded in between Mei and Bee. The waitress appeared with menus, took the drink orders, and cleared the previous plates. She seemed a bit perplexed; the restaurant was filling up.

Tina shrugged off her jacket. "This is a lovely place, Mrs. Zan."

Wendy leaned back in her chair and glanced sideways at her daughter. "What is it Captain America says: 'Avengers, assemble?'"

Mei glanced at Jojo, who nodded. "She's agreed," she said, beaming.

"That's fantastic." Mei laid both hands on the table. Bee thought that even in her yoga pants, hoodie, and black tennies, Mei gave a forbidding air. She was getting her lawyer on. She said to Wendy, "Thank you so much. This is fantastic for Bee. We've all talked about it, and I'd be happy to handle the legal agreements between you two." She straightened and raised her chin a little. "I know you and your husband's representative is Sebastian Cole. I have worked with him before, but in this situation, I'd like to suggest that my association with Bee, and her fashion line, not to mention our joint history with Zan Enterprises, gives me the advantage of being more familiar with the aspects of this deal than Mr. Cole."

One of Wendy's eyebrows drew up. Bee glanced at Jojo, who had a confident and almost proud expression on her face. Well, at least Jojo didn't seem to be at all fretting about how Wendy was going to react to Mei's little speech.

After glancing over at Jojo and seeing Jojo grinning back rather smugly, Bee thought, Wendy turned to scrutinize Mei. They were all staring at her. It was impossible to figure out what she was thinking.

"Well, I've always known Jojo was a leader," she said. "I just didn't realize she was the general of an army."

Everyone tried to laugh, but they all sounded as if they were choking.

"I don't see how I can refuse, Mei. I can find no argument with your proposal."

Tina, who was decked out in a bright red T-shirt, tight jeans, and her signature heels—this time Blahniks—clapped her hands. Just then the waitress brought the drinks, giving Tina a startled glance.

Tina laughed. "Oh no, I wasn't summoning you, don't worry. Thanks!"

Smiling, the waitress left their drinks and swished away.

Raising her wine, waiting for the others to join in, Tina said, "Here's to Pinky B at TORS. Hot and divinely delicious Drive-by Dumpling will be served."

Chapter Thirty-Five

The Aunties, Drive-by Dumpling's crack dumpling-makers, supplied the special order of *jiaoxi* for the Pinky B launch, and on the Saturday before the Sunday launch party, it was waiting at the Lus' food truck in Flushing. Tina, dumpling mastermind, roped Raj into driving across the river and bringing the rest of the Leftovers along for the ride and hot pork and shrimp dumplings. It was time, she told him, that he meet the family.

The April morning was clear and breezy; the East River glistened in the morning sun, and fresh wind swept away the pungent river odors. Traffic choked the Queensboro Bridge. In the shotgun seat, Tina listened to Bee—Wan Pi on her lap—Jojo, and Mei laugh like hyenas high on weed as they riffed on what kind of rewards Dick Doran, Mei's misogynistic and racist boss, deserved to win.

Jojo offered, "The Darth Vader award?"

Bee snorted. "Ten days in a Chinese hell, all expenses paid from his hacked bank account."

"No!" Mei turned from her open window. The wind had blown

strands of hair loose from their combs to flutter in her face. "Forced labor at a diversity retreat. A year's participation, I would say."

Tina flung her arm over the back of her seat. "You guys are making Raj nervous."

Raj gave her a quick smile. Jojo leaned forward. "The prize for Raj should be the Hugh Grant award for cuteness."

Bee and Mei both said, "Eww" at the same time.

"I'm talking about the Hugh Grant of *Love Actually* or *Notting Hill.*"

"That was before he was getting blow jobs from hookers," Mei said, while Jojo's cheeks grew red.

"Oh, shit, I forgot about that."

"You don't, do you Raj?" Bee asked, and Jojo poked her in the ribs. "Sorry, probably way outta line with that one."

"I wish Hugh Grant had never been born, let alone in England," Raj said, and everyone laughed again.

By the time they arrived at Drive-by Dumpling's Corona Park location, just after noon, the line already stretched almost to the edge of the bocci ball pitch. Seeing all the people through the window, Wan Pi began to bark hysterically.

"I don't know if he wants to play with them or eat them," Bee sighed, pulling him back. He stared up at her and whined beseechingly, licking his chops as if confirming the latter motive.

Dropping the girls off, Raj drove off to seek parking. Tina and Mei grabbed out two large coolers from the back seat before he left.

"I hope he comes back," Mei whispered to Tina.

Watching his black SUV navigate into the traffic and turn a corner, Tina sighed. "Me too. He seemed a little nervous, didn't he?"

"Honey, a deer in headlights. C'mon, let's go load up and beg prettily for some *jiaoxi.*"

"I'm only a little famished," Bee called over her shoulder. She,

Wan Pi, and Jojo were already halfway to the shaded seating area, with every table filled.

The Lus kept a private table at the front end of the truck. Hidden behind two rattan screens, this is where the Lus would grab a few minutes' break between the rushes. Discreetly, Tina motioned that the girls should slip behind the screens.

Tina's heart buzzed in her chest. Having spotted her, Dad waved from the window, and Tina wished Raj were here so she could introduce him quickly and get it over with. Bringing him to the truck was so much safer than bringing him to the house. Here, Lian and Tai, especially during the lunch rush, would be way too busy to start peppering him with questions.

"Mom," Tina called as she rounded the screen, "I'm here for the *jiaoxi.*"

Lian poked her head out the truck's side door, open to cool the always-sweltering kitchen. The aroma of pork and spices flowed from the door with her.

"Ah, Tina. Good you can help. Come in."

"Mom. Wait a minute. I have to—"

"No, no, wait, help us get these people fed so we can sit and talk."

Mom vanished back inside, and Tina felt a heavy lump in her chest. *What am I so worried about? What's the big deal about introducing Raj to Mom and Dad?*

This worry, and Raj not being here to offer his beaming smile and easy hand, made Tina's chest tighten. There was the other thing. The reason she had been so desperate to persuade him to come today. But she couldn't think about that right now.

Tina set her cooler down on the one Mei had stationed by the wooden steps leading to the door. She'd tell her friends she'd be occupied for a bit but renew the promise of food. Turning, she saw that the table was occupied, and not just by her besties. The ladies were talking animatedly to Web Martel, who got to his feet as soon as he saw her.

"Your mom insisted I sit at the captain's table," he said, grinning. "I'm done, though."

"He says he's here every day." Jojo grinned too. "He liked my sweatshirt, so we had to talk about how many times we've each seen *Black Widow*."

"Hi, Web." Tina was happy to see him. He might not only distract her from her worries but would entertain her noisy, restless friends. The considered opinion of the Leftovers Club was that Web looked enough like Idris Elba to be his younger brother.

Much younger, Tina thought. There wasn't even a hint of gray in his midnight-black hair and goatee. "What'd you have today?"

"My favorite. Pork and chives."

"That's *my* favorite too," Bee declared. "But Wan Pi prefers the plain pork." She leaned over to rub his head, and he barked in agreement.

"Listen, guys—" Tina started to explain her commitment to helping out for a while, when Raj peeked around the screen. "Oh, whew! I knew I was in the right place when I heard Bee declaim about pork and chives."

Seeing him, fortunately, made Tina tense about her crazy scheme. "Okay, come on. Time to meet the parental units." Grabbing his hand, she pulled him toward the back door and called in from the bottom step. "Mom, I want to introduce you to my friend, Raj."

Why couldn't I say "My boyfriend, Raj"?

If this omission bothered Raj, he didn't show it. Behind her, though, Tina could hear the girls making impatient sighs and mutterings.

Like a German shepherd guard dog, Lian was at the door in a flash. A small lady, stocky and undeniably strong looking, she extended her hand to Raj. "Ah, Rash. So nice to meet you at last. Please, sit down and I'll bring you some *jiaoxi*." She waved a vinyl-gloved hand at Tina. "Tina, come in. Get some drinks for everyone. Hello, girls. My best girls ever!"

Waving eagerly at Bee, Jojo, and Mei, Lian vanished back inside, and Tina, shrugging, gave Raj a quick peck and hopped up the steps into the kitchen.

Inside, the swirl of spices and heat hit Tina hard, but she loved the familiar smells. Tai, her father, stood at the window, bagging up orders that he gracefully pulled from the warmers, stuffing napkins and packets of garnishes and Chinese relish into paper bags. Tina had insisted they move from plastic to paper, and to her surprise, her parents had relented easily.

"Two waters, one mango, one Coke," Tai ordered, and Tina, without a second thought, opened the cooler, pulled the drinks out, and handed them to Dad.

Lian was at the counter now too, taking orders, scanning iPhones, and taking credit cards. In Cantonese, without looking at Tina, she asked, "Is he the boy you've been seeing? Why do you bring him here when we are at our busiest? No time to talk."

Tina understood Cantonese enough to get the gist of Mom's questions. She answered in English. "Yes, Mom. I'm sorry the timing is so bad, but we had to pick up the *jiaoxi*. You know, for Bee's big fashion party tomorrow. I still would love you to come."

She knew Mom would turn her down. Although she was disappointed, she understood. Wednesday was the only day Mom and Dad took off, and they managed to be plenty busy on Wednesday, too, visiting friends, doing the weekly shopping, and getting the truck serviced.

Lian shook her head. In English this time, she said, "No time for fashion shows. And to go into Manhattan. Your father is too tired to drive all that way."

"No I'm not," Tai retorted in Cantonese. "I would like to see the pretty clothes on those pretty girls."

Mom muttered something in Cantonese under her breath that Tina understood as "men are pigs."

Tai laughed out loud. "The smartest animal in the celestial heavens."

Web appeared at the end of the window. "Are they arguing again?" he asked with a smile.

"We never argue," Tai replied, handing three bags to the patient parent of one of the many baseball players in the park today. "This is the language of love."

Web laughed. "Hey, Tina, your friends are crazy—in a nice way, I mean. They kept me entertained."

Leaning past her dad, Tina gave a mock sigh. "Now you see what I have to put up with."

"Well, at least they're not as nuts as my family. See you on Tuesday, Lus." Waving, he left, jogging slowly along Meadow Lake Drive toward downtown Flushing.

"Such a nice boy," Tai remarked, taking the next drinks order from Tina. "Do you know he read the *Book of the Dead*? And he made a record. Songs, you know. Or was it a CD?"

"I had no idea, Dad." She did know that Tai looked forward to Web's visits, and they watched Web round the curve at the bottom of the lake; he was quite fit, jogging here in the park every day, as far as she knew. He had a bright, friendly smile and a soft, articulate voice, and treated Tai with respect he too often didn't get from other patrons.

The crowd had thinned a little. Tai loaded Tina up with dumplings for her hungry friends. Taking off her gloves and cap, Lian washed her hands and gathered up the drinks to take out. Tai followed her, lingering in the truck doorway to listen.

Raj was sitting on an empty beverage crate because there were only three chairs. "Tina," Lian barked, waving her hand, "go get three more chairs. From that table right there. People don't like that one so much."

Getting up, Raj went to help her. "She knows her own mind, doesn't she?"

"I warned you," Tina breathed, bumping against him.

Tina didn't feel in the least bit hungry, which was unusual for her, she knew. But the rest of the girls plunged into the bags. Lian opened up a bento box of fried rice, chicken, and chopped enoki mushrooms. She shrugged as the girls gaped at her. "I smell those dumplings all day. Good to have something else."

She peered inquisitively at Wan Pi. "You named him Naughty One?" she asked Bee. Lian frowned as Bee tried to think of a reply that was at least a little respectful, but Lian added, "He looks like mischief. Mr. Mischief."

Bee said, "He's the king of mischief. I've had to hide all my cushions—and his favorite toy is plastic bags."

Tai, sitting on the top step in case a customer appeared, sipped a cup of tea and giggled. "I would give him some, but my daughter makes me use paper."

"Mrs. Lu, no wonder these dumplings are so famous. They're incredible," Raj said after taking a bite.

Tina was relieved to see the pride on Mom's face. "Very old, secret recipe." She tapped her head, as if the recipe resided there. "In my family for generations."

"What part of China is your family from?"

The conversation between Lian and Raj commenced. Tina, leaning forward with her chin propped on one palm, exchanged glances with Mei, then Bee, and finally Jojo. They all nodded, silently, with approval. Raj had charmed Mama in the snap of a finger.

Personal histories were exchanged, as well as how the dumpling business was started, and how Raj came to be a publisher. Tai asked about the books, wondering if he'd read any of them. Relieved, and suddenly extremely weary, Tina leaned against Mei.

She saw that Bee seemed impatient, and Tina knew she would have to break off this romance between her parents and the charming Raj soon.

"It's just that I need to be back at the hotel," Bee whispered, a wrinkle in her forehead. All week, leading up to her big debut, Bee had been more freaked than a cat on a bicycle. Wan Pi, lying next to her, got up and stared at her, his rear end wiggling his missing tail.

Even he wanted to be on his way, Tina thought. She was saved from seeming rude and in a hurry to leave by the appearance of an entire baseball team at the window.

With the excuse that she had to get the frozen dumpling order to TORS today, Tina kissed her mother, hugged her father, and rounded up the girls to help load the coolers, already filled with ice bags. They walked to the car, roughly a block away, carrying the coolers between Tina and Raj, and Mei and Bee. Jojo said something about straining her back.

"By the way, that Web guy? Wow. I forgot what a nice ass he has," Mei told Tina in a soft whisper.

Tina, having watched Web jog away, had to agree, and wondered if that was why she'd watched him until he was out of sight.

As Raj pulled onto I-495, he reached over and took Tina's hand. "That went pretty well, I thought."

Tina, leaning back in the leather seat, gave him a smile. Inside, though, her thoughts tangled her up. She had to face the problem: lately she'd been having second thoughts about Raj.

Maybe I hoped this meeting with my parents would wash this garbage out of my head, she thought. It didn't seem to be working.

Chapter Thirty-Six

I f it weren't for Bucky Gerardo, Alex thought as she hefted a bundle of Pinky B dresses inside the elevator rising to the TORS penthouse level, Bee's big launch scene would never have gotten out of the gleam in Wendy Zan's eye. Jojo, Alex's elevator companion who was carrying the ball gown, deserved the credit even more, because she was the one who'd called him to propose the joint venture.

Catching Jojo's eye, Alex winked at her, and Jojo laughed. "I have the jewel in the crown in my arms," she joked, eyeing the lovely pale fabric inside its plastic protective casing.

"And, as usual, I'm number one gofer." Alex had another reason, however, for winking at Jojo, and she wondered if Jojo knew what she suspected, but Alex kept it all discreetly to herself, except for keeping a watch out for Jojo's safety in small ways.

When the elevator doors opened, the rising sun streamed through the endless open glass, floor to ceiling, that encased the penthouse level's crowning venue: the Tower Room. Sharing the penthouse level with the Zans' flat, the event space formed a fan-shaped platform floating over Lower Manhattan, with views of the East River and the Williamsburg Bridge. Alex had no doubt that the views from the rooftop garden she could see beyond the glass would be even more spectacular.

An open staircase curved up the interior wall over the elevator. It led to a broad gallery that swept around the southern end of the large space. This was where the caterers were setting up the buffet and social area, using an upstairs conference room as a pantry and kitchen. The gallery, too, led out onto an outdoor space—a teak deck with a scattering of umbrellaed tables.

In the huge main room, music, a babble of voices, and the squeal of racks being wheeled across the shiny charcoaled teak flooring met Alex's ears. The show, scheduled for one p.m., was in full start-up mode.

Alex marveled at the technician's lighting, which had gone up yesterday, and the five-foot-high scaffolding of the runway jutting out into the room like a breakwater, with seating being set up on both sides and in curving rows around the end. The New York skyline served as a background, visible through a clear mesh hung across the eastern window walls for reflection prevention. A giant Pinky B logo—courtesy of one of Bucky Gerardo's copious contacts—hovered over the catwalk, suspended by invisible wires.

Until Bucky had gotten involved, all Bee had hoped for was a short, two-foot-tall catwalk composed of every stage component TORS possessed. Bucky knew people. Turned out, he knew more people than Cindi Koh. Alex still had the uneasy feeling that Cindi was going to show up. She was just the type to be nervy like that.

Joseph, in white tennies, tight black jeans, and a black T-shirt emblazoned with the Pinky B mascot, sailed over to them and relieved some of Alex's burden. "At last," he crowed to Jojo, juggling three hangers and their clothing into his arms, "the Audubon dress is here! This way, ladies."

He sailed away to the right, leading them beneath the southern gallery, past the steps up to the runway, and into the lower-level conference/dressing room where the models would be made up, coiffured, and dressed. Just inside the doors, a trio of TORS staffers unboxed Pinky B T-shirts, socks, bags, and buttons—all swag that Bee had made weeks before that would be given to guests as they filed in.

After helping Joseph hang the clothes, Alex wandered out into the Tower Room, gravitating toward the windows to get a better look at that view—the East River, the sparkling towers of Lower Manhattan. She supposed that the Zans' apartment, which was on the other side of the interior wall, had some pretty spectacular views of its own—possibly even glimpses of the Hudson. Light crept over the great city, which Alex never tired of staring at. She'd left Bee's studio early with Jojo and the last of the clothes, mostly to give herself some space from Bee, who was clinging to the proverbial ceiling with all four paws.

"Listen, Jojo and I will take this stuff over," Alex had told Bee this morning. "We'll get an Uber. I think you and Wan Pi need to walk over. In one hour."

Bee had been pacing between her bedroom and the great room, Wan Pi on her heels, in a tizzy about what she should wear. Nothing Alex said could soothe her. Staying overnight with Bee when she was so wound up was impossible for Alex, who had worked four twelve-hour shifts in a row so she could have plenty of time to help. So Alex had come by early. She'd stay the night afterward to help her poor girl recover when the show was over.

"What about this dress?" Bee had pulled a cap-sleeved, shirt-waist, short but full-skirted dress of striped cotton. "I'll wear one of the Trilbys with it. And those seventies platform shoes I found last year at Thrift Jungle."

"That'd be fantastic," Alex concurred. She liked Bee in

anything. She might quail at seeing Bee in a business suit of sky-blue wool, but to Alex, Bee could pull an outfit out of a dumpster and look great.

Throwing down the dress, Bee, sorting through the pile on the sofa, had lifted up a black mini pencil skirt. "Or this Pinky B silk-screened tank, and, and—I know, the red silk cape!"

From her seat on the side chair, Alex leaned forward. "The platforms for this one for sure."

"No, no, no. Boots! Wish I had some thigh-high ones." She'd dropped the skirt onto the coffee table, forgetting it as soon as it landed.

Bee had next focused her panic on what Alex should wear. Usually, Alex liked her to suggest ideas, but this time Alex knew exactly what she planned to wear. In the moment the discussion started to evolve into a fight, Bee's cell rang. Alex had literally been saved by the bell.

When Jojo showed up, Alex's relief had been profound. Bee hadn't wanted her very best clothing hanging at TORS all night due to unfounded fears of thievery. Nothing Wendy suggested in the way of locks and staff oversight was safe enough; the only option was for Alex and Jojo to ferry the fashions over this morning.

Alex had let Jojo into Bee's apartment, whispering, "Let's get outta here, quick. She's about to go atomic."

Jojo, nodding in a knowing way, gave Bee a wave as she listened to Bee rattle off a litany of worries, such as food being late, elevator jams, music mix-ups, and one of the models calling in sick. Jojo had led Joseph, Cam, and Bucky in getting this show off the ground, then turned the event over to her hubby. Things seemed well in hand. Still, Bee had followed Jojo and Alex around her place as they got the outfits into garment bags and the accessories into large, lidded containers. She'd nattered at Jojo, and Jojo had responded with soothing replies like: "I'll check as soon as I get there" and "Do you really think so?"

Now, as Alex took a minute to enjoy Gotham's amazing vistas out the window, Jojo came to stand beside her. Dressed in a knee-length red sweater over a black tunic and leggings, Jojo glowed. She was, Alex thought, having the time of her life. Wendy, Jojo's dreaded Dragon Mother, had even tactfully let Jojo have the spotlight, only making the odd suggestion now and then about who and how the hotel could offer assistance.

"The walk will calm her, I hope," Alex said. "I'll bet she'll be here in less than an hour, though. She won't be able to stand the suspense."

"And the models don't show up until ten." Jojo gazed into her phone as if it were a crystal ball—which, in many ways, it was. "Let's see, at one, or a little after, when hopefully even the chronically late people wander in, Joseph introduces Bucky, who speaks briefly and who introduces our Bee!"

"Is she going to introduce the looks?"

"Oh *God*, no." Jojo gave a short laugh. "We want the chatter to be clean and coherent. No, Joseph will do it. He's fantastic."

Alex nodded. It warmed her to think how many people had Bee's back, especially her three best friends, Jojo, Mei, and Tina.

Jojo scanned the area. "I heard they have baked goods around here somewhere, and the TORS bakery makes quinoa muffins. I wonder where they've got the food stashed."

As vegetarian as she was, Alex had no love for quinoa unless it was drenched in sauces. She pointed up at the gallery. "Upstairs, I think. Let's go check it out. I'm famished."

"I never had quinoa until recently. It's actually really good. I wish I could find it more places."

"We better find you some, then."

They did manage to score some baked goodies in Tower

Conference Room 2, which was stacked on top of TC Room 1 and shared its footprint. They carried their loot back up to the dressing room to nosh. As they sat on folding chairs before the makeup tables, marveling over the array of tony makeup the models would get to use today, a slender man, bearded, wearing a gray double-breasted coat over a vintage jean jacket—an odd combination, Alex thought—sat nearby.

"Hey, Bucky," Jojo called out to the man.

"Jojo! My favorite promoter!" Grinning, Bucky pulled up a chair and sat facing them. "Wow, the set looks big, really big." He glanced over at Alex and held out his hand. "I'm Bucky. You a friend of Jojo's?"

"She's Bee's friend," Jojo said. Alex shook Bucky's hand. "This is Alex."

"Wow. You're Alex! So great to meet you." He nodded at Alex as if he approved.

Alex wasn't sure she liked him yet; he seemed rather full of himself, but he had been a tremendous help to Bee, so she decided to give him the benefit of the doubt.

While Jojo and Bucky went over the lineup together, Alex took her coffee and the elevator down to the mezzanine. Pinky B's debut outlet was situated on the mezzanine-level skywalk that ran between the hotel's open-air carpark and a smaller boutique hotel the Zans had purchased. This was currently undergoing renovation to bring it up to the standards of the "mothership."

The basic construction of the storefront that was to house Pinky B had been completed, and the specialized fixtures and decor were going in now. The shop wouldn't be open for two weeks.

Alex had had to talk Bee down from "borrowing trouble," which was the way her grandmother referred to worrying about the future that you couldn't foresee, much less do anything about. Bee had fretted every day since Wendy's offer of a launch party about finding an adequate manufacturing stream for her off-the-rack clothes. The flagship store, Pinky B at TORS, would feature couture sewn in Bee's studio; she'd been able to talk Sheila into helping out two days a week on spec. And of course, there would be one-offs, tailored upon purchase.

As this was Sunday, the shop's wide glass door was locked, but Alex had the code. Brown paper covered the glass walls that opened onto the skywalk, which was eerily quiet. At the other end from TORS, the entry to the other building was boarded up, as if barring strange creatures from escape. Sunday morning traffic on Rivington, which would be visible once the paper came down from the exterior windows, was more of a muted hiss than a roar. Almost spooky, Alex thought, as she pushed the heavy doors open.

The shop floor was a midtone bamboo, cushioned for "give." The painting hadn't begun yet, though ladders and scaffolding were in place. Pinky B would be hand-painted onto the left-hand wall, the dressing and measuring rooms just behind it. Floor-to-ceiling windows would have thin mesh shades against the bright sun; an observer would be able to see for blocks along Rivington toward Bowery. Against the right-hand wall, the desk had been installed— plain white ceramic on maple. In the space between the dressing rooms and the desk would be where buyers and friends could lounge in plush chairs and view the fashions.

Bee had painted all these images for Alex, according to her suggestions. But today Alex felt rather melancholy. What if she and Bee drifted apart? Bee would quit her day job and vanish into the world of fashion. There would be no place there for a hardworking ER nurse. Bee's career was taking off, like the Dreamliner. Alex wondered if it would ever be coming back.

Hearing the rattle of paper behind her, Alex turned quickly from the windows. Being here alone with no one around did feel weird, and her heart ticked up a beat or two.

A man was peeking in through the open door, his hand on the anodized steel push bar. Stiffening, Alex stood still, bit her lip, and said, "Hello? Can I help you?"

The man, who Alex could see now was Asian, squinted at her through gold-rimmed glasses. "Oh, so sorry to disturb, but—wait. Aren't you Alexis?"

Alex hesitated. There was something familiar about this man, but she couldn't quite place him. "Yes," she said carefully. "And you are . . . ?"

The man didn't move. Still squinting, he didn't answer right away. "No. Sorry, sorry. I am disturbing," he said and disappeared.

A flash of recognition hit Alex, and, darting after him, she yanked open the door and ran out into the hall. "Mr. Lin! Mr. Lin! Wait."

Bee's father stopped on the gently sloped ramp leading down to the TORS mezzanine and turned back.

"It's so nice to see you again." Alex rushed, stopping a few feet from him. "Do you want to see Bee's store?"

Mr. Lin gave a quick shake to his head. "No, I— No, thank you."

"Oh, come on, please. I'd love to show it to you. Bee isn't here right now, though. She's . . ."

Mr. Lin turned to go, then stopped. "Okay, yes. I would like to see it, but just a few minutes."

As she led him back inside, Alex wondered if he knew about the launch upstairs. Her heart raced as she thought how strangely wonderful this was. Bee's father, whom Bee had been feuding with for months, had actually snuck over here to see what was going on. No doubt Mama Xing had told him all about it.

She couldn't read his face as he studied the area, ran his hand along the ceramic desktop—even though it was still covered with plastic film, and peeked into the dressing rooms.

Nodding, he said, "Big. That's nice. Big space, and right in New York City. Good."

"Bee's very excited about it." Alex stood a few feet behind him, near the windows.

"Mrs. Zan. I have heard about her and her husband. Very wealthy Chinese."

"Yes," Alex swallowed. "Yes, they are."

"They must think there is profit in Bee's business." Mr. Lin glanced up to study the ceiling's recessed lights.

Nodding, at first Alex didn't know how to reply. Then she said, "Bee's been working so hard on this. She's getting well known in the New York fashion scene."

Turning, Mr. Lin made his way toward the door. Alex wondered if he knew about the launch party. "Um, there's a launch party for Bee's line in the penthouse today," she said, trotting after him as he pulled open the door. "Starts at one. You know you are invited."

Standing just outside the door, Mr. Lin said nothing but stared at her for a few moments. "Thank you, Alexis, for the tour."

Then he walked quickly away, disappearing into the luxe hallways of TORS.

By the time Alex got back up to the Tower Room, the place was starting to buzz like a beehive. The models had arrived, and as Alex poked her head into the dressing room, she saw Bee's usuals: Beautiful Bettie, Darling Dorothy, Sassy Simon, and Freakin' Felix. Squatting at Bettie's feet, a pedicurist painted her nails as she stood barefoot on the floor. Dorothy, in big curlers, saw Alex and winked, while someone swirled a giant makeup brush in her ear.

Felix was having his black wavy hair blow-dried while studying his phone and, Alex thought, secretly taking selfies. And, standing on a chair, Simon waved at her as Sheila hemmed up the black silk shorts he was to show off as part of the streetwear section. The odors of polish, hairspray, gels, and blush were almost nauseating. Alex wondered how the models and the dressers could stand it.

Backing out of there, Alex felt relieved that Bee was not in the dressing room. Music pounded on and off as the DJ made her sound checks. Alex felt a headache starting and went up to the outdoor deck, trying to stay out of the way of the caterers setting up tables.

She thought about Mr. Lin's strange visit. Having not seen him since the disastrous Fashion Week debacle which seemed like a century ago—she was surprised, and relieved, that he had been so polite and curious about what Bee was up to. That had to be a good sign.

"Oh, goldie foxy, I'm so glad I found you!" Bee grabbed her from behind, and Alex, feeling inexplicably happy, turned and gave her a big hug and kiss.

"I've been wandering around, trying to stay out of people's way."

Bee was beautiful. The excitement and attention made her glow. She had dyed her hair, which was buzz cut over her right ear and spiked in all directions on top, a bright orange with green tips. She wore the cutest little strapless bustier, crazy quilted with pieces of Chinese silk, and a full-flowing black cotton miniskirt, appliquéd with Pinky B.

Grabbing Alex's hand, Bee tugged her toward the doors. "Come with me. I have to get back to the dressing room. I was just talking to the DJ, making sure she had the sound list."

"I don't think I can go into that dressing room. It's insane and filled with carcinogens."

Bee rolled her eyes as she led Alex down the stairs into the main showroom. "You are such a weenie. I should have bought you a gas mask."

"Bee, wait a minute." Alex tugged at her hand, and they moved under the open stairway to stay out of the staff's way. "You dad came by."

Blinking, Bee stared at her. Her lips parted. "Here? He's *here*?" She turned her head jerkily, as if afraid to find him walking straight toward her.

"No." Alex pulled her closer. "He came to the shop. I happened to be there, just checking things out, and—"

Bee's hand tightened on Alex's arm. "You *talked* to him?"

"Well, sure. I gave him a little tour of your space."

Bee processed this news, her eyelids blinking like an overloaded mainframe.

"He liked it," Alex added, feeling worry crawl up under her ribs. "'Nice, big space,' he said. He's heard of the Zans and seemed impressed."

Now Bee was shaking her head. "Does he know about the launch?"

Hesitating a moment, deciding not to tell Bee that her father turned down Alex's invite, she said, "I don't know. Maybe."

"He'll never come," Bee said sharply and took off rapidly toward the dressing room. Alex didn't try to tell her she was wrong or urge her to call him. Right now was the worst time to bring up all that.

By that time the guests had started to arrive, visit the bar to order drinks, schmooze, and find seats. Cam had lined up photographers behind everyone and to the side and in the front aisle, and the music had swelled into rumbling expectancy. Alex climbed up to the fourth-stair step and sat down with her feet dangling over the edge and with a bird's-eye view of the catwalk. Jojo, Tina, and Mei found and joined her; the four of them sat, one to a step, peering down from beneath the maple banister. Jojo waved at Jim, who was standing near the elevators with his cell phone in hand, coordinating events, communicating with runners in charge of getting the models lined up, and monitoring how the caterers were doing as they set out the treats, wines, and *jiaoxi* in a social space across from the runway.

They had agreed beforehand to wear Pinky B tees, each a different color. Tina's was blue, her skirt yellow, and her high heels —Prada—were bright red. In a red T-shirt, Mei had added a bluish tint to her black hair and wore tight black capris with white Stuart Weitzman open-toes. Only Jojo, in typical style, wore an oversized white Pinky B, slim denim jean leggings, and pink Merrell tennies. Alex's was black; she wore Bee's blue and green-ribboned hiking skirt and her Doc Martens.

Joseph, in a red tux and trousers—Bee told her Elijah had designed it just for this show—jumped onto the stage with his mic. Alex half listened as he gushed about the setting, thanked Jojo's parents, and finally introduced Bucky Gerardo. At the very edge of the stage, Cam Lobo, in a skin-tight Pinky B long-sleeved tee and attractive shorts tight over his bottom, aimed his iPhone on a selfie stick. Alex could see him deftly zooming in and out on Joseph, then following Bucky as he came on stage.

People actually leaped to their feet when the author trotted onto the catwalk. Still in his jean jacket and slim jeans, Bucky graciously praised Bee's designs, thanked her for her generosity in allowing him to pump his next book—he raised it into the air amid cheers— and then pointed to the open stairway where Alex and Bee's besties were seated.

"And I owe this fantastic opportunity to Jojo Zan, editor at Gray Ghost publishing—"

"Oops," Mei whispered to Jojo. "He just gave you a promotion."

"And folks, check out Jojo's blog, *Book Brew*, where you can read all about me"—he gave a sheepish bow—"and all about the fantastic line of Gray Ghost books!"

Next to Alex, Tina groaned and muttered, "I'm glad Raj couldn't make it."

Joseph hopped back onto the stage, much to the relief of Alex and the others, and Bucky trotted off to applause, while Joseph touted the Gray Ghost sales desk in the north corner of the room, where they could purchase his book.

Jojo squeezed out of her place. "Better get to work." She was in charge of the "Bucky" book table.

Turning, Mei told her, "Be sure and shame anyone who goes up to buy a book during the show!"

And, oh, the show! It was fabulous: a glitz of music, strutting models, and perfect lighting. Not a glitch in timing. With mixed feelings, Alex felt tears behind her eyes as the viewers gave the finale, where Bee joined her models in a row on the stage—a standing ovation, whoops, and cameras flashing photos every-where. Mei and Tina, on both sides of her, squeezed Alex tightly with hugs, and this affection warmed Alex through and through.

"Time to get out of the way before the buffet stampede begins," Tina murmured, and they scrambled to leave the stairway. Alex sought out Jim, thinking she could stand back beside at least one sympathetic viewer who felt a little outside of things, but he had disappeared—probably to be at the back table where Jojo was selling books.

Journalists, fashionistas, and fans mobbed Bee as she came off the stage. Alex totally lost sight of her, as small as she was among her admirers. Leaning against the wall in the back, near the stairs, Alex felt very alone. Would Bee have any time for her at all today? Why should she even stay around? She could go back to Bee's studio and wait, but likely Bee would be wanting to go out with her besties and a crowd of her new friends.

Poor pitiful you? Don't be daft, she told herself. *Give Bee her Moment, Al. This isn't about you.*

Feeling a touch on her shoulder, Alex turned to see Wendy Zan, elegant as always in a lilac wool suit and her strings of fine gold necklaces. Her face looked kind, and Alex could see she was pleased with her little show.

"You stand here like a wallflower? You should go push your way through the mob to stand with Bee."

Alex, who had braided her golden hair and flung it over her right shoulder, flung it back and laughed a bit. "I'm not one for getting trampled by the fans. Let them have her for a while."

Nodding, Wendy surveyed the crowd; by now, many were heading upstairs where the food, drink, and *jiaoxi* awaited, along with a delicious view of the city. "My son-in-law is doing well, I think. He's got this all under control."

Alex knew, only from rumor, that it had taken awhile for Wendy to warm up to Jim, especially after learning he was only half Chinese. "I've always liked him. He and I know how it is to be a partner of this tight club who call themselves the Leftovers."

Wendy gave her a sharp, curious look, and Alex wondered if she'd blabbed something that Jojo hid from her mother, but Wendy said nothing, just nodded.

"Jim is a smart young man," Wendy mused as she watched him across the room where he was urging one of his gofers to get more Pinky B swag from the conference room. "You are smart too. I think Bee relies heavily on you, from what Jojo tells me."

Alex felt her face grow warm. She wished she could feel as confident about that as Wendy. Saying nothing, she just smiled.

Wendy went on, "You know, I am so proud of Jojo. When she says she's going to do something, she does it and follows through." She waved her hand. "All this. Jojo did this. I did very little, actually. Jojo and Jim. Their show."

Turning to Alex, Wendy shook her head in wonder. "And how she does that blog thing. I don't even know how to get to it on my computer. Lang, Mr. Zan, had to show me!"

Before Alex had to come up with a reply, one of the hotel managers grabbed Wendy's attention. Alex couldn't hear what he told Mrs. Zan, but as soon as she heard it her lips tightened and she rattled off a string of words in Chinese before stomping off, the manager trailing after.

Finally, Alex realized she had to satisfy her growing hunger, so she climbed the stairs with the crowd and, after waiting only a few minutes, had a plate of vegetarian *jiaoxi*, roasted red peppers, fresh figs, and provolone bruschetta. She took a glass of white Riesling outside on the terrace and found a place at the railing overlooking a distant Wall Street.

She'd seen Mei and Tina taking loaded plates back inside to Jojo and Jim; they invited her to join them, but she declined, saying she wanted to enjoy the view a little longer. But really, she just wanted to be alone with her thoughts.

"Oh, there you are."

Turning, wishing this were Bee but the voice was wrong, she saw Sheila coming through the crowd, holding up Wan Pi's leash.

"Please take him. He's already peed twice in the conference room toilet. I think he misses his mom—and his aunt," she added, as Wan Pi danced around Alex's legs and then hopped up to paw her knees. Around them guests laughed, and Alex heard many "awws" and "cute dog!" He wore his bright yellow Pinky B dog tee.

Taking his leash, Alex knelt and nuzzled his soft head. "You are so naughty, Wanna Pee. And I'll bet you're hungry." She gave him a nugget of bruschetta.

Sheila sighed, almost sagging. "Thank you! Boy, I sure could use a drink, but they're on my trail—someone has to take measurements. You wouldn't believe the people who want to buy!"

"They feed you back there, right?"

Touching her chest, Sheila laughed. "I have such heartburn. Yes, we are well fed!" With that she was gone into the crowd.

As Wan Pi had several admirers to distract him, Alex leaned against the rail and answered the usual questions: "Boy or girl?" "What does Wanpee mean?" "How old is he?" "Where did you get him?" Finally, Alex realized she would never have any peace. She was careful not to tell them who she was, even though it would probably mean nothing to them.

Oh, yes, I'm Bee's girlfriend. She felt better about the words, these days, but she had to wonder how long their relationship would last.

Finally, after checking her phone for the sixth time to see if there were any texts from Bee, Alex texted Bee, asking her where she was and if she could get away.

A reply came back immediately. *In the main room. Near stage. Save me from these people!*

Chuckling, her spirits lifting, Alex picked up Wan Pi and threaded her way through the terrace crowd. It would be so nice to see Bee at last, and maybe they really could get away and find a nice place nearby to tuck in for a celebratory drink before going home.

As she went down the steps, watching her feet and managing Wan Pi, she heard a familiar voice say, "Hello. It's Alex, isn't it?"

Shock ran through Alex as she recognized Cindi Koh's face.

Cindi glanced down at Wan Pi. "You're the dog-sitter now, huh?" She smiled, but Alex didn't see any warmth there. "Do you know where the star is? I've been looking for her everywhere."

"Nope," Alex said, moving downward rapidly, getting away from Cindi as fast as she could. At the bottom of the stairs she scanned the theater space—most chairs were empty, with some moved together by several people who wanted to chat. Beyond was a milling group, and finally Alex saw the flash of Bee's currently orange hair.

Putting Wan Pi down, she dashed through the chairs, moving them aside, pulling Wan Pi behind her. It seemed to take forever to reach Bee's side, where she was standing in a group of admirers demanding to know when her shop was going to open and if they could get on a waiting list. As soon as Bee saw Alex, her tired face lit up; she waved at everyone and muttered something like, "I need to talk to Alex here," took Alex's arm, and steered her through the black curtains the staff had set up to mask the dressing room door and steps up to the runway from the audience.

Wrapping her arms around Alex, Bee nuzzled her head into Alex's shoulder. "It was like the Zombie Apocalypse out there. I was sure they were gonna rip off my arms and eat them. Gah, I'm turning into Jojo."

With Bee's warmth, aromas of oolong and cinnamon, and the touch of her body next to hers, Alex hated to break the moment, but she had to warn Bee.

"Cindi Koh just walked in. She's looking for you."

Stiffening, Bee stepped back. "Da bitch."

The next moment she was off, Alex following with Wan Pi. "Where?" Bee barked as she exited the curtains and turned toward the stairway.

"She passed me on the stairs, going up."

Marching to the foot of the stairs, Bee gazed upward, her Chinese dragon face sharpening her features. Breathing fire would be next, Alex thought.

"How long ago?"

"Maybe five minutes." Alex thought quickly, wondering what Bee was planning to do, if she had a plan at all. *I can probably call*

911 if a fight breaks out. I wish I knew where Jim was right now. Or maybe Jojo. She did martial arts.

Nodding to herself, Bee stood at the bottom of the stairs. As people went up and down, greeting her and complimenting the show, Bee nodded politely but kept her gaze upward. Stepping closer, Alex decided she could at least shoo away people who lingered a bit too long.

Alex saw Bee's eyes narrow. She saw a pair of tiger-striped high heels stepping down the treads. Long, shapely legs, the lavender pencil skirt. Stepping back, Alex watched, feeling a niggling of doubt. *What if Cindi lays on her heavy charm? What if Bee falls for Cindi's waspish flattery?*

"Oh, there you are," Cindi cooed as she descended to stand on the lowest step above Bee. "I've been looking for you everywhere."

Cindi had the gall to give Bee a big smile. "What a fantastic place, Bee. And oh my, don't you look adorb in your electric outfit?"

There was a tick of seconds as Bee gazed up at Cindi. Alex took a step closer, thinking she could grab Bee and get her to safety if things got really nasty.

A smile crept across Bee's lips and she sighed loudly.

Alex cringed inside. She barely stifled the urge to reach for Bee, to guide her away, like a bodyguard would.

"Alex," Bee said loudly without turning her head, "would you call security, please, and ask them to escort Ms. Koh off the premises?"

The far corner booth at Molly's was dark, if not quiet, and Bee snuggled against Alex as they sipped their drinks together. Finally escaping the hubbub of the day, shooed away by Jim and the hotel staff ready for cleanup, Bee and Alex had Ubered to one of their favorite taverns.

Alex could never have described the vast joy she'd felt at seeing Cindi Koh's face when Bee told her to call security and have the woman evicted. That had taken mere seconds; Joseph, spying the Cindi/Bee standoff, had grabbed Cam, and the two of them were already hurrying over when Alex intercepted them with a request to page security and have them get Cindi out of there.

In the end, the eighty-sixing was a bloodless act that Cam and Joseph performed themselves. After a silent but deadly exchange of looks, Cindi, chin raised, ignoring guests who had clearly figured out what was happening, stepped off the stairs and stood toe-to-toe with Bee and with a venom in her eyes that had made Alex's fists clench all on their own.

"Sorry you feel this way, Bee, darling," Cindi growled, then as Cam and Joseph descended on her, she raised a hand. "I'll let myself out, thanks."

Ever the gentlemen, Cam and Joseph had insisted on riding down with her.

"Did you think you'd be welcome here?" Bee called as the doors closed on Cindi's furious face. "How bloody clueless can you be?"

"I can't believe the balls on that girl," Bee said now, picking at her french fries.

Alex, her head leaning against the wall, answered, "If this was Jojo's movie, you'd have spat fire on her and burnt her to a crisp, leaving a little smoking crater in the travertine floor." She made an O with her fingers to show just how little.

Laughing, Bee raised up to kiss her. "God, I love you," she said.

Alex stiffened, and Bee apparently felt it. Sitting up, she faced Alex straight on, her eyes glistening. "It's true, Alex. I do love you.

I think I've been in love with you all along but was too dense to get it."

As every muscle in her body relaxed, as if she'd just finished a long run or a heavy yoga workout, Alex felt her mouth fall open. Her eyes stung with tears.

"Oh, Bee." She didn't know what else to say.

A glimmer of worry showed on Bee's forehead. "You love me too, don't you?"

Alex sighed and almost laughed out loud. Throwing her arms around Bee, she crowed, "*Are you kidding?*" and wrapped Bee in a deep embrace.

A few heads turned toward them, then away. This was New York, after all, where anything could happen and probably did.

Chapter Thirty-Seven

The Pinky B grand store opening had gone well, was exciting and busy and everything Bee had hoped for, but she was so glad it was behind her. Today, at the very end of April, the New York City weather had had enough of beautiful, fragrant spring days and invited a rainstorm into town. Rivington Street wavered behind the sheet of water that drenched the glass at the back of the store. Traffic was jamming up because of the wetness, and a line of cars snaked slowly down Rivington toward Bowery.

Bee had a feeling there would be few shoppers today, which would give her time to stock and read more of *Business for Dummies*, one of the many books Alex had bought for her. She also was looking forward to seeing Alex, who was coming by after she woke up after working a nightshift last night; they were going out for dinner afterward. A special dinner, Bee hoped.

Getting up, she went back to the window, standing behind her sales desk and next to the two pink upholstered swivel chairs, to enjoy the rain. Wan Pi, snuggled in the corner on the old fisherman's sweater that Bee had had since middle school, opened one eye, stretched, and sighed.

After she had told Alex to her face that she loved her, Bee worried it would change their relationship, that Alex would either reject her—*what sense did that make?*—or become clingy and demanding. Bee knew clingy and demanding were not Alex's MO, and she hadn't seen it in the ten days that followed. Straightening the Pinky B poster behind the sales desk for the tenth time this morning, she tried to settle down with her book, but the words held no meaning, no matter how many times she started over.

Two customers wandered in, girls who appeared shy and young —high school? Browsers, Bee thought unkindly, but came around her desk and asked what sort of clothes they liked to wear, and when. They relaxed immediately and launched into descriptions of jeans and jackets and swimsuits. Bee often posed these questions to people who came in; it was certainly less off-putting than giving a "can I help you?" greeting to shoppers who only wanted to browse.

She allowed them time to feel the fabrics of the samples on the racks, point to the shoes they especially liked, and briefly consider, until they saw the price tag, one of the Pinky B rayon scarves. They were soon gone, thanking her as an afterthought. *Teenagers*, she thought, refolding the scarf and fanning it out with the others.

Still, teenagers grew up, and if Pinky B can keep up with new designs, teenagers could become adult customers.

Lunch was leftover Thai in her Bento box. She fed Wan Pi half of it as he waited eagerly beside her stool. She hoped that soon she could hire a salesperson so she could take a real break. She really wanted to spend this time in her studio, looking at fabrics, cutting out fabric pieces, and sewing. She often sketched her designs; she hoped people would ask about a certain look or request a modification—within reason—and she had placed a corkboard on the wall toward the back, where she could tack quickly drawn sketches inspired by customer descriptions.

The afternoon hours seemed to stretch endlessly, and more than once she considered closing her doors early today, but she was only open Wednesday through Saturday and hated to miss a good customer. Two more browsers came, then Sheila dropped by to chat for a while.

Alone at last, Bee was browsing on her laptop when she heard the shop door open. Closing the computer, Bee checked to see who had entered. Her heart nearly stopped, or at least leapt into her throat, giving her a spasm of coughing.

In a weave sports jacket, white shirt with no tie, and tan slacks, Dad stood just inside the door. Carefully inserting his umbrella into the umbrella stand, he walked a few feet in and studied the shop, avoiding eye contact with Bee.

Bee opened her mouth but nothing came out. Wan Pi, sensing something was wrong, got to his feet. She heard a soft growl.

"Very nice shop. For ladies, I think." Zhen noticed the Pinky B poster.

"We have a men's line, too. Street wear and formal." Bee made her voice loud and confident, hiding her shocked confusion. "Over here."

As if he were a customer, Bee came around the desk and led him to the rack of men's clothing.

Dad touched the red brocade jacket. Bee knew this lavish male look was a long way from Dad's button-down style, so she pulled a tony butter-shaded unisex trench coat from the rack. "This looks like something you might prefer," she said boldly, expecting him to scowl.

He reached for the sleeve, felt it, then lifted it to peer at the hem of the cuff with a thoughtful and at the same time critical expression. Nodding slightly, he let the cuff drop, turned toward the windows, and nearly ran into Wan Pi, who was sniffing the back of his pants leg.

"Oh, who? What is this?" Dad blinked down at the dog, who tilted his head and then tentatively wiggled his little docked tail.

"This is Wan Pi. I haven't had a chance to introduce him to you." Bee watched Dad's face. They had never had dogs growing up. She wasn't sure he even liked dogs.

"Oh," he said before stepping around the dog and walking toward the windows "You need some male mannequins in here. More customers, from a big hotel like this one, are male, I think."

Bee felt a small blink of hope, like a broken lamp flicking on, proving it was not dead. "I know. I have a couple on order."

A few minutes of silence strolled uncomfortably by. Zhen peered out the window. "We're still seeking a location," he said. "Is this a good neighborhood?"

"It has potential. New development, and increased shopping. This hotel will help with that." Bee was grateful to have a shop an easy walk or scooter ride from her studio, even though the location, Lower Manhattan and the Bowery, was clinging by its fingers to chic.

Turning, Dad nodded and touched the back of one of the chairs.

What is he doing here? Bee fumbled to find something to say, a banal observation about the weather, or directly ask why he came. Was his visit an offering of the peace pipe? He still hadn't looked her in the eye, when all the time her gaze was on him, trying to see the invisible, but Zhen's placid face offered no clues.

When he finally spoke, one hand on the back of the chair, the other adjusting his glasses, Bee could barely hear him. "This is a beautiful shop, and the fashions are . . . striking."

"Thank you," Bee managed. She was still beside the men's clothing rack, trying, without any success, to pull her thoughts together. She felt as flustered as if the mayor of the city had just walked in.

Removing his glasses, Zhen cleaned them with a tissue, put them back on, and finally met her eyes. Now he saw her, as if for the first time, she thought, his hands folded in front of him.

He said, a little gruffly, "I am proud of you, daughter."

Bee couldn't stop a sudden intake of breath. Her surprise even seemed to close up her throat. *No tears, damn it!*

But Dad wasn't finished. "I love you more than you will ever know. You were right; I should have listened to you. I should have trusted you." He bowed his head. "Can you forgive me?"

Again, Bee was speechless; Bing Lin without a retort or a snide remark was a Bing Lin she didn't know very well. And a Zhen Lin actively apologizing? That was unthinkable. *This must be a play and we are pretending to be ourselves.*

What did it mean that she had finally done something her dad could be proud of?

Maybe it's because I've been all talk and wannabe and never did it. Never pulled it all together.

Alex's voice came into her head. *Do or do not; there is no try.*

"I think so, Dad," she said. "Yes, I think so." She went to him, opened her arms, and gave him a hug.

Responding stiffly, he folded his arms around her then quickly broke free. "Have you talked to your brother?" he asked briskly.

Bee actually felt relieved to hear the old Zhen come back, leave behind the mournful, uncertain man he had just been, and get back to business. Bee turned, straightening the business card holder on her desk.

"Bing, yes, did you talk to Hao?"

Turning at the sound of her mother's voice, Bee saw Xing Lin approaching. To Bee's utter surprise, her mom wore a Pinky B bomber jacket that Bee had given her last year as a sort of joke, with a pair of white slacks. With her Fendi handbag hung over one shoulder, Mom was a comical mishmash of styles, and Bee loved her for it. Wan Pi trotted up to her immediately. Mom stopped, her mouth agape and eyes wide, then reached down to pat the wriggling little brown dog.

"Ah, so sweet. So cute. A shop dog!"

Behind Mom, Bee saw Alex peeking through the open glass door, both amused and quizzical. Bee waved her in, feeling every tense, spiking nerve in her body relax at the sight of the golden fox.

"Hi, Mom." Bee gave her mother a kiss on the cheek. "Yes, I've talked to Hao."

Mom's eyes, wide and blinking, glanced across Bee's shoulder at Dad. Then she said softly to Bee. "He knows."

This could mean only one thing—that Dad knew Hao was bailing out of the business and following his dream girl to Australia.

"I know he's leaving for Australia this Saturday," she said, facing Mom but loud enough for Dad to hear.

Alex moved past the family, as if trying to be invisible, but Bee grabbed her arm. "Hey, wait a minute. Hang with us a bit."

Raising her eyebrows as if to ask *you're sure?* Alex shrugged and sat in one of the swivel chairs, clunking her backpack beside her.

Alex's being here, Bee knew, would force Dad to be on his best behavior.

Nodding politely at Alex, Dad pressed his hands together. "I don't understand my son. Why would he give up everything we have given him and run after this red girl?"

"Maybe it's for the best, Dad," Bee answered, even though Dad's question was purely rhetorical. "You have to admit that Hao was never very enthusiastic about working in fashion."

"What is he enthusiastic about, except skirts?"

Bee swallowed back a laugh. "I think he has an eye for business, but it's not fashion, that's all. He's got his MBA. He can work in finance, anything he wants pretty much."

"Always good with numbers," Mom added, shrugging off her jacket.

Going around Bee's desk, Dad picked up one of her business textbooks. "What is this book for dummies? You're not a dummy."

"I have a business now, in case you didn't notice." Leaning on her elbows on the desk counter, Bee pointed to her laptop. "I need to put those economic classes they fed me at Central St. Martin's to use."

"Good." Setting down the book, Dad gazed at her solemnly. "Hao said you want to help run Lin Designs."

Bee opened her mouth and shut it again. *Is this an offer, an opening? A challenge?*

"We need someone in our family to help, to learn," Dad added carefully. "I think you have told me you want to be this person."

Now. Here it is. The offer I've been waiting for. Do I say yes? No? Yes, with certain compromises? I mean, I'd love to work with the design wing of the business, but I want nothing to do with the day-to-day running of it.

"Wow, Dad. I don't know what to say." Bee stuck her fingers into her hair. "Let me think about it, huh? I mean, I think I want to, but I've got this now, and—let me think about it for a few days."

She thought she saw a movement in Dad's lips, of disappointment, but she couldn't be sure. Mom touched her arm.

"You think about it, yes," she said, patting Bee's sleeve. "Maybe you do design—you are so good at that, and your Dad and I manage the manufacturing. You can see good designs for us, I know."

Bee warmed inside and gave her mother a thankful smile. She

could immerse herself in design, for her own Pinky B line, and for Lin Designs as well. "That might work," she said aloud.

"Good." Dad nodded and almost smiled as he acknowledged Alex over Bee's shoulder. "How are you , Alex?"

Bee stared at him and saw that he *was* smiling, and it was at Alex. Her head swiveled back and forth like she was watching a tennis match.

Alex, squatting on the floor, petting Wan Pi, was almost blushing. "Oh, I'm great, Mr. Lin. It's good to see you again."

Dad now turned to Bee. "Daughter, your mother and I would like to take you out to dinner tonight." He waved a hand. "And Alex too, of course." He paused. "And the naughty one. Can he come to a restaurant too?"

If Bee were a fainting person, she would have been flat on the floor. At a complete loss for words, Bee gazed open-mouthed at Alex. She was saved from replying by Xing, who pulled on her arm.

"Yes. You finish up your shop, and we meet you in the lobby in an hour. Come, Zhen, Bee has business to do." Shouldering her purse, Mom waved at Dad to follow, and he obeyed without a sound. Just then, as if the Chinese gods had ordered it, a young couple came into the shop.

Alex pretended to be browsing through the racks while Bee helped her customers. Overjoyed that the wife was interested in being fitted for the red silk sleepwear and kimono, after trying it on for her husband, Bee took measurements and promised a version to be ready by early next week. She could have done it sooner, but she thought she might look too eager, as if she didn't have enough business.

After they left, hand in hand—they verified that they were newlyweds, as Bee had already guessed—Bee went to where Alex was examining a sleeveless silk shirt with embroidered appliqué pockets and put her arms around her.

"I could give you that, if you like it," she breathed in Alex's ear, knowing what Alex would say.

"Nope. I pay for it. You're in business now."

Walking over to her desk, where Wan Pi had obediently retired to his sweater, Bee finalized the sleepwear order in her laptop, while Alex leaned her elbows on the desk. "Wow. Your Dad. I saw your mom outside, and she urged me to wait until you two had said whatever you had to say to each other. She had all her fingers crossed. Probably her toes, too."

Sighing, Bee still felt wary; she also should feel triumphant, she thought, because Dad had made the first move. She folded her hands. "I wish I felt better about it. It's what I wanted, for him to grovel. But now that he has, sort of, it doesn't feel as great as I thought it would."

Alex slid her hand along the counter, covering Bee's with hers. Bee was grateful she didn't say anything—no lectures, no urging to smooth things over, as much as she might want to say those things.

Bee's fingers began to tingle, and she felt a loosening inside, as if a knot had untied itself deep down. Now or never, she thought, and gripping Alex's hand, she reached down to the first shelf to find her backpack.

It wasn't there.

Crap!

Still holding on to poor Alex, who was trying to pull away, Bee crouched down. The shelf was empty. Her brand-new tiny Pinky B backpack was gone.

"Where is it," she whined, feeling her throat close. The worst possible moment for her to misplace it.

"What?" Rubbing her arm where it had chafed against the edge of the desk, Alex had broken free.

"My backpack. I put it here when I got in this morning."

On her knees now, Bee rummaged through the rest of the shelves, through clothes in need of mending, scarves she took off display because they didn't look right, and her pile of business books.

"Oh, it's got to be here somewhere." Alex joined in the search, peering behind chairs and under racks.

Oh why. Why now? Bee kept her tears at bay, knowing they erupted from anger at herself, at the Chinese gods, at stupid pink chairs. Coming around the desk, she stiffened.

Those teenage girls. Did I let them out of my sight for a minute?

The Pinky B small pack wasn't up for sale yet. Bee's was the prototype. It would be just the accessory a teenage girl would want and might even steal.

"No," she said, covering her eyes. "It can't be."

"I found it," came a voice from the fitting room.

Relief flooding her, Bee ran into the fitting room, Wan Pi at her heels, and saw Alex walking toward her, holding up the backpack.

"It was behind the table. Must have fallen there somehow."

Now. *NOW!*

Bee held up her hands, palms out. "Stop!"

A little stunned, Alex halted, then extended the backpack toward Bee.

"No, I mean." Bee felt a crazy laugh crawling up her throat and squelched it. "No, open it. I mean, look inside. The front. Look in the front pocket."

Alex's eyebrows drew close together in a skeptical frown. "Okay," she said warily and unzipped the tiny pocket, the one emblazoned with the Pinky B likeness. Her fingers crept inside and stopped. Alex opened her mouth as if to ask a question, closed it, and looked down as she drew out the tiny little box covered in pink suede.

Bee closed her fists under her chin. She felt herself trembling. "Open it. Go on, open it!" Wan Pi, sitting beside Bee as if he sensed her agitation, began to whine.

Alex seemed unable to move. Slowly she set the backpack on the table and held the box in her hand.

Her voice hoarse, Alex murmured, "Is this—?"

"No questions. Just open it," Bee squeaked as she white-knuckled her hands.

Opening it, Alex closed it again and squeezed her eyes shut. Bee forced herself to wait.

Don't think. Don't say a thing.

Alex gave her a quick glance before she opened the box again. "Oh. My. God."

"If you want it, try it on," Bee managed, keeping her voice steady and calm.

Bee watched as Alex's mouth twisted; her chin wobbled. "You bet I want it," she croaked, lifting the ring out of its nesting box. The diamond seemed to capture all the light in the room in order to sparkle for Alexis as if she held a tiny star in her hand. Starting to put it on her finger, she stopped, turned to face Bee, and, hand trembling, held the ring out to Bee.

Swallowing, Bee tried to speak as she took the ring, but her voice squeaked and stumbled as she muttered, "Will you marry me?"

She slipped the ring onto Alex's finger.

"Oh, fuck yes, Beetle. Fuck yes. I thought you'd never ask."

Wan Pi tried to squeeze between their legs as they hugged each other. Then, on his hind legs, he pawed them, barking, his little round butt waggling his entire stocky body.

"Wan Pi approves," Alex said into Bee's ear. The sound of her voice buzzing was like music.

"You'll adopt him? Become dog step-mommy? Sign the papers?" Bee replied, nuzzling Alex's neck.

"It's what he and I have been planning for months," Alex said, and Wan Pi whined and yowled, as if he was telling them, *Get on with it!*

"C'mon. Let's go tell my parents."

Alex pulled away. "You sure?"

As soon as Alexis said the words, Bee knew she couldn't tell them, not yet. Taking Alex's hand, where the ring glittered, she said, "Yeah, you're right. One thing at a time. Poor Dad."

Nodding, Alex pulled off the ring, snapped it into its box, and stowed it in her backpack. "I'll put it back on when we get home."

"Yeah. Home. You *are* going to move in with me, right?"

Alex gave Bee a wry look. "Well, duh."

Hand in hand, like the newlyweds who had just left, they locked up, turned off the lights, and went off to dinner with the Lins, Wan Pi trotting proudly at their sides as if to say, "And they lived happily ever after."

-END-

About the Authors

Vincent DeFilippo: Starting as a daydreaming 13-year-old in a humble classroom, I envisioned a grand future of wealth and success, contrasting sharply with my reality of selling newspapers on the Verrazano Bridge. This vision fueled my transformation into a determined businessman, traversing the globe, leading teams, and achieving academic excellence, all driven by the desire to lift my family to a life of comfort and joy. Now, as an educator, I impart lessons learned from my journey, emphasizing the importance of understanding behavioral finance and cognitive biases, and aiming to equip others with the knowledge to achieve sustained success and growth.

To learn more, visit Vincentdefilippo.com

Yazhen "Bowie" Feng deFilippo was born in Guang Dong, China. She has her MBA from Manchester University and worked for Montpelier Asia (Wealth Management), Saudi Aramco, and Pfizer. She is currently a renowned antique jewelry dealer, collector, wife, and mom.